Because
We Are Here

To My home boy
Jeffery Yems,
with best wishes,
Chuck

Also by Chuck Wachtel

Joe The Engineer

The Coriolis Effect

The Gates

Because
We Are Here

Stories
and Novellas

Chuck Wachtel
4/22/05

VIKING

VIKING
Published by the Penguin Group
Penguin Books USA Inc., 375 Hudson Street,
New York, New York 10014, U.S.A.
Penguin Books Ltd, 27 Wrights Lane,
London W8 5TZ, England
Penguin Books Australia Ltd, Ringwood,
Victoria, Australia
Penguin Books Canada Ltd, 10 Alcorn Avenue,
Toronto, Ontario, Canada M4V 3B2
Penguin Books (N.Z.) Ltd, 182–190 Wairau Road,
Auckland 10, New Zealand

Penguin Books Ltd, Registered Offices:
Harmondsworth, Middlesex, England

First published in 1996 by Viking Penguin,
a division of Penguin Books USA Inc.

10 9 8 7 6 5 4 3 2 1

Some of the selections in this book first appeared, in whole or in part, in the following publications: "St. Ralphie" in *Active in Airtime*; "Sleeping Beauty" in *Arts Indiana*; "News" in *Sycamore Review*; "One Week," "Documentaries," "The Funeral," "Real Dreams" (numbers 1-4), and "The Beginning of the End of the Cold War" in *Hanging Loose Magazine*; "Here" in *Flatiron News* and *VIA: Vistas in Italian Americana*; and "Wednesday" in *First*.

Grateful acknowledgment is made for permission to reprint excerpts from the following copyrighted works:
"Thirteen Ways of Looking at a Blackbird" from *Collected Poems* by Wallace Stevens. Copyright 1923 and renewed 1951 by Wallace Stevens. Reprinted by permission of Alfred A. Knopf, Inc.
"Catastrophic Birth" from *Collected Poems 1939–1962*, Volume II, by William Carlos Williams. Copyright © 1962 by William Carlos Williams. Reprinted by permission of New Directions Publishing Corp.

PUBLISHER'S NOTE
These selections are works of fiction. Names, characters, places, and incidents either are the product of the author's imagination or are used fictitiously, and any resemblance to actual persons, living or dead, events, or locales is entirely coincidental.

LIBRARY OF CONGRESS CATALOGING IN PUBLICATION DATA
Wachtel, Chuck.
Because we are here: stories and novellas/by Chuck Wachtel.
p. cm.
ISBN 0-670-83887-X
1. Manners and customs—Fiction. I. Title.
PS3573.A29B4   1996
813'54—dc20   95-39988

This book is printed on acid-free paper.
∞
Printed in the United States of America
Set in Goudy
Designed by James Sinclair

For three colleagues:

Brian Breger, Cornelius Eady,
Robin Tewes

Acknowledgments

The author would like to thank Donna Brook, Beena Kamlani, Jocelyn Lieu, Joan Silber, and Paul Slovak: caring and careful readers; and Howie Michels and Francine Prose, in whose guest house the first of these stories was written.

Contents

Contents

News

. . . in some respects my account differs from what you will read if you look up the old newspaper files. I have told the truth of what I have told in the words and the truth of what I have not told which resides in the words.

E. L. DOCTOROW

St. Ralphie

When Ralphie Leo wakes, he finds himself thinking of the faces of people sleeping on TV. It is in their sleep, he has realized, that they are the most unlike the rest of us, because they wear on their faces the same expressions they had when they were still awake. If they fall asleep happy, their faces sleep happy, if they fall asleep angry, their faces sleep angry. They remain assembled. If Ralphie Leo lived with a TV family, he could wake in the middle of the night, whenever he wanted to, wander the rooms of his house, and find his wife and his many children, all of them gracefully composed in sound, gentle, eloquent sleep.

These thoughts are not the remnants of a dream but the first thoughts of his slow waking. Lying beside him, not yet awake, is Deedee Cohen, and it's only the second time they've shared a bed. Last night, after they made love, and after he was certain she had fallen asleep, he took his dentures out. He slept uneasily. Mostly he just lay there, wondering what she would think if she were to wake up before he did, and watch him, his cheeks so deeply sunken they nearly touched on the inside. Ralphie is fifty-eight years old and has not shared a bed with anyone—up until first sleeping with Deedee last month—since Brenda, his wife, passed away four years ago. It's six-thirty A.M.

He slips out of bed and walks to the bathroom. Standing in front of the mirror, he opens his mouth and sadly rubs his fore-

3

finger over the stubbled pocket of his left cheek. Out of a clear
sky it occurs to him that perhaps, up until very recently, the
first thing children realized—the first thing from the world of
liquid images around us to solidify into fact—was that each
toothless man was not the same toothless man, and each toothless woman not the same toothless woman. Young children
could easily believe otherwise. The concave cheeks, the lips
curling back over the jaw, give toothless people far more in
common than brothers and sisters of the same family.

His sadness gives way to the sense of connection this notion
gives him. It's as if the brief experience of a thought has shaken
him loose from his own singular life and connected him with
nearly everyone who has ever existed on the planet.

This is how his day, a Friday in mid-July, begins.

At seven-thirty Ralphie and Deedee are having raisin bread
toast and coffee and watching *Good Morning America.* Above
the newscaster's head is a visual aid: the words "A New Apartheid" followed by a question mark and set on an upward angle
like the bar of a fraction, separating two stick figures with circles
for heads.

"I thought that was all over," Ralphie says. Then he points
at the screen. "Doesn't that look like a percent symbol, you
know, like the one on your calculator?"

"Oh *yeah*," Deedee says. She pushes back her plate and lights
a cigarette. She's wearing a yellow quilted housecoat. "Tell me,"
she then says, "is there a single thing in this world that doesn't
remind you of something else?"

For the last six months, Deedee, two years younger than
Ralphie and a divorcée, has been doing the books, part time, in
his hardware store on Jerome Avenue. He's beginning to become
relaxed with her, and the more he does, the more beautiful he
finds her.

The newscaster says that a Senate panel has accused the New
Millennium Task Force, whose report on U.S. cities was released

last week, of being thoroughly irresponsible, and calls its findings a volume of undocumented lies. "In particular, the panel took exception to the report's warning for the dawn of the new century, that if current economic trends continue, the walls now rising in our major cities will reach unscalable heights and will, as in South Africa under apartheid, separate an elite minority from an economically disadvantaged majority."

"If I live to be a hundred, I'll never understand this world," Ralphie says. "They got the Berlin Wall down in what, two weeks? It's unnatural to separate people. That guy Mandela showed us that." He shakes his head. "I just don't know. . . ."

Deedee pours herself and Ralphie another cup of coffee. "Who are you, you should know anything?" she says. The level in the glass pot goes from the four-cup line to the two-cup line.

He doesn't mind her saying this. He's been a widower for four years. His daughter, Randi, has lived in California nearly twice that long. Deedee's saying this implies a continuum of people being near enough to him to say such things.

As the newscaster announces a station break, the visual aid over his head is replaced by footage from the stories that will follow the commercial: a young man, pulling the gray hood of a sweatshirt over his face, being walked by two plainclothesmen toward the open rear door of a police car, followed by the words "Mets Do It Again" moving like a train across the screen. Then a beautiful pair of hands appears. They are washing dishes. Beside them, on the edge of the sink, is a yellow plastic squeeze bottle, shaped vaguely like a standing human.

"That's the lemon-scented kind," Ralphie says to Deedee. "*You* use that."

"So does half the world," she tells him. Then she asks, "Aren't you late?"

"I'm going in a minute." He doesn't want to leave yet. He likes sitting at this Formica table. He likes the toast crumbs on his plate, the taste of his coffee, the sound of the TV. "I'll wait until they finish giving the news."

On Friday mornings he plays a round of golf with his friend

Eugene on the Forest Park Golf Course. They tee off at eight-
thirty. Eugene owns the video rental club next door to Ralphie's
hardware store. Friday morning golf has been their ritual for the
last five summers.

As he drives toward the golf course, Ralphie imagines a young
child discovering that his toothless grandfather and the toothless
man next door are not the same person. As it did earlier, the
thought makes him feel connected.

This often happens to Ralphie. A thought he has—not one
he thinks up, one that occurs to him—can suddenly become a
link to someone, sometimes everyone, else.

Last week he was at the store, sorting out an order of drill
bits, when he heard, through the wall, the steam whistle on the
electric teapot Eugene keeps behind the counter. All at once
his mind filled with the image of an old man sitting in a
parlor somewhere in London, reading a newspaper and half
listening to his teapot whistle. In the kitchen, his wife turned
off the flame, and as the pitch of the whistle decreased, a
spasm of terror hit the old man's body. He dove onto the
floor. "Helen," he called to his wife. "Get away from the windows!" He heard bombs falling. *Ralphie* heard bombs falling. In
half a century, this man's now old body had not forgotten the
Blitz.

The whole thing happened in a second. The time it took to
unwrap a three-eighth-inch mason bit and find its proper drawer.

Ralphie was a child when the Second World War ended, and
he never drinks tea. Where did this old man come from? How
could he suddenly flare into life? Into *his* life? Ralphie felt he
had loosened his grip on his own, local moment and briefly
connected to this man he could never have known.

Immediately after these experiences, Ralphie decides he must
have a second sight, some kind of vision other people don't
have. But then, as the world around him crowds back in, he
begins to doubt it. Who am *I*, Ralphie Leo, to have such a

power? Nuthouses are filled with people who see things that aren't there. Such thoughts are as present as a clock's ticking and should be given as much importance.

Ralphie and Eugene smile at one another when Eugene overshoots the green of the fourth hole by less than twenty feet, the best drive either of them has made all morning. Ralphie has driven his ball into a small stand of pin oaks less than halfway down the fairway.

As they walk toward Ralphie's ball, Eugene points a golf club toward the sun. "Nice morning," he says. "Could get hot, though. Then again, it could rain."

Ralphie looks up. Although it's a bit cloudy, the sun is strong enough to lift a fresh smell off the grass. It reminds him of the smell that came out of the open top of Deedee's washing machine as he passed it, less than two hours ago, on his way out the back door.

He wedges his ball out of the trees and onto the fairway without getting it any nearer the hole. On his third swing he drops the ball just beyond the green, exactly where they imagine Eugene's to be.

They smile again.

As they walk toward the green, a low-flying plane passes over the fairway.

Eugene suddenly dives onto his stomach. He covers his head with his hands and laughs.

Ralphie starts to duck, quickly looks around, then straightens up again. "What?"

"Remember the crop-duster scene in *North by Northwest?*"

Ralphie shakes his head and smiles.

"Hit the dirt!" Eugene says, then rolls over, hugging his stomach, in tears with laughter.

On slow afternoons they watch Alfred Hitchcock films over and over on the four monitors in Eugene's store. He tells Ralphie they have hidden meanings most people cannot see.

"Come on, Cary Grant." Ralphie helps Eugene to his feet, then looks up at the sky. "It's getting cloudier," he says.

They both complete the fourth hole in three more strokes, making it a five on a four par for Eugene, and a six for Ralphie.

On their way to the fifth hole, Eugene tells Ralphie that to-day, and maybe from now on, they shouldn't use the showers at the club.

"Why not?"

"AIDS," Eugene says.

"From a shower?"

"It's possible."

"You're crazy."

"The guy who's not careful is the crazy one. It's more than possible."

Ralphie doesn't answer. He watches a bank of clouds cover the sun. The wind is beginning to reveal the undersides of the leaves. It will rain today. Probably soon.

"It isn't just AIDS," Eugene says. "It's everything. Everything has changed. And it's changing because we wanted it to. Only no one seems to remember just *when* we decided to make these changes. Even the weather's different, you know what I mean? And how does *weather* get different?"

Ralphie nods. He's still looking at the sky.

"Disease has changed too. Normal contagiousness—you know, somebody sneezes in your face on the subway, you catch their cold, you go home, kiss your wife hello, and she catches it too—that doesn't exist anymore. It's a thing of the past. AIDS is like something we all got already. That's what it feels like. And once you realize it, you start showing the symptoms."

"I think it's going to rain," Ralphie says.

"You better listen," Eugene continues. "Just suppose some guy with AIDS pisses in the shower and you step in it and later, in the locker room, you scratch your foot, and afterward we have lunch. . . ."

"You're crazy," Ralphie says again. He taps the side of his head with the tip of his forefinger. "Impossible."

"Crazy, huh? You remember *Vertigo*?"

"Of course. We've watched it like a dozen times."

Eugene smiles as if his point were already made.

"So . . . ?" Ralphie asks. He feels a drop of rain hit his forehead; another, his nose.

"If you watched that movie closely, you'd know that *anything* is possible."

"We'd better head back," Ralphie says.

"You know what I'm saying," Eugene says. They turn and begin to walk back toward the club. "Am I right, or am I right?"

"You're right," Ralphie says.

"You knew I was right all along."

"Absolutely," Ralphie says. It's growing dark as night. The rain is really beginning to come down.

They walk faster. The rain quickly soaks through their light summer clothes.

Suddenly a bolt of lightning leaps across the sky. Not ordinary lightning, but a long, liquid streak, like a child tracing an arc with a sparkler. An earth-shaking clap of thunder follows.

"Ever see anything like that?" Eugene asks.

"Never," Ralphie says.

"We better move." Eugene runs ahead, bouncing his cart behind him.

Ralphie keeps walking. He can't get any wetter. The rain is cool.

Eugene is now some distance ahead. He turns, looks back at Ralphie. "Move it!" he shouts.

Ralphie waves his arm forward, in a *not to wait, keep going* motion.

Another bolt of lightning flings itself through the dark sky like a long, solid burst of tracer fire, passes directly over Eugene's head, and strikes Ralphie's outstretched hand.

Ten years ago, Ralphie, his wife, Brenda, and his daughter, Randi, spent a rainy autumn night sitting on the living room couch, watching TV. At that time Randi, who was in high school, had a cat, which she had given the family name: Leo. Ralphie wasn't interested in the program. Instead, he was watching the cat, lying on the carpet, reaching over his back to lick himself in long, diagonal strokes.

That night Ralphie had a thought, and had it with such suddenness that before he knew it he'd spoken it aloud. "There are *two* cats!" he said.

Brenda kept watching the screen. Randi looked around the room for the other one and then smiled, sadly, at her father, thinking this a silly, inept attempt at making a joke.

But there *are* two cats, Ralphie said again, this time to himself. The back and rump being licked are one cat, and the head, neck, and tongue are the other. If I'm putting a Band-Aid on my knee, he thought, I am two people. The knee is a friend I'm helping. The hand applying the Band-Aid, and the mind and eye that guide it, are me.

"It almost seems too simple," he said aloud.

"You're right," Randi said, referring to the show they were watching: *The $25,000 Pyramid.* "It *has* to be rigged. Hardly anyone ever gets to the top."

As Ralphie stands on the wet fairway, watching Eugene, who is frozen with shock, staring through the distance between them, he remembers that night ten years ago. He knows Eugene cannot see him. The moment the bolt struck, Ralphie became totally invisible.

His discovery, the night he watched Leo the cat, however simple, was a true discovery. With his thoughts, over the years, he has been gradually shaking loose the local, attached-to-one-place Ralphie from the other Ralphie. The lightning has burnt away the one; the other still remains.

He sees Eugene is coming to his senses. Ralphie looks at the ground at his feet to see what his friend will find: golf cart and scattered clubs, tatters of burnt clothing, dentures.

Eugene now begins to run toward him. Ralphie feels a deep

sadness when he realizes how hurt he will be when he discovers
what has happened.

It takes two hours of explaining before Eugene even begins
to answer him as if he is really there.

"Things have changed," Ralphie tells him. "But it's okay."

"They sure have changed."

Eugene looks up at the sky. "They sure as hell have changed,"
he says. "Now I'm *talking* to you."

"It was you who said anything can happen. Remember?"

"Yeah, I remember. And look what *did* happen. . . . You
get struck by lightning, and I start hearing voices out of
thin air. Ralphie, this is not the kind of *anything* I had in
mind."

"You're fine, Eugene. There's nothing to worry about." He
pats his friend's shoulder.

Eugene steps back so suddenly he trips over Ralphie's golf bag
and falls onto the wet grass. "I can feel you!" he says.

"There's nothing to worry about," Ralphie says again.

"*Right. . . .*" Eugene stands up again but keeps his distance
from Ralphie. "*Nothing* to worry about. You might even be dead.
What does that make me—Cosmo Topper?"

Ralphie laughs. He can't help it.

"Funny, huh. We saw that movie together." Eugene begins
to weep.

Ralphie steps toward Eugene, then takes him in his invisible
arms.

As Eugene comes to accept the situation, he begins to think
of solutions.

"Maybe we should talk to a priest. Maybe you have to get
struck by lightning again."

First one, then several shafts of light slip through the breaking
cloud cover. As the day brightens again, other golfers return to
the course.

"I got it," Eugene says. "The emergency room. You need a doctor. A doctor will get you back."

"But I haven't gone anywhere."

"They'll get back the rest of you. The part I can see."

"It's no use."

"Try it, Ralphie. Do it for your old golf partner. We'll walk in there like Cosmo and George. It'll be all right. You'll see."

Ralphie watches a reception nurse drape a blanket over Eugene's shoulders. He finds it interesting that she can be maternal, yet impersonal and severe, all at once.

"You must have a lot of experience with hysterical people," he tells her.

She looks at Eugene, then at the empty space beside him. "What are you, a ventriloquist or something . . . ? Here." She pats the seat beside her desk. "Sit down."

There are children's crayon drawings on the walls. Mostly of children and grownups standing beside houses. Trees, clouds, suns with spoky rays coming from them, birds that are rounded, upside-down double U's.

"You ought to know enough to come in out of the rain," the nurse tells Eugene. She takes a form from the file stand on her desk. "What's your name?"

When they first arrived, Ralphie made Eugene wait until they attended to a man with heart palpitations and a small boy, asleep on his mother's lap, with his left hand wrapped in a blood-soaked towel. Eugene then shouted to the nurse that his friend had been struck by lightning—and was now invisible. That was when the nurse wrapped the blanket around him.

Again he tries to explain it to her. This time in a calmer voice.

"It's just not possible," she says. She writes something down on the form.

"Not possible, huh?" He's starting to cheer up. "Anything's possible. Show her, Ralphie."

"Maybe we should just leave," Ralphie tells him.

"Hey, you *are* a ventriloquist," the nurse says.

Eugene insists that they stay. "They can help you here."

"No one can. But there's nothing to worry about."

"*I* get it," the nurse says. "It's an act. You come in here with this story about your invisible friend. Then you throw your voice." She's laughing now and shaking her head. "It's like a singing telegram, only crazier. Who sent you—Rhonda? This is the *best*. . . ."

"She thinks *I'm* crazy," Eugene says to Ralphie.

"Ssshhh," Ralphie whispers back.

"You *are* great," she says. "You know that?" She gets up. "Just wait a second." She passes through a set of swinging doors. A moment later, she comes back in with a doctor and another nurse. "This guy's incredible," she tells them. "In-*cred*-ible. Do it some more, will you?" she says to Eugene, then turns to the doctor and the nurse to watch their response. "You *have* to see this."

Ralphie's friend is suffering, and he will not let him be humiliated. He walks up to the doctor.

"What he says is true," he tells him.

"He *is* good." The doctor smiles at Eugene, then looks through Ralphie.

"Listen," Ralphie tells him. "I *was* struck by lightning, and I am invisible."

"I can't believe it," he says. "How do you do it?"

"You better believe it." Ralphie grabs his lapels and begins to shake him. "My friend's not a ventriloquist and he's not crazy."

The doctor howls, then faints.

Eugene sits back in his chair and smiles. "See," he tells the nurse. "Anything is possible."

With her left hand she slowly opens her desk drawer. Then quickly pulls out an automatic and holds it on Eugene. With her right hand she pushes a button hidden on the underside of the desktop.

Two security guards appear from nowhere and head for Eugene.

"Not *him*," the other nurse says. "It's that other one. He's invisible, and he's got the doctor."

They look around the room and finally locate Ralphie because he's holding up the doctor by the lapels of his smock. They each grab a wrist they cannot see and drag him through the swinging doors.

Ralphie is sitting on the mattress of a single bed, the only furniture in the windowless room in which they have locked him. "It's so dark," he says, aloud, "that *I* can't even see myself."

Where am I, he thinks, sadly.

He then thinks of the mess he's made for Eugene. . . . And what about Randi and Deedee? "They'll probably tell them I've died. I should have taken my thoughts more seriously. Maybe I could have prevented all the trouble I'm causing."

Suddenly an image fills his mind: a green towel hung over the railing of a sunporch to dry. A vision so beautiful, so comforting, that tears fill his eyes.

And, as suddenly, Ralphie finds himself in blinding sunlight. He is no longer sitting on an unmade bed, but on the webbed seat of an aluminum deck chair. And next to him he discovers, to his astonished delight, Randi, in a terry-cloth robe, combing out her wet hair.

Of course, he thinks. *It's still morning in California. Randi always loved to swim in the morning.* He smiles.

He now begins to understand the full meaning of his bisected life. He no longer connects, simply, with thought. Without the old, fixed-to-one-spot Ralphie, he can follow the vision to its source. And he can aim! Just by his thinking of people, they become a destination. He can sail inside the beam of his thought and arrive in their company.

This is more than happiness.

He watches Randi. She will soon get an official phone call

with news of her father. But he can be there and, somehow, help her. He can be with Deedee when she finds out, too. Then—he quietly rubs his invisible hands together—he can visit the old guy in London. He's never been to London.

But first he must go back to the hospital and spring Eugene. On his own, he'll never get out of there. Then he'll convince his friend there's nothing to worry about.

There's a soft breeze blowing in California, and the sky is clear. Ralphie decides to remain there, sitting in his chair one moment longer, before thinking himself back to the hospital. It gives him such pleasure, being with Randi. He remembers that night, ten years ago, when she hadn't seen the second cat. Leo, what a perfect name. He watches her smile slightly at a thought she has. He watches the comb glide through her long, wet hair. Imagine all of us, including the cat, having the same name.

Sleeping Beauty

1

Larry watches the blood in the thin plastic tube that tapers into the boot of the metal needle that cuts into his wife's forearm. He then checks the plastic bag that hangs from the aluminum rack beside the bed to see if the level has gone down any. If the space on top has grown, the part he can see light through, time has passed. He rubs the stiffness out of the back of his neck. He has just woken up, and in this last period of sleep his head had drifted over the cool back of the aluminum chair until it rested against the wall.

Four days ago, when she came out of surgery and he first saw her, he thought the blood in the tube wasn't moving. He knows gravity will impel its downward motion, but he also knows it can't flow unless her body allows it to enter. One of the nurses told him it looks that way because it never changes color. But it moves, she told him, slowly, like the hands of a clock. That's when he stopped trying to discern the blood's passage from the elevated plastic bag to Marlene's motionless body, and started measuring the empty space on top.

There are also tubes running into her leg and through the bandage that enwraps her midsection. An electrode plate, attached to two thin wires, is taped to her chest. Her entire body, where she is not covered with the bedsheet, or the bandage, is

black and blue. When he first saw her, he was sure she was
already dead. Since the blood wasn't moving, he couldn't believe
the electronic life signs were messages sent from within Marlene's body; he thought they were manufactured by the
machines.

He has since come to believe she is alive but not, yet, fully.
It's as if four days ago, when she had the accident, she went
somewhere else, and since then only a small part of her has come
back: the part that can cause the lights to throb and the hands
of the dials to move back and forth.

Larry has gone home only twice in the last four days. Not to
sleep—he's been sleeping in the chair in the hospital room. He's
gone home to change, and then gone to see the children, who
are staying with Ruby, Marlene's mother.

Ruby has come every day but has only stayed briefly. She's so
angry at Larry, and he at her, that she's too uncomfortable to
stay very long. Larry gets uncomfortable as well, but he won't
budge. They haven't spoken since the day after the accident,
when she told him she'd given permission for the local newspaper to use the picture of Marlene from their high school
yearbook.

2

Marlene and Larry began dating twenty years ago, less than
a month after he got out of the service. They were soon spending
all their free time together, and within a year they were married.
Neither Ruby nor any of Marlene's friends could understand it.
And none of them made any secret of this. Ruby said Marlene
was twice as good-looking as Larry. Marlene had a high school
diploma and had just finished the courses for her certificate in
dental hygiene. All Larry had was an honorable discharge. He
had just begun working as a projectionist in the Florence
Theater.

Before that, they'd hardly known each other. That was also
part of everyone's surprise. He'd always been in the slower classes

and, out of school, kept mostly to himself. The only times they were in the same classroom were when Marlene's class was seeing a film. Larry would set up the screen and operate the projector. He was already good at that.

Marlene was petite and wore her thick brown hair short and cut straight at the sides. She was articulate and pretty. During her high school years, everyone who knew her envied the life they were certain she would have.

Larry was tall and slouched into himself when he stood still. And there was this odd change in his voice. When he came back from Vietnam, he spoke with a Southern accent, like someone from Georgia or Alabama. He was the only one in Florence, New Hampshire, to speak that way. He'd lost a lot of hair in the two years he was in the army, and in their wedding portrait he looks ten years older than Marlene.

They didn't have a child until the fourth year of their marriage. When Ruby pressed her on this, Marlene told her she was still too young and that she liked it being just the two of them. Women wait these days, she told her mother. Where have you been? Then, after the first—Asa, named for Marlene's father, who died when she was in the fifth grade—she had the other two, Darla and Melanie, barely more than a year apart. This week—the week of Marlene's accident—falls in the one month of the year when their ages follow one after the other: twelve, thirteen, fourteen—Melanie, Darla, Asa—like three steps on a flight of stairs as long as their marriage.

After the births of her three children, Marlene never got her looks back. She'd gotten heavier. Her eyes grew tired, and softer, and sometimes gave the impression that she was farther away than she actually was from the person she was looking at.

Ruby had told everyone that Marlene had done this—let herself go—on purpose. She knew what she was doing. She wanted to equalize their value in the economy of beauty. Ruby never forgave Larry for this.

3

No one knows how Marlene could have fallen from the cat-walk that encircles the upper level of the Florence Lumber yard. The railings that surround the walkway are three feet high. One of the men on the floor below caught a glimpse of her just before she landed on the ten-inch platform saw. He said her body, as she was falling, was stretched out, almost relaxed, as if she were lying on a mattress.

Ruby works as a shipping clerk in the yard. Marlene had come to meet her for lunch, as she often does, and afterwards had walked her back to her desk. The shipping office, like the other offices, opens out onto the catwalk. Often, while waiting for Ruby, or after they'd had lunch, Marlene would lean against the railing and watch the sawyers below cut the rough lumber into boards, stack them onto pallets, then wrap the heavy neat piles in tight bands of aluminum.

The elevated, insular walkways always reminded Marlene of a prison cell block. She had never been in a real prison but had built a strong, clear image of one from the memory of two different movies, one starring Sissy Spacek, the other starring Robert Redford. She doesn't remember their titles—she never remembers the titles of movies—but she imagines they were filmed in the same prison because the concrete catwalks and the metal railings were the same. They are also the same as the ones in the Florence Lumber yard.

What Marlene likes most about movies is how they grow to be a part of her after she's watched them. Sometimes, when she sees them again years later, she is disappointed to find how different they are, or have become, from the movie she remembers. There is always more silence, and the people seem less connected to each other. In her memory, the characters understand each other's inner thoughts with an easy fluency, and they keep talking during all the times the audience can't hear or see them.

Each year on midsummer night, the Florence Drive-in would have a dusk-till-dawn special. For the same price they'd run as

many movies as they could before the sun came up. The year
before her father died, he and Ruby brought Marlene along, and
all the movies they showed that night were about people running for their lives. Dean Martin and Jerry Lewis were running
from gangsters, so Jerry Lewis, who looked really young anyway,
got dressed up like a teenager. Dean Martin pretended he was a
teacher, and they both hid out in a school. Tony Curtis had
escaped from prison with Sidney Poitier. No place they hid was
safe for long, so they had to keep moving. Their arms were
shackled together, which made it hard to run, and besides that,
they didn't like each other, so they decided to go their separate
ways when they got a chance to cut the chains. However, when
they finally did, near the end of the movie, they stayed together.
Then Tony Curtis and Jack Lemmon were musicians who had
to get out of town because some gangsters wanted to kill them.
They got dressed up like women and joined an all-women band
that had Marilyn Monroe in it, too. She played the ukulele. No
one knew who they were, though everyone in the audience
could tell they were men.

Once, at lunch, Marlene asked her mother if she remembered
that summer night. She wanted to tell her about how the films
keep changing and getting all mixed up together. She sometimes
remembers Sidney Poitier running down a hillside, shackled to
Jerry Lewis. They are both frightened because men and dogs are
chasing them, and Jerry Lewis keeps crying in fear. At first Sidney Poitier gets angry with him because the noises he makes are
so silly, but then he becomes tender, like a father, and tells him
not to worry, they will get safely away and then everything will
be all right.

"Films never remain the same," she told Ruby.

"I forget them, if that's what you mean. The only one I remember from that summer is *Some Like It Hot*. That's the one
with Marilyn Monroe. And you know why, don't you?"

Marlene shook her head.

"Because Marilyn and Marlene are really the same name."

"But what I mean is the stories keep changing. The stories don't hold still."

"Of course," her mother said. "That's why they call them moving pictures."

4

Papers from Boston and New York have already called the hospital, and Larry is imagining the newspaper accounts as the knowledge of his wife's accident is carried farther and farther away from them, out into a world where no one knows who they are.

He and Marlene had once seen a documentary on TV about how humans have changed over the years. We used to have longer arms, the narrator had said, and our memories have been getting worse and worse since the invention of the written word. These changes took a very long time. But somehow—maybe just in the years since Larry was a teenager—people have changed in another way. They no longer have any way of understanding the things that happen at a distance, to absolute strangers, other than to imagine seeing them lit up on a screen. This scares him. No matter how many times he's seen them, the people Larry sees in the films he shows every day are as unlike him as trees are unlike him, as cars are unlike him.

A reporter from Texas has left three messages on their answering machine at home. He wants permission to reprint the picture Ruby had given to the Florence *Courier*, which has already used it two days running. It's the one from their high school yearbook. Ruby cannot understand why this has made Larry so angry.

Didn't he agree, she asked him, that she had protected Marlene by refusing to give them a more recent photo? Larry has not said a word to her since. The Texas reporter said they've already got permission to use some of the other photos the local paper has run: the one of the surgeon who'd flown in from Min-

nesota, and the one of the platform saw, already back in operation at the lumber mill.

They will hold his wife captive in their vocabulary, use the
same words as the tabloid headlines that hover in front of you
while you're waiting on the checkout line at the supermarket:

WOMAN SAWED IN HALF
IS SEWN TOGETHER BY DOCTORS

He imagines a line of strangers staring through these words
as if through a window, into their lives, into this hospital room.
But he can't imagine what they'll think, reading such a thing
and looking at the picture of his beautiful wife when she was
seventeen years old.

Everyone in Florence is wondering how it happened. Larry
doesn't care *how* it happened. What people should realize at
times like this is that we don't know how most things happen.
What he's doing is waiting.

Ruby told him that Marlene probably fainted. She'd done it
at least a half-dozen times when she was growing up. And she
didn't care where, either. In the car, at school, it didn't matter.
Once she just swooned and slipped off a stool at the Florence
Diner. The woman working the counter said she never made a
sound.

Marlene had just walked her back to her office after lunch,
then stood outside, leaning against the railing, looking down
onto the work floor. Ruby's desk faces the side wall, not the
window, so she only saw her out of the corner of her eye. It was
the sudden movement that caught her attention. She said it was
as if the top half of her daughter's body had suddenly become
heavier than the bottom half. The weight just lifted her feet off
the walkway and she toppled over. Fainting is the only possible
explanation, Ruby said.

She was in surgery sixteen hours. Everyone said it was a miracle that she hadn't died instantly and that her spinal cord had
not been severed. They put pins into her bones, they reunited

the walls and inner tissues of damaged organs. With microsur-
gery they reconnected arteries and veins.

For Larry, it's not a time to understand anything as being a
miracle. They are in this moment, *in* their lives, and this is what
has happened. It's not a time to understand things; it's a time
to wait.

5

Marlene says hello to Larry. She's awake.

He's been standing beside the bed since her eyes opened ten
minutes ago. Her eyes were dark and completely still until this
moment, when she focused on him.

Larry's in tears and cannot, yet, go any nearer to her. Ruby
and the doctor are standing beside him.

"I had a dream," Marlene says to Larry. She then falls silent.
A moment passes.

Then she notices Ruby and says, "We're having lunch today."

The doctor leans over Marlene. For a moment she glances
toward him, but she does not see him. Larry, slowly, pushes him
aside.

He then kneels beside the bed and takes her hand in both of
his. She seems unaware of anything else in the moment but this.

"What did you dream?" Larry asks her.

"My body is getting older," she says.

"Whose isn't?" Ruby says softly, then smiles.

"No. In the dream my body is getting older. That's how it
talks to me. The wrinkles . . . it gets heavier . . . other things.
And it's getting tired. I didn't understand at first."

The doctor begins to approach Marlene, and again Larry motions for him to stop.

"I was afraid to understand," she says. "It all meant the opposite of what I thought it meant. My body told me that getting
older, it was really getting younger. More like a child each day.
And *I* would have to grow up again. I'd have to start taking
care of it, more and more. It would be like Asa and the girls,

and that scared me. . . ." Her fingers move slightly in Larry's hand. "Because it will never grow up. Only get younger and younger . . ."

She takes in a short breath, falls silent for a second, and looks back at her husband.

"Larry," she then says. She slowly draws in another small breath. "Larry, I've been so afraid."

News

"He had just made up his mind," the Assistant D.A. said.
"He wasn't going to be arrested for murder."
New York Times

Now I say that the peace the spirit needs is peace,
not lack of war, but fierce continual flame.
Muriel Rukeyser

Ronald, her son, had been watching the man sleeping at the other end of the bench until finally, sinking into the space against her and beneath her arm, he, too, fell asleep.

When they first sat down, Ronald didn't speak or point at him, he just watched, and she followed the beam of his vision as if it was a line somebody had drawn through the air. At first his focus tightened, pushed back the passing traffic, the buildings and sky, and found the sleeping head at the far end of the bench. He then slowly gathered in the unshaven cheek that filled slightly each time the man exhaled, the three ballpoint pens, bound together by a rubber band, in his shirt pocket, the stiff, grimy pants bottoms, the legs scissoring the armrest, reaching into the middle section of the bench. She watched him discover the six little half-and-half containers, the kind you get in coffee shops, at the seat-back behind his feet, one empty, five still unopened.

Throughout, Ronald said nothing. He's four years old, and she knows when he comprehends what he sees.

It's getting chilly, and his head has fallen deep inside the fur-lined hood of his green winter coat. It looks just like her brother Charles's flight jacket, only smaller. Last year, when Charles first gave it to him, it was much too large. Since then, he's nearly grown into it.

A bus stops in front of them. No one gets on or off. She and
Ronald do not stir, and the bus moves on.

All she knew about what was happening, she knew from the
gunshots. When the police started firing, she was already too far
away to see anything, but she knows the sound. Everyone does.
Harder and rounder than firecrackers, and in a rhythm like people talking to each other: speaking, listening, speaking again.
She knew they were firing in the hall outside the door to her
apartment because Charles was in it. And when she heard the
louder shots, she knew they were firing from outside at her living
room window. This bench was the first place where she could
stop beyond hearing distance, and the farthest point she would
let herself reach. When it gets darker and cold, she'll have to
go back there. She's afraid of what she may see, and she's afraid
she may never find out what actually happened inside that storm
of noise, which is what usually happens when it's this far away
and it's not happening to anyone you know.
She knew, there were four policemen standing just inside
the building. They watched her come through the door into the
entryway, holding Ronald's hand, then pass through and out
onto the street. Instead of looking back at them, she set her eyes
on the spot they'd all held their eyes on until they raised them
to look at her. It was the tip of a finger, at the end of a blue-
uniformed arm, repeatedly pressing one of the downstairs bells.
It was her bell, and they'd all fixed on it as if their convergent
stare would force whoever was hearing it, inside an apartment
upstairs, to buzz them in. She acknowledged them only briefly,
as she was swinging her eyes forward again, like they were just
any four people coming into the building and she just happened
to be passing them on her way out. On the stoop, a policewoman
spoke into a walkie-talkie, then held it close against her ear,
and while she listened to whatever was being said back to her,
she smiled at Ronald.
There was a line of double-parked squad cars with their lights

spinning. She picked up Ronald so she could walk faster. She looked straight ahead. On her left, the gray-brown fronts of the buildings slid by. From her right, the lights sliced her with their red and white blades.

Then the shots started, and more sirens at a distance. Suddenly there was a tide of people pushing past her to get down the street and see what was happening. She kept walking until she couldn't hear the shots anymore. No one on the last two blocks she'd walked on seemed aware that anything was going on.

It was less than an hour ago that Charles came over, but it feels like much further away in time. It makes the other things she was doing earlier today seem longer ago, too. She was drying Ronald after his bath when Charles walked in. He was wearing the blue Pepsi-Cola jacket he'd had on the last time she saw him. That was on Columbus Day, and they had watched the parade on TV. Ronald laughed at the Superman float, and Charles told him he'd better not laugh, because Superman was real. Ronald said he was just a balloon, and Charles was surprised that Ronald knew to say that. So he said, Yeah, he's a balloon, but he's a *real* balloon, and Ronald laughed again. It's been almost two months since then. There must have been times he was cold, just wearing that Pepsi-Cola jacket.

The first thing Charles did when he came in was to set his bag of Chinese takeout on the coffee table and look out the living room window. Then he walked into the other room, her bedroom, where there are two heavy cardboard boxes, filled with his things, on the floor in the closet. He'd left them there last spring when he lost his apartment downtown. He's never said where he's been living since. When he came back into the living room he was carrying his flight jacket over his arm.

He asked her if she'd been watching the news and if they said anything about some crack dealers getting killed in an apartment over on Willis Avenue. She hadn't heard anything. He told her he hadn't heard anything about it, either. But it was something the police had cooked up so they'd have an excuse to go around asking questions about him.

Why would they think such a thing? she asked him.

He told her he didn't know. Not for sure. With cops you can never tell; they're always coming up with all kinds of strange shit.

He sat down on the couch then and started eating his chicken in garlic sauce and fried rice. He kept giving mouthfuls to Ronald, who loved the chopsticks and how good Charles was at using them. That was one of the things he'd learned in the service. That, and electronics. But since he's been back, he's mostly worked at other kinds of jobs.

These things feel like they happened a long time ago, in a different, earlier part of her life. It's as if an hour ago is when she was only a teenager, and Charles was as small and young as Ronald is now.

The last year or so, he's been around less and less, and she isn't sure what he's been doing for a living. Even before that, he rarely talked about his jobs. One day last summer, he brought them a bonsai tree in a green bowl with small pebbles covering the soil. Ronald loves it. He calls it the mouse tree. Sometimes Charles would leave them some money, and those were the times she knew he was doing all right.

When he got up again to look out the window, he let Ronald use the chopsticks by himself. He dug them into the fried rice, one in each hand, spilling it onto the coffee table. Charles sat back down on the couch and smiled at him. She told Charles he'd better clean that up when they were done.

Charles kept smiling at Ronald and then at her, and then he said, right out of nowhere, Where would you ever find another brother like *this* brother? and he pointed at himself.

And she smiled at him and said that and a broken leg would be *all* she needed.

Then Charles told her she was going out for a while. Just like that. *She* and Ronald.

He didn't ask her, he just said it. Go to Tisha's, he told her. He asked if she still lived down the block, or had she gotten married again and moved someplace else?

She was about to ask him if he'd gone crazy, but then she looked at him. He was still smiling, but the smile no longer had any reason for being there. His mouth just hung that way, as if he'd left it there—the smile—and then backed away from it.

He knew Tisha had moved to New Jersey over a year ago. She remembered telling him. Her tongue was dry, and she tasted her lipstick for the first time since she put it on that morning. She never tastes her lipstick once it's on. That's when she went into the bedroom and came out with Ronald's coat and her own. When she left, Charles was looking out the window again.

Charles would always seem changed when he arrived on one of his visits. Sometimes he'd put on airs, like some kind of uniform, and it took a while to find him inside it all. It was like seeing the shadows of what he'd been doing, and who he'd been doing it with. She once asked him if he acted different so she'd be busy watching him, trying to figure out *what* he was up to, rather than just ask him about it. He told her that no one, in all the places he's been to, ever said to him the kinds of things she did. No one.

What she did know was that the older he got, the more his outside self could spin freely from his inside self. Each time it took her longer, more watching, to find the Charles she knew. There were times he came back really changed. Like when he came out of the service, and like this last time. Something had really changed this time, and she knew it.

She herself never seems different. Whenever Charles shows up, he finds her unchanged. No one she knows ever registers a look of surprise, or even curiosity, when they see her after not seeing her for a while. That's what she does for people: remains the same, and no one expects otherwise.

The only changes she does undergo are in accordance with

the changes that occur in the people around her. Her mother, Ronald, Charles. One store closes, another opens, so she'll walk a different route to buy groceries, pass different mailboxes, different storefronts with different people hanging out in front. Changes happen *to* her. People notice that winter is coming, but not that she's started wearing her coat again.

She could have been different. She is certain of that. Not act different, which is what Charles usually does, but *be* different. And *not* like these calm, happy mothers on diaper commercials, or the ladies in office clothes who get on the bus every morning. That's just living your life for the moments other people see you doing it. She could have been a *better* different.

She watches an old family-size Pontiac, riding low on its shocks, roll to a stop across the street. Its white paint is dust-shadowed to a cold, soft gray. The trunk is tied down over a load of cardboard boxes. The man driving it gets out, unties the sisal cord, lets the trunk hood rise up, and begins to unload the boxes, one at a time, and carry them into a storefront across the street. She watches him walk in and out of the doorway. With her eyes, she traces the arc of faded Hebrew letters that crosses the store's window until it's eclipsed, at its midpoint, where one of the wide panes has been replaced by a sheet of plywood.

Time has passed. The late afternoon smells like dead leaves, cold brick dust, and smoke. Ronald lets out a small, breathy cry in his sleep.

This is her life? The thought, its suddenness, startles her.

Not a new thought, one she's had before, but it strikes like something new. Like something that suddenly leaps from the roots of a tree up into its branches.

This life out here, this life around her, is her life?

This collection of people and things and noises and smells always closing around her like a fist?

This half-living, half-dead thing on the other end of the bench—*he* has something to do with it. And this sad fool, driving around in his sorry-ass car, lugging all his cardboard boxes like he's on some kind of mission—he has something to do with it, too. Not that they bought tickets to get into this afternoon along with her; they're just passing through, each in his own drift between one moment and the next. But they're here, and whatever else they're doing, they're in on it.

Maybe that's what those old Hebrew letters are telling her: Look around. *This* is it.

"Charles." She speaks her brother's name before she thinks it.

Every day some crack dealer gets his ass shot off. It's like the weather report, it's like the bus going by, it's like wallpaper, it's like leaves. Why did he want to know if *she* heard anything about it? Would it matter if she did? Damn him.

Another bus passes. The man across the street comes out to his car and swings another box onto his shoulder. When its weight settles, he lets out a long steamy breath.

There was something she used to say to herself, never knowing exactly what it meant. She first heard it over twenty years ago, in a sermon given by a radio preacher on the stage of the RKO movie theater. She and Charles and her mother were there. Just sitting in the old velvet seats gave her the same happy, expectant feeling she'd get waiting for a movie to start. But once the sermon began, she got bored. She couldn't understand a thing the man was saying. She understood the words, but not the thoughts he was building out of them. Charles was much too young to understand even that much, and he fell asleep. She just sat there, bored and annoyed, as a wind filled with words passed by overhead. Then she heard him say, *Your life is just one of the things your soul could have dreamed of.* Just *one* of the things. She used to say it over and over to herself like a jump-rope song. She knew if she said it enough times, she'd come to understand what it meant.

———

Earlier, when she and Ronald were waiting for the elevator, she thought about the time Charles fell off the kitchen chair, hit his arm against the radiator, and broke it. He was four years old. He had been standing on the chair, reaching across the table toward a pair of scissors, when their mother walked into the room. When she saw him, she gasped. Then, to stop him, she called his name. *Charles.* He turned toward her, frightened, and then fell. Things happen so easily, and when they want to. You can't stop them.

She remembers her mother sitting on the kitchen floor along with Charles and the both of them crying. Then she started, too.

That was a long time ago, all three of them on the kitchen floor. Charles has always been her younger brother, but he hasn't seemed younger for a long time.

When they left the apartment before, and got into the elevator, she lifted Ronald up so he could look at the round sticker advertisement on the wall over the floor buttons. *Gallo's Car Service.* It has Roadrunner on it, and Ronald likes to look at it because he remembers him from TV.

What does he say? she asked him.

Meep-meep, Ronald said.

He touched it with his finger and laughed. Roadrunner was racing along a road that spiraled up a mountain. He had climbed halfway, leaving loops of pink dust in his wake.

Wile E. Coyote was nowhere in sight, but you can only see what's on this side of the mountain. He could be on the other side. He could be waiting there, for Roadrunner, and nobody on *this* side would even know about it.

Ronald ran his fingertip across Roadrunner's tail, his long neck, his face. He kept his finger there but leaned away from her so he could turn and look directly at her. He looked at her mouth and then at her eyes. She mimicked him, looking back at Ronald's mouth and eyes. She then smiled, and he returned his attention to the sticker.

Something bad had happened that hadn't finished happening,

and whatever it was, Charles had to be alone with it in her apartment.

Meep-meep, Ronald said again, and lifted his finger so he could see Roadrunner's whole face. He was smiling at him.

In this last minute before she wakes Ronald, she traces, in advance, the route they'll walk back on. Each block leading to the one their building is in the middle of, the entryway, the hall, the elevator. It's dark now. Enough time has passed for it all to have changed back again. This late in the afternoon, they could cover the entire distance, right up to the door of the apartment, and not pass another soul.

Now, seeing herself back there, she remembers a moment that all the events and motion had crowded out of her mind. She had just heard the elevator door roll shut behind them, and when she took Ronald's hand, he tried to pull it free. This was the last moment before she knew what was about to happen. She was thinking that Ronald has been doing this, wanting to walk on his own, more and more. He's begun to be hungry for the world, and has grown to the age when you first know that to move freely in it is for it to be yours.

She then saw, on the other side of the Plexiglas door, the policemen crowded into the entryway they were about to walk through. The elevator banged hard against the wall of the shaft as it began its ascent, and one of them, his hand above his eyes, looked into the dark hall. She tightened her grip around Ronald's hand and pumped a wave of herself through it, which must have filled his small body with her fear. She would not let his hand breathe this air, and if it were possible, she would keep it there, inside hers, until so much time had passed that the life that has begun to gather around him, that he's so hungry to meet on its way toward him, *her* life, would be something so far removed, so immeasurably distant, he could never remember he'd even begun to live it, not even in his dreams.

One Week

Wednesday, May 29—Tuesday, June 4, 1968

Wednesday

Joe Lazaro's sitting on his front stoop. His left sneaker, gym bag, and loose-leaf notebook are on the step next to him. He pulls a thick yellow-white sweat sock off his foot, gyrates the foot slowly, and examines the reddish, slightly swollen ankle. A 707, beginning its descent into Kennedy Airport, thunders overhead. He's humming "Shake Me, Wake Me," by the Four Tops, and as the jet's roar lessens, he begins to hear his voice from the outside again, not just from inside his head.

He's been working out all afternoon in the high school gym, practicing the same tumbling pass over and over: round-off—back handspring—piked back somersault—landing in a straight split. It's the opening of his floor exercise routine, and he hasn't thrown it right all season. He can clear five feet in a back sommy anytime, when he's landing on his feet. But when he's landing in the split, something in his body, probably in his balls, doesn't want him returning to earth from all that altitude. So he keeps throwing low, causing his left foot to take the fall before the slide into the split. The ankle's swollen, but not too badly. Next Tuesday's meet against Jamaica High School is the last of the season, and he wants to throw it right. Tonight he'll soak the foot. Between now and the meet he'll have to get through three days of work and, since this is Memorial Day weekend, four of

34

school. That's the distance in time. In terms of space, he esti-
mates thirty miles of bike riding and twenty more of walking.

What matters is that his ankle holds out through the rest of
his routine, the eighty seconds that follow his opening pass. On
Tuesday, before the meet, he'll wrap it tightly in surgical tape.
Unless he really hammers it into the floor, it should hold.

His father walks out the front door, down the stoop past Joe,
and over to his truck, parked in the driveway. He reaches into
the driver's window, lifts a pack of Pall Malls off the dashboard,
and walks back into the house without saying a word.

His father's name is Vincent, but he is known to everyone as
Jimmy. The name of his employer, Elgan Decorating Company,
is painted in red script along the side of the truck. He hangs
buntings and strings of pennants for supermarkets, car dealers,
restaurants. He hangs black-and-purple mourning drapes on police stations and firehouses and government buildings when
someone important dies. When Sixth Avenue became Avenue
of the Americas, Jimmy was one of the guys who hung up the
disks on the overreaching arms of the lampposts with the names
of all the American countries on them.

For as long as Joe can remember, his father has had an upside-
down triangle of darker, reddish skin, which begins at his
second-to-top shirt button, spreads along the opening collar, and
ends at the base of his neck. It was always there, as Jimmy, his
father, was there. As a child, he thought of it as something all
grown men had, something he, himself, would later have, like
pubic hair or a deeper voice. It wasn't until he was twelve that
he realized it was simply from working out of doors.

An oil truck eases down the block and double-parks in front
of the Healys' house across the street. Four of the Healy sisters
are sitting on the stoop. They seem completely unaware of the
truck being there, of the steady metallic growl of the idling engine. Nor do they notice the man climbing out of the cab, un-
reeling the oil hose, setting the small *Watch Your Step* sign over
it where it crosses the sidewalk, and dragging it into the alley
beside their house.

The four of them aren't doing a thing. Not even talking, just staring out into the space in front of them. They don't need a real object to mark the far end of their vision's reach. To Joe, it appears to stop a yard or two in front of them. If he were wearing only his jockstrap, or if he stood up and waved his arms, they wouldn't notice. They'd adjusted their eyes like lenses, set them to span the distance between a couch and a TV and no further. Their only activity is lighting cigarettes. Every so often, one of the younger ones takes a drag from a cigarette held by one of the two who are over fifteen. All four of them can snap their jaws and launch dense, clear-edged smoke rings.

The Healys are a mystery. The whole family. Mother, father, six sisters, and two brothers. Every room of their house smells of rotting milk, laundry, and cat shit, and none of them seems to notice. The only one you can actually talk to is Richie, but he's not around anymore. As soon as he turned seventeen he quit school and joined the army. He did it to get out of that nuthouse. He's so happy to be out of there that last Christmas he sent a card to every family on the block. He's an MP in Saigon.

The oilman pulls a lever that shuts the spigot on the back of his truck. Then slowly reels in the hose, picks up his sign, closes the rear door, and climbs back into the cab. The Healy sisters frighten Joe. He's afraid they might be most people. And if that's the case, most people never think about things like how oil gets there. For most people there is no history to the heat in their living room. Nobody pumps the oil into the tanks in their basements, nobody drills for it, nobody refines it.

That goes for everything around them, too. It's all just there. A world without origin. People driving into the A & P parking lot would look up at the pennants his father had put up the day before, point at them, and say to their children, Look, aren't those pretty, and never give a thought to the fact that between the last time they were here and now, someone climbed up the lampposts and telephone poles and reeled out these strings of bright colors between them and the sky over their heads. Who paved the streets they just drove on? Who put up the light they stopped at on the corner? If not for the pennants, they might not have otherwise looked up.

Joe's got a copy of the original plans for the Brooklyn Bridge on the wall of his room. How *it* got there is all he thinks about. All day people drive both ways across it, staring at the world through a beautiful dense web of suspension cables, unaware that the man who designed them died while seeing to it that they got there. And without them to absorb stress and sway, the first piddly-shit little wind to come along would dump two hundred cars and trucks into the East River. *Let them drown.* It took nearly fifteen years to build. A third of a mile from end to end. *Mile* being, if anybody gave a shit, from the Latin *mil* for a thousand, measuring a thousand steps. And *feet*, 1,595 of them. People don't even think about that word, even when they trip over their own. If you see the bridge's construction in terms of distance covered, not just time, that's barely more than one hundred feet a year. All that work so people can pass from Brooklyn to Manhattan in less than a minute. Like there never was a river between them.

Joe leans back and stares up into the leaves of the thick Norway maples, already teased out to full size by a week of pre-summer heat. He hasn't stopped humming.

He can smell the faint oil smell and the cloud of diesel exhaust left behind by the truck. The air that he and the Healy sisters are breathing is filled with dinosaur molecules.

Joe's sister, Jeanette, appears just behind the screen door. "What do ya need," she asks, "an engraved invitation?"

"What?" Joe turns. He sees only her shape, molded into shadow, and the pale fingertips of both hands, pressed outward against the screen.

"Dinner's on the table. You didn't hear me call you?"

"I didn't hear shit."

"That's cause you're sittin out here hummin your ass off. You forget the words?" She shakes her hips like a hula. *"Wake me-ee, shake me-ee, when it's over-er . . ."*

Joe hurls his sneaker against the screen. Jeanette slips further back into the house.

He picks up the sneaker and, as he's about to put it on, notices the words *Made in Hong Kong* stamped on the white canvas inside. He's had them six months but never noticed till now. He looks the sneaker over, top and bottom. He examines the stitching and lace grommets, tongue and sole, and then decides they held up pretty good anyway.

Saturday

Joe's sitting in the window of D'Aurio's Meat Market, waiting for the heavyweight Schwinn, chained out front, to fall over. Anyone passing would simply see an old bike, propped carelessly against a parking meter, but that's just what they're seeing, not what is there. This careful arrangement of objects, one fixed, one movable, is actually an experiment in the environmental aspects of structural engineering. The passing el trains will have the same effect on the bike, leaning without the support of the kickstand, as an earthquake, registering tremors of only one or two on the Richter scale, would have on the Brooklyn Bridge if its span were supported solely by fixed structures rather than hung from suspension cables. Three Jamaica-bound trains have rumbled past since Joe came back from his last order. He figures the one after the next will do the trick.

Saturdays are usually busy, but when the weather gets warmer, people buy less meat, and when they buy less at D'Aurio's, Joe has less to deliver. Sal's in the box, cutting a leg off a side of lamb for his own Sunday dinner.

The inside of the window is decorated with little plastic cows, pigs, and sheep, knee-deep in a field of green cellophane paper shredded like coleslaw. Along the top, salami and prosciutto wrappers, stuffed with paper, hang from an aluminum meat rack. The reflections of the passing cars remain on the window for a fraction of a second after they pass from sight. Then they peel off the glass and slide past the faces of the soldiers, brides and grooms, high school graduates, and babies in the window of Mati's Photography Studio next door.

For the last two years, Joe has spent all his Thursday and Friday afternoons, as well as his Saturdays, delivering meat, scraping the blocks, emptying fat and bone buckets, endlessly wiping down the stainless-steel counters, and sweeping the saw-dust, which is his favorite job because it's always the last. Before the month is out, he'll be a high school graduate. He starts

Queensborough Community College in the fall. He's outgrown riding bicycles and sweeping floors for a living.

Sal comes out of the box, and Joe heads for the back, in case Sal thinks up something for him to do, like washing his car or sweeping the sidewalk. But Sal, holding the leg of lamb like a baseball bat, heads him off.

"*Ti piace a-ves?*"

Joe stops and turns toward the front door.

Sal whispers it again. "*Ti piace a-ves?*" *Do you like cunt?* Sal's way of announcing that a woman who rates being looked at is about to walk into the store.

He turns back to Sal. It's Mrs. Catalano, a seventy-year-old widow who Sal is sure has the hots for him, because she dyes her hair, wears lipstick, and comes in at least three times a week.

"False alarm." Sal drops the leg of lamb onto the block and starts laughing. Joe laughs, too.

Sal teases Mrs. Catalano whenever she comes in. And his being fifty-nine, which, from where Joe sits, is nearly seventy, puts a vengeance in his teasing. She never seems to notice or, at least, never lets on if she does.

She walks up to the counter, and they're still laughing.

"You boys . . ." She waves her bare arm. "You always laughin."

They laugh harder. Sal doubles over.

"C'mon. What's so funny. You tell me, too. . . . Hah? . . . Joe? . . . Be a little respec . . ."

"It's nothin, Mrs. Catalano."

He begins to feel embarrassed. Sal keeps laughing.

"What can we do for you?" Joe asks.

"Just two sausage, an half the poun 'merica cheese."

Joe slices the cheese while Sal cuts and weighs the sausage. When she takes the bag from Sal, he starts to laugh again. Joe stares out the front window, trying not to.

"You boys . . ." She spins her finger beside her temple. "Maybe you drink while you workin. Maybe that's why you always laugh."

"If she looked as good as she thought she did," Sal tells Joe after she leaves, "she'd be a ravin beauty."

Joe asks Sal if he could start cleaning up early, since it's slow. But Sal tells him if he had intended to close up at four, he would have put four on the door.

"An besides, when it's slow is when you have ta stay open. You gotta get every dime in the register you can. Joseph, there's a lot you have yet ta learn about business."

Sal calls him Joseph in the moments when he sees their relationship as master and apprentice, rather than boss and part-time employee. When Sal wants to feel more mainstream American, or more normal, something most people in the neighborhood comprehend as the same thing, he'll use words and phrases from the vocabulary he gained from TV: *slacks, can do, the very essence, cook to a turn.* Joe wants to ask him where this sudden business sense came from but holds back, not wanting to hear the whole story, starting with Salvatore D'Aurio, Sr., *Che è nato a Palermo,* who opened the shop in 1917. He has come to understand that Sal, like many of the men Joe knows his age, has developed the ability to find reasons, when asked, for doing the things he has always done, for no reason other than habit. Besides, he's the boss. At least until the end of the month.

The phone rings and Joe answers it. It's one of Sal's girlfriends. At the moment he has three. Joe knows all their voices over the phone but has never met any of them. None of them live in the neighborhood, and they're not allowed to come to the shop. Sal calls this *not shitting where you eat.*

It's Marie, who, according to Sal, is thirty and a real piece. She's just had some kind of operation, and they can't sleep together for at least six weeks. Marie is the youngest of Sal's girlfriends, and Joe's more curious about her than about the others. What could she possibly find in a fifty-nine-year-old butcher who's married and wears a hernia belt?

When Sal takes the phone, he puts his hand over the receiver and tells Joe to go into the back and pick up the extension.

"I want you ta learn how one is supposed ta talk to a woman."

"No, thanks. I already know."

"Go on. It's your chance ta learn somethin new."

It's a dumb thing to do, but his curiosity is aroused. In the back, Joe picks up the *Daily News* Sal left on the sausage table, where he has his coffee, opens it to the sports page, then gently lifts the receiver off the hook.

He can't see Sal. It's like listening to him over the radio.

"Hello, Marie?"

"Yeah, Sal?"

"Yeah. How are you?"

"Much better. The stitches are out."

"Good."

"I'd like to see you. Maybe tonight?"

"No can do. You remember what the doctor said . . . six weeks."

Joe watches a roach climb up the drab green wall that hasn't been painted since the days of Sal Sr. Once a month Sal lights a sulfur bomb, but you can never get them all. He tries to distract himself, to semi-listen, but he's too curious.

"Monday maybe?"

"The doctor said six weeks."

"But we don't have to do *that*. Sal . . . I just want to see you."

"Yeah, but you know what'll happen."

"No, Sal, I don't know what will happen."

"You'll give me a blow job or somethin . . ."

"*Sal* . . ."

"And then you'll get all hot . . ."

"Cut it out."

"And then you'll want me to put the tip in and I'll say, Okay, but just the tip, and you know if I put the tip in I *gotta* go all the way."

Joe knows Sal is showing off. But he's surprised to find out that he actually talks to his girlfriends the way he says he does.

"*Sal.* Just come over."

"Let's wait a few weeks. . . . Till you're better. Besides, I'll be real busy around here with people havin barbecues an all."

"You don't want to see me."

"I do. I swear."

Joe closes the *Daily News* and reads the headline. HELEN KELLER DIES. He'd heard it on his clock radio that morning. Next week it'll be a big thing at school. He'll probably have to do a paper on it. Maybe he can recycle his old book report on *The Miracle Worker*. He props the phone between his chin and shoulder. The first paragraph of the front-page article is in much bolder print than usual.

```
Helen Keller, who overcame blindness and deaf-
ness to become a symbol of the indomitable human
spirit, died in her Westport, Connecticut, home
at the age of 87.
```

Joe stops listening for a while and reads on. Then he starts listening again.

"Marie, I gotta go. I'll call you next week. Okay . . . ? Monday. Okay . . . ? Marie?"

"What?"

"Okay . . . ? Monday. Yeah?"

"Yeah, what?"

"Okay?"

"Yeah."

"Monday?"

"Yeah."

"Okay. Bye."

After reading his horoscope, Joe goes back out front and sits in the window. He unfastens the Ace bandage wrapped around his ankle, unwraps the first layer, pulls it as tight as he can, and reclasps it. Sal's in the box, and Joe's glad he's gloating in there rather than out here where Joe can see him.

Out front, a woman in a gray dress stops to let her dachshund lift its leg on the front wheel of the bicycle. He feels a slight tremor, hears the sound the train pushes ahead of itself. Suddenly a Brooklyn-bound train is dragging itself through the narrow strip of space between the sky and the elevated tracks. Joe looks up at the blur of rocking cars. He heard only one pass when he was in the back. This one's the one.

The bike splatters onto its side, but he can't hear it because of the rumbling overhead. The dog yelps without a sound. It's like watching a silent film through the window. The leash snaps tight, the woman tugs back. She repeatedly shouts something, perhaps the dog's name, that has two syllables—*Ya-hoo* or *Harold*—but the dog pulls her all the way to the curb, in scatter-legged, hoppity steps, pissing the whole way.

Sal comes out of the box and assumes the smile on Joe's face has something to do with the phone conversation. He gives him a proud nodding smile. Instead of opening conversation, Joe walks out front, unlocks the bike, and wheels it into the back. There are no more orders today.

When he comes back out front, he begins scraping the block. He wonders why she takes this kind of crap from him. What it is he has that she needs so badly. Why she ever slept with him in the first place. She can't *not* know how little he cares about her. Maybe she doesn't like him, either. Maybe he gives her money.

At the same time, there was something that left Joe in awe. The control. She knows what he wants from her because he tells her, directly: to fuck and then go home to his wife. Simple. That's all. And she gives him that. She almost needs to give him that.

Diane, who Joe's been seeing since October, never really seems to need anything from him, sexually or otherwise. Sometimes, when they're together, she pushes his hand away. Other times, she unzips his fly. The times they've gone all the way seemed great favors on her part. His desire for Diane is constant. He hasn't actually told her this, but she knows it.

Last Friday night, they drove up and down Liberty Avenue in her father's Biscayne, arguing over what movie to see. Diane's preference was *Elvira Madigan*, Joe wanted to see *One Million B.C.* Diane said it was a dumb film and that all he really wanted was to see Raquel Welch running around half naked and grunting like an animal. She had him there. But the rolling argument continued until it was too late to see either film.

So they went to the Pits, a parking lot near the carousel in Forest Park, where couples can pull over until midnight, when the cops drive around with their brights on and everybody goes home. That night she wouldn't even let him reach under her blouse, a bridge he had first crossed months ago.

When he got home he figured it probably had something to do with the movie. The next night they went to see *Elvira Madigan*. He couldn't follow the story. He hated all the slow motion and hadn't realized it ended until the credits began to roll down the screen. But he did not tell her this. Afterwards, they went to the Pits, but the same thing happened. Maybe she had her period. He never found out for sure.

It wasn't actually the control that surprised Joe into feeling something like envy, but the clarity. Sal knows exactly what is happening at all times because he decided he knows what Marie is all about, and she, by behaving in kind, proves him right. It's as if she could be no one else. Had she, a formed adult self, walked into the space that happened to correspond with what he needs her to be, or had she remade herself to fit his will? Sal knows her as someone who needs to have sex with him on a semi-regular basis. Someone who will want no more than that but will want it steadily. And she—in Joe's listening in on their life together, as if it were a dream he was having—rose to the terms of that identity and became that person: herself, a woman he knows only by the soft, tense voice he can still hear.

Joe finishes scraping the block and begins washing down the counter.

Sal asks him what he thought of the conversation. "You see, you can't give em too much," he says, "cause they'll take it. She's lucky I'm callin her on Monday. You can come by an listen in then, too, if you want."

"No, thanks." Joe's whole answer.

They don't speak again until Joe finishes sweeping the saw-dust and is piling up his tips to exchange them for bills.

"It's Saturday night," Sal says. "Gonna get your end wet?"

"Six even," Joe says. He slides six stacks of quarters, dimes, and nickels across the countertop and lines them up beside the cash register.

"Aren't ya goin out?" Sal asks.

"Nah."

"Joseph, it's Saturday night and you ain't goin out?" Sal sets a five and a single beside the change. "I don't believe it."

Joe takes off his apron, folds it, and sets it on the inside edge of the front window. "We're just gonna baby-sit, Diane and me. Her parents are goin out. She has a little sister."

"Aha, Joseph . . . The kid's asleep, no one else in the house. . . . Such opportunities don't arrive often. The perfect time for nooky."

"Leave it, Sal."

"What? Diane won't let you in?"

Joe doesn't answer. Sal laughs. Joe grabs the bills and heads out the door.

He doesn't like the sound of Diane's name when Sal pro-nounces it. He may want Joe to know all about *his* sex life, but what he and Diane do is none of his fucking business. Any influence he allows Sal to have over him begins and ends with working hours. After that, Joe goes back into his own life, a life that's miles away from Sal's, and will be light-years away long before he's half Sal's age.

He'll be a successful engineer. He'll have a home somewhere in the country, and an apartment in the city, overlooking the

Brooklyn Bridge. He won't smell like pork and tell other people to listen in while he makes an asshole out of himself over the phone. He'll have a family. And no kid of his will ever work in a fucking butcher shop. He's going to be miles from here. Miles and fucking centuries.

Although it's only six o'clock, and the sun is still high, it already feels like a Saturday night. Joe enjoys the feel of taking the first step onto the span of time that will reach all the way to Thursday, the next day on which he'll have to work. It's a clear, warm night. The first members of the group of guys, most of them younger than Joe, that assemble on weekend nights in front of Bill's Candy Store, across the avenue from D'Aurio's, have already shown up.

Their first business of the evening will be to organize enough money for a night's supply of beer. Then to find someone with proof of age, or in uniform, willing to buy it for them. After that they'll head up to Forest Park, take over the half-circle of benches that surround the World War I monument, an enormous bronze soldier in a soup-plate helmet, frozen in an uphill charge, carrying a long Springfield with fixed bayonet. Joe remembers a lot of late-spring and summer nights when he's done the same thing. A case of beer can transform a few park benches into a whole world. A place where dreams that drift toward the future encounter walls that cause them to bounce back into the moment, keeping it densely soaked with pleasure.

A train passes overhead. Joe looks up and watches the sparks shooting through the moving wash of its black undersides. After it passes, he sees the bars of clear sky between the ties.

He turns off the avenue and heads down the street. First thing after supper, he'll take a shower and wash off the fat and sawdust. Whenever he first enters a side street from Jamaica Avenue, he feels lighter. As if his own shoulders had been helping the thick, riveted steel columns support the elevated track, and hadn't even known it until being freed of the burden.

Joe is walking south. To the other people on the street, and the people living in the row houses that line it on both sides, he's walking away from the bus stop and the mailbox on the corner, away from the liquor store and the el tracks, or toward Mrs. Catalano's house, or the hydrant Mr. D'Rienzo's dog always pisses on, or the manhole cover that wobbles whenever a car drives over it but won't even budge if you jump on it, or the stoop where the Healy sisters are endlessly lighting cigarettes and listening to their portable radio. They could give a shit less that where they are exists in fixed relation to everywhere else. The four cardinal directions reach outward, from any given location, sending coordinating lines all the way to the stars.

The world quiets down and empties as he walks deeper into the maze of side streets. Most of the people who live on Joe's block are inside, eating. He can smell the various suppers from the houses he passes. By midblock the street is dead silent, not even a passing car. The only other person out-of-doors is Mrs. Rizzotti, who is standing in front of her stoop, in a clean white shift, washing the sidewalk with a hose.

Tuesday

The dozen or so members of the Richmond Hill High School gymnastics team are standing in two groups on the 114th Street el station. Joe, captain, floor exercise and tumbling; Ralphie Fitzgerald, tumbling and side horse; Tony Pugliese, high bar and rope climb; Eddie Dietz, high bar and long-horse vaulting; Artie Lucarelli, high bar and parallels; and a half-dozen interchangeable team members who fill in the empty spaces left by the guys who don't show up. The best members are all there except for Ron Pozzi, who said he wasn't coming because Tony Pugliese couldn't get his car, but usually made an excuse, such as this, when his mother couldn't spare him from the liquor store she ran alone. Diane and Camille, the only two audience members from Richmond Hill, will drive out later with the coach, Mr. O'Hare.

Tony Pugliese walks to the edge of the platform, then begins doing deep-knee bends, facing the tracks and humming to himself.

For away meets, the team members are freed from eighth-period classes so they'll have enough time to travel to whatever part of Queens they're going to, warm up, and be in whites by three-thirty. They were the only students not in classrooms at two o'clock. Ralphie, enjoying the privacy, stopped at the top of the stairs leading to the exit and drew a cock, poking into the mouth of Snoopy, lying on top of his doghouse on a poster captioned: *Howard Gold's Got My Vote for G.O. President.*

In one group, six guys are playing salugi with Eddie Dietz's gym bag while he runs back and forth trying to catch it before somebody throws it onto the tracks. Ralphie's standing in the center of the second group, holding his crotch with both hands, humping his hips back and forth, and chanting *Whah Whah Whah* in rhythm with the fucking motion.

Joe smiles at him. Then he asks Ralphie why he hasn't been put away years ago.

"Cause Mrs. Pug likes me free to come and go as I please."

Tony Pugliese, who's been facing the other way, turns and heaves his gym bag at Ralphie's crotch.

"How come you ain't got your car today?" is Ralphie's response.

Pug is the only team member with a car, a 1964 Grand Prix that they've crammed with more guys than the clown cars at the circus in Madison Square Garden.

"If I had it, an asshole like you wouldn't be ridin in it."

Joe picks up Pug's gym bag and brings it back over to him. It's the kind of thing a team captain should do.

"What happened?" Joe asks him. "Breakdown?"

"My father needed it to go to a job interview. His transmission blew last week."

Everyone knows Pug's father, who used to be a fireman, would never go back to work. Three years ago, he fell through the roof of a burning house and broke his back. He can walk, even drive, but can't bend or reach or lift anything heavier than a lunchbox.

"Did I hear right?" Ralphie says from behind them. "Your father's workin? Does that mean your mama's home all alone? What am I doin here?" He pretends to walk toward the station exit in a hurry. "Wish me luck, boys. Here I go. *Destination: Mrs. Pug.*"

Pug clenches his fists.

"Forget em," Joe says. "You know he's fuckin crazy."

"Crazy or not, he won't live out his last month of civilian life."

Ralphie has already joined the Marines. However, he has to graduate high school before his induction.

Ralphie starts humping the air again. This time he starts singing "Bring It on Home to Me," in a faster, flatter imitation of Sam Cooke's voice.

> *"Bring it to me . . .*
> *Bring your sweet lovin . . ."*

He intends it to taunt Pug, but when the other guys start singing along, the words and melody take over. They slow the song down until *it* becomes the message, briefly transforming the whole moment.

> *"Bring it on ho—ome to me . . .*
> *Ye—eh—ah,*
> *Ye—ah,*
> *Ye—eh—ah,*
> *Ye—ah . . ."*

A Brooklyn-bound el train rumbles into the opposite side of the station. The platform shivers and sways.

"I hate when it does that," Pug says. "It feels like the whole thing'll collapse. That's why I prefer travelin by car."

"If it didn't shake," Joe tells him, "the whole thing *would* collapse."

"Joe the Engineer," Pug says.

Ralphie calls Pug's name, but Pug ignores him.

The train pulls out of the station.

Ralphie starts chanting *Whah Whah Whah* again.

Joe leans toward Pug. "Marine Corps material," he says.

"I'll fuck em up," Pug says.

For the most part, the meet will be a joke. There will be fifteen audience members, which will include two coaches, and three judges who will pretend this is a serious sporting event as they dole out scores like 3.5 and 4.0. In the schools out in north Queens, filled with smart, clean-cut students and serious athletes, half the school shows up. The home team members shake your hands and give you a bucket of orange quarters to suck on like they do in the Olympics.

For Joe, the meet will be serious business. Especially the ninety seconds of it that will elapse during his floor-ex routine. If nothing goes wrong, he'll walk out of there division champion in the event. If he throws his opener with enough height, he stands a good chance of breaking 8.0, a score he's never gotten in four years of high school gymnastics.

The opposing team usually boos anything members of the Richmond Hill team do. But when Joe's waiting for the judges' nod, there's silence. When he finishes his routine, everyone applauds.

The windows of the Jamaica High School gymnasium are covered with thick metal screens to protect them from weekend break-ins and rock throwers. The afternoon sun pouring through spills a neat grid of light across the taped-off free-exercise floor.

Joe's pacing just outside his starting corner, hyperventilating, concentrating, bouncing on his toes, feeling the floor. The surgical tape feels like a hand firmly gripping his left ankle. This is how it should feel—as tight as a cast—so it will stretch only in moments of extreme exertion. Otherwise it won't continue its support throughout the whole routine, and it's in the last seconds, during his final pass, that he'll need it most.

He hears Ralphie's loud, echoing voice carrying a string of words over the gym floor toward the other team.

"Keep your eyes open, folks, and your mouths shut, cause Joe-the-Fuckin-Engineer's gonna give you all a lesson in class."

Joe walks to his starting point inside the tape. That spot is the one thing always there, in every gymnasium he's ever been in. He knows it as a small, fixed light. In the moment before you do a routine, the forty-by-forty-foot patch of floor looks like a neon blueprint. It looks like your future. His starting spot will leave him four steps to juice up for his round-off, leave him three feet inside the opposite corner when he hits the split.

Almost blind with oxygen, climbing out of his body, he stands at ease. He can no longer hear a thing outside his own head. The judge nods.

He lifts to his toes, leans into his run. *Slow.* Don't rush. Use each step. *Now* fast. Round-off—*whip*—back handspring—*lift,*

lift—don't reach for calves—*stall*, they'll bend toward the chest—*pike*—*open*—split. The somersault comes close to five feet easy. He hits the split with maybe six inches to slide. Best one he's thrown all year. His ankle? *What* ankle? It's downhill from here. No more thinking. Let the body take over. *It knows.* The horse knows the way home. Press out of split to handstand—easy hold—*it knows*—roll into one-leg rise—*easy*. The second pass does itself. Must have. Already sitting in jam, legs in spread-eagle, chest on floor. Now second handstand—fall to straight scale—*hold*—*whip*—back walkover—take it on ball of right foot—slight bend of right knee—return to scale—*easy now*—like lifting wings—swing left leg under—hold it out front—arms still wings outstretched. Now last pass. Use *all* that's saved up. The horse knows the way. Round-off—back handspring—full twister. It *knows*.

Now pull arms slowly to sides and make it look easy.

Deep, low bow to judges, to audience. Thank you. *Easy.*

Joe walks back to the bleachers and puts on his warm-up jacket. *Sit. Zip.* Let the room slow down. *Easy.* Wait for score.

"*Seven point* nine . . ." It's Ralphie's voice. He's standing on the seat. "Them motherfuckers are blind."

The coach isn't satisfied, either, but he tells Ralphie to calm down, then walks over to the judges to talk it over.

The score stays. They never change it.

Ralphie looks at Joe. Joe looks back at him, lifts his hands, palms upward. Then smiles.

His breathing slows. It now feels as if hours have passed since he stood looking out onto the sunlit free-exercise floor, as if it were an ocean he was about to cross. He's slipping back into the moment everyone else is in. It has an entirely different feel than the moment he left two minutes ago.

The meet goes pretty much as expected. Richmond Hill could never lose to Jamaica, which has a newer and even more disorganized team. Joe, though dissatisfied with his score, took first in floor ex. Pug, who could have gotten an easy first in rope climb, got disqualified. The judges said he didn't touch the wooden disk that hangs at the top of the rope. Pug swore up and down that he'd touched it—it's covered with black chalk to mark the climber's fingers—but his fingertips came up clean. When they offered him a second climb, to settle the matter, he kicked over the white chalk stand and walked away. The final score was eighty-two to sixty-eight. An easy win. If Pug had gotten his first, it would have been ninety to sixty.

Joe's standing with Diane, Camille, and Pug at the el station. The rest of the team is further down the platform. Mr. O'Hare was furious with Pug for getting himself disqualified. He told Pug he behaved like an asshole and that he could have beaten their best climber on his tenth climb. He said it was attitude the judges care about. Hadn't he learned that by now? Yeah, right, Pug said. Then how come it was the judges that copped the bad attitude, not him.

"Fuck it," Joe says. "We wiped their asses anyway."

"Watch your mouth," Diane tells him.

A Jamaica-bound train, which had been held on the opposite track, pulls out of the station, shaking the platform and sprinkling sparks onto the traffic below.

"A month from now none of this will matter," Joe says.

"But I touched," Pug says. "Those motherfuckers were deaf, dumb, *and* blind."

"A month from now," Joe says, "you'll be happily experiencing a-goddamn-dulthood. No school, no judges, no Ralphie . . ."

"What are you talkin about?" Pug says.

Camille takes his arm. He shakes it off, walks to the edge of the platform, and looks down.

They suddenly hear shouts. The cluster of guys further down the platform scatter as if a hand grenade had landed in their midst.

Eddie Dietz comes running over, bent forward and limping from laughing so hard.

"Ralphie's pissin off the station."

Joe leans over the railing to see what's going on. A man carrying a plastic dry cleaner's bag over his shoulder walks right into a stream of piss that's pouring out of Ralphie, who's got his cock poking through the support posts, twenty feet over his head.

The guy stops and looks up. He then starts running toward the station entrance.

Joe and Diane, Pug and Camille, pair off. The rest of the guys form groups of two or three innocent-looking high school students, holding books and athletic bags, on their victorious way home from a gymnastics meet.

The guy runs onto the platform and right past Joe and Diane: a guy with his girlfriend would never piss off an el station. He's big and heavy and already panting. The clear plastic bag, which has a pink dress in it, is streaked with yellow runnels of urine. He lumbers toward the guys further down the platform.

Joe lets out a quiet, breathy laugh after he passes. Diane asks how he could think such a thing was funny.

The man stops at each group of guys, who shrug, shake their heads, and hold up their empty palms. Then he gets to Ralphie, the only one standing alone, who says something to him and points toward the exit at the far end of the platform. The guy heads toward it, no longer running, just walking fast.

They stay in separate groups until the train arrives and they get on. Then they work their way through the cars until they're all in the same one.

Ralphie's leaning against the picture of a big yellow policeman on the inside of the door at the end of the car. The cop's wide yellow palm is thrust forward. Over his head, it says: *Do Not Ride Between Cars*.

"What'd ya tell em, Ralphie?"

"We thought shit-sure this guy wasn't leavin till he killed *some*body."

"*Maron*, he was a big fuck."

"I just told him there was a couple Moolinyams standin here a minute ago. Then they just start runnin like they were scared of somethin." He laughs.

Joe feels Diane slip out from under his arm and take a step away from him.

"I tell em, They went thataway, and I point to the exit. So he says, Nigguhs, huh? like he shoulda known it all along. Then he takes off after them. I wouldn't wanna be the first two Moolys he runs into."

Most of the guys are now stomping around and doubled over with laughter. Eddie Dietz does a bird's nest on the strap handles.

Diane is staring with disgust at Ralphie.

"What . . . ?" Ralphie shakes his head, still laughing.

"I *swear* . . ." She then turns to Joe with the same anger.

The rest of the guys are still laughing.

Joe takes a step toward Diane.

She walks halfway down the car and takes a seat facing the other way. Camille joins her.

Joe watches them. They hold themselves rigid and still. Neither of them is speaking.

"Hey, Joe," Ralphie says. "C'mon."

Joe is still looking away from Ralphie, toward Diane and Camille. He's thinking that he's dreaming. He's not on the QJ train. No one else is there. It's yesterday, and today hasn't even happened yet.

"Hey, fuck me," Ralphie says. He pokes Joe in the back.

Joe swings around, then just stares at Ralphie.

Ralphie takes a step back. "What am I supposed to do," he says, "grin that fat motherfucker to death? Whatamy, Davy-Fuckin-Crockett . . . ? Fuck *me*."

The train stops. No one gets on or off. The laughing subsides.

Joe stands there a minute longer, then walks over to where Diane and Camille are sitting. Camille slides over so Joe can sit next to Diane, but he remains standing. He holds on to the

strap handle and looks out the window. The train heaves slowly
into motion. A wall of soot-brown bricks, another of asbestos
siding, a neon hardware sign, not yet lit up, a cat sitting between
parted curtains in an open second-floor window, drift by, not
five feet from the elevated track. He begins to relax as the train
speeds up. He doesn't turn his head or try to hold his focus on
any one thing and can feel his eyes flicker and quake until the
quickening procession of different things becomes one thing,
and soon, when the train breaks free of the drag of acceleration,
reaches, then holds at, cruising speed, there will be no sense of
movement inside the car. The calm absence of motion will hold
long enough for him to take a single breath before the train
slows again, and each building, each window, each brick, begins
to reaffirm its separate existence, and the weight of his life, as
he will always know it—a resistance his body must constantly
oppose; a growing mass of words that cannot speak themselves
—will reassert itself, and he will again lose all awareness that
this presence, this force, is a thing apart from himself.

Joe walks in at five forty-five. Supper's always on the table at
five-thirty. He knows it's meat loaf because it's Tuesday and
because he smells it. When he walks into the kitchen, Carmen,
his mother, removes the upside-down plate that had been keeping his dinner warm. Joe sits down and, for the first time, feels
the hot, aching throb in his ankle.

The only sound is the metallic bleeping of submarine sonar
coming from the living room TV. *Voyage to the Bottom of the
Sea* is on, but no one is watching it. Jimmy, Joe's father, likes
to leave the TV on when they're eating so he can hear the six
o'clock news.

Jeanette is waiting for Carmen and Jimmy to get tired of
watching her stare at her half-eaten meal.

Joe tells Jimmy that they won today.

Jimmy picks up Jeanette's plate and scrapes what's left of her
meat loaf onto his. She knows she's gotten her freedom and

heads for the television. Jimmy looks at Joe, nods slightly, and smiles.

Joe tells him he threw his back sommy–split better than he has all season.

The news comes on. Jimmy shouts to Jeanette to turn up the sound. What he wants to hear is the weather, because he works out of doors.

"After a North Vietnamese rocket attack on Saigon that left thousands homeless, cut off supply roads, and forced merchants to leave the city, the prices of everything from haircuts to rice have risen more than one hundred percent. . . ."

"They don't give the weather till the end," Joe reminds him.

Carmen begins clearing the table.

Documentaries

So proudly she came into the subway car
all who were not reading their newspapers saw
the head high and the slow tread. . . .
                                        Charles Reznikoff

1
Something She's Wanted
for Years and Years

Lassie wakes and starts barking, then jumps onto Timmy's bed. It's the middle of the night.

Downstairs, in the dark kitchen, the motor in the new electric refrigerator, their first, has begun to rumble and knock.

Timmy, in his robe and slippers, follows Lassie down the stairs.

His father switches on the lamp on the night table between the twin beds. His wife sits up. He swings his feet onto the floor.

"What is it?" his wife asks. The clamor of barking and mechanical thumping has grown louder. "What *is* it?" she asks again.

Downstairs, Lassie stands on her hind legs with her forepaws against the door of the rocking refrigerator, barking. Timmy stands beside her.

His father switches on the kitchen light as he rushes into the room. Timmy's mother enters right behind him, then stops, just inside the doorway, and lifts her hand to her cheek. "What's wrong with it?" she asks.

"Lassie," Timmy's father shouts. "Stop that barking." He presses his hands against the refrigerator the way a doctor presses the abdomen of a patient. He tightens his eyes into focused thought. Timmy and his mother watch him closely. Lassie is silent.

Suddenly the throbbing stops. There is a moment of waiting, during which no one says a word.

Then Timmy's father says, "I think it's okay."

"You think so?" his wife asks. She walks to the refrigerator and presses her cheek against the door. "I'll die if anything happens to it. I've wanted this for so many years."

"I think it's okay," her husband says again. "Why don't we all go back to bed," he then says. "I know *I* have a big day tomorrow."

He heads out of the kitchen, followed by Timmy.

Timmy's mother then slides to the floor, her cheek still against the clean white enamel door. Her soft hair flows over the shoulders and back of her nightgown. She is possessed of a gentle, radiant beauty.

"Lassie," she says.

Lassie begins to lick her cheek.

"Please don't bark at my refrigerator anymore."

Lassie sits back on her haunches and cries softly. She hates the refrigerator. She prefers the old wooden icebox Timmy's father brought out to the barn that morning. She's been barking at the new refrigerator all day. She wouldn't even eat her food after it had been kept inside it.

"Please don't bark at it anymore," Timmy's mother says. "I wouldn't bark at anything you wanted for years and years."

2
Single Parents

We see the walls of the delivery room. We see the young mother, lying on her back, and we see the nurse, in a surgical mask, help her lift her legs, one at a time, and bend them at the knee. We are hearing the disembodied voices of the father and the man interviewing him, which have trailed through from the previous scene: a park in Newark. "I show up every morning," the father says, ". . . every morning, and they just say, Come back tomorrow."

In quick succession we see a stainless-steel hospital cart, in motion; the legs and white skirt of the woman pushing it to the mother's bedside; the legs of a doctor passing through a swinging door and arriving at the same bedside. Then a full-body shot of the doctor, smiling, followed by the back of his head as he leans over the mother.

"Can you support any of your children?" the interviewer asks the father.

We see the small, dark head emerging. We see the hands, enormous, in wet clear gloves, waiting to receive it.

"You can't give what you haven't got," the father says.

We cut to the park. The back interviewer, seen from behind, is in the foreground. The young father faces him. The tops of cars, climbing an ascending highway, mark the farthest reach of our line of sight. Behind the father, three young men, standing in a line against a hurricane fence, are playing steel drums. We hear the sounds of passing cars, voices, the fast, thudding, hard-soft notes of the drums. The father holds his hands in his pockets. He has not been asked another question. He smiles.

We cut back to the delivery room, and we see the mother, lying still, looking up at the nurse. We hear the cry of her new baby.

Now the father is with her. Time has passed: the light source has changed. He stands beside the bed. The doctor tells him he has a new daughter. He looks directly at us. "I'm the king," he says. He smiles and taps his cheeks with his fingertips. "Teedee, teedee, teedee . . ."

We see him bend over the bed and embrace the mother. He leans heavily on her shoulders and chest, causing her to gasp and say, "I'm in pain, Timothy. I'm in pain, Timothy."

3

Most of What Happens
in Any Given Moment
Is About Frailty

He says no, he doesn't want any help. He's bent forward, a
man well into his seventies, unable to regain his feet, both arms
against the bumper of a parked car. His wife holds his upper
arm in both hands. "We'll be all right in a minute," she says.
"He just fell." Four or five other people have stopped to watch.
Orthodox Easter Sunday, late afternoon. Avenue B at East Elev-
enth Street: the slow cooling that first occurs in the pavement
and brick and car metal just before it begins to get dark. At a
distance, a basketball stomping the pavement.

Blood begins to drip onto the fingers of his right hand and
onto his hat, lying on the ground beside his keys. Two gold
charms, one shaped like a saxophone, the other, a top hat, are
on the chain along with his house keys, car keys, and a smaller
one that might be for a padlock. I step nearer and take his upper
arm, gently at first, since he'd wanted no help. However, the
slight lift causes him to sway, first toward his wife, then back
toward me, at which point she loses her grip and his head and
shoulder push into my stomach. I try to lift him to his feet.

"My finger's cut," he says, looking at his hand. He's heavy,
and I have to bend my legs and press my shoulder under his
armpit. I then help him turn so the back of the car can take
most of the weight. At that moment I notice that the words I'd
been hearing, but not listening to, are an argument going on
between a man and a woman who had stopped to watch. They're
young, probably a couple, and both hold large takeout cups with
straws coming through the holes in their lids. He calls her a
motherfucker. She shakes the ice in her cup. "*You're* a motherfucker," she says. She has a round blue mark on her cheek the
size of a quarter.

The man who had fallen is now sitting on the bumper. He

closes his eyes with the effort of lifting his head. I can see that the blood is coming from his nose and mouth. "You haven't cut your finger," I tell him. He opens his eyes and turns to look toward the young couple: although they're both looking at him, they're still arguing, and their voices have grown louder. His eyes fix on the blue mark on the woman's cheek. I imagine that he is wondering, as I do, if it's a tattoo, or a bruise, or a birth-mark. "You haven't cut your finger," I say again. I pick up his keys and hat and set them on the trunk. His wife then steps between us and begins wiping his face with a handkerchief.

4

The Aunt and the Grandfather

A wire-mesh door swings open and a young man walks through. He approaches a picnic table where his aunt and grandfather wait, seated. They're in a large gymnasium. At a distance are a backboard and hoop, its shape stretched and echoed in a dark beard of shadow, against smooth, white-painted brick. They both stand and hug the young man closely, and he joins them at the table.

The young man, who is seventeen years old, has been convicted of killing his parents and younger brother. His aunt and grandfather visit him every week in the psychiatric ward of the maximum-security prison where he is serving a sentence of twenty-five years to life.

The grandfather is in his mid-seventies, and his daughter, the young man's aunt, is close to fifty. They are allowing themselves to be filmed for a television documentary on teenage murderers.

Throughout, we hear the voice of the aunt, and of a man we do not see who is asking her questions. When she sits down again, after embracing the young man, we hear her tell the interviewer that she and her father are the only ones who stood by her nephew. The rest of their family have washed their hands of the whole experience.

We now see that on this visit they have brought with them a little girl, who sits cross-legged on the table. (We did not see her earlier, and it becomes possible that they have joined to this moment footage of another visit, perhaps of several visits.) She could be the daughter, or even the granddaughter, of the aunt or, possibly, the young man's sister. The child laughs and gesticulates as she says something to the young man. The three of them watch her with amusement.

The voices of the aunt and the interviewer hold together each separate moment we see and cause them to come one after the other: she and her father at their kitchen table, the sun rising above the roof of a house, the two of them driving in a car, the two of them walking toward the gates of the prison.

We see them sitting with the young man again at the picnic table in the gymnasium. This time the little girl is not there. The aunt tells the interviewer that she and her father feel deeply saddened that they were unable to better acknowledge the apparent signs of the young man's troubled, painful adolescence. At thirteen, he twice attempted suicide, once by hanging, and once by an overdose of antidepressants; he later told everyone in their family that a another world war was coming, much, much worse than the other two, and that it would bring about a series of changes that would finally result in *his* becoming president; he's had long periods of insomnia, and still does, caused by what he said were thoughts that would keep growing into new thoughts, one after the other: I will go to the department store. . . . I will have to have money if I want to buy something. . . . I will have to earn that money at a job and work every day until payday. . . . I will have to find that job. . . .

5
You're So Impatient with Clasps

A young woman wearing a gold ring in her nose, six rings in one ear, and none in the other, slowly paces a small circuit around a palm plant set in the center of an oval carpet in the waiting area of an HIV clinic. Her black jeans are as tight as skin around her flat pelvis and skinny, childlike legs. She will widen her orbit to the aisle of wooden floor between the carpet's edge and a circle of aluminum-and-canvas chairs, or tighten it so she can touch the pointed leaves of the plant.

Aside from her parents, there are four other people in the room. One man leans his head backward, his eyes closed, into the curve of his friend's arm. He's sweating profusely, and the red bandanna he's wearing as a headband is soaked through. His friend continually wipes his hair, temples, and eyelids with paper towels. He keeps a roll on the empty chair beside him. Two other men sit quietly across from them. One of them appears jaundiced, perhaps from hepatitis.

Her parents sit in the arc of the circle nearest the door. The mother holds her daughter's black denim jacket folded on her lap. They're both in their mid-fifties, and both are wearing blue jeans and white jogging sneakers.

The young woman stops in front of her parents, bends toward them, and shows them the clasp on her chain necklace. It has been broken and replaced by a yellow Twist-Em, the kind that hold closed the tops of plastic bags.

Her father, carefully examining it, says, "I'll bring it into the jeweler's, and *this* time I'll have them fix it right."

When she stands up straight again, her long brown hair, thick and evenly trimmed, falls nearly to her waist like a cape.

She begins her slow pacing again, and as she walks, she tells them about a silver choker. It's on her dresser. The clasp on that has broken, too. Her cheeks and mouth hang in a loose scowl but clench tightly when she speaks. Her eyes are withdrawn and unfocused. Her voice is constricted and nasal, yet deep, and grows louder as she speaks. Much louder than necessary for her parents to hear her. She has been, and perhaps still is, addicted to heroin.

The music that has been softly playing stops. She falls silent. Her parents look around, as if they have just now realized there had been music in the first place. Then it starts again. Something sweet and waltz-like and barely audible.

The young woman rocks one way, then the other. "I know that song," she says.

Her mother smiles. "It's 'Lara's Theme,'" she says. "From *Doctor Zhivago*."

Her daughter, now swaying, doesn't answer.

Her father tells her to give him any jewelry that's broken, even any she's afraid might break soon. He'll bring them in along with the necklace.

She steps backward and begins to walk a close circuit in front of her parents.

"You're so impatient with clasps," her mother says. She shakes her head, smiling to her husband, then to her.

A woman in a nurse's uniform crosses the circle of chairs and hands a prescription bottle to the friend of the man in the red bandanna. The young woman stops pacing for the few moments it takes for the man to help his friend into his scarf and coat and for them to leave. She holds the tip of a palm leaf and looks down at it.

She takes a few steps again, but then stops. "Oh yeah," she says, and walks back to her parents.

They smile at her approach.

"I forgot but I been wanting to ask. How did Aunt Lilian like Jackie Mason?"

"Oh," her mother says. She pauses, thinks, then says, "She didn't like him at all."

"Really? Huh . . . We were on the avenue together and a bus came by with this big ad . . . *The World*, or something or other, and it had Jackie Mason." She sticks her tongue out and removes something from it, looks down at it, rubs her fingers together.

"*The World According to Jackie Mason?*" her father says, careful to make it a question, creating a small and welcome place into which she can speak her answer.

"Yeah, that was it. She had tickets. She was going with her boss."

Her mother laughs. "She didn't like him, either."

"When was that?" the young woman asks.

"When was that?" her father asks her mother.

"I think it was like . . . six months ago," the young woman says.

"That sounds right," her father says.

"I remember," the young woman says. "It was really hot that day, and she was wearing shorts."

Here

"Thought leaps on us" because we are here. That is the fact of the matter.

. . . The self is no mystery, the mystery is
That there is something for us to stand on.

We want to be here.

The act of being, the act of being More than oneself.

GEORGE OPPEN

Here

Rose Lazaro, trying to legibly fill out her deposit slip on the soft surface of her leather shoulder bag, looks up and is pleased to find that the line is much shorter than usual. Nine bodies including her own, all contained within the home stretch of the cord-and-stanchion maze.

Every other Tuesday for the past two years, Rose has spent the better part of her lunch hour waiting on this teller's line to deposit her paycheck. She presses in her account number, the ten letters of her first and last names, then flips the two leaves to make sure the carbon is readable.

When she counted the people ahead of her, she made it a point to look at them only briefly, giving each one no more attention than it would take to discern from the little men and women on the doors of public rest rooms which is which. She did this because it's been one of those days—they come infrequently, but inevitably, like a recurring dream—on which some gland, for reasons of its own, releases something into her bloodstream that causes her to watch people too closely. First she'll notice an earring, the wing of a shirt collar, the small shadow on the side of someone's nose. Then the whole person attached to the particular feature briefly takes on a furry, sort of radiant aura, like the light surrounding Our Lady of Guadalupe. When that fades, they begin to stand out, as if they'd been magnified yet remained the same size. Finally, they start to look familiar, which, by this point, they are, since she's been looking at them so long.

She focuses her attention on the deposit slip. This week, the last in the month, her entire salary goes into her checking account. She imagines a federal budget pie chart. In place of military spending, the largest wedge has her landlord's name on it. The others carry the words *telephone, student loan, winter coat—fourth payment.* Nothing that will add anything to the life she was living two weeks ago, when she began earning the money. None of it is hers. None of it is real.

This morning, on the Lexington Avenue uptown local, she noticed that the two women sitting across from her were making lace. What first caught her attention was that both their dresses were cut from the same bright green and red material. The dense jungle of leaves on their sleeves and bodices bounced and trembled in unison.

This is the usual quantity of information gathered by a single glance on an ordinary morning, strangers being a mystery she is happy to leave unsolved, a forest she walks around in, knowing with an easy certainty that she exists more fully than the trees. Then she saw their dark, muscular fingers working the needles.

At first she thought they were older than they actually were —they had to be—but gradually, watching them, she realized that, like herself, they were in their late thirties. They spoke Italian, and both had white bands of lace climbing to their fingers from the plastic shopping bags on their knee-spread laps.

Rose grew up hearing her parents and grandparents speak to each other in Italian. She understood few of the words but understood their intonations, hand movements, and facial expressions. They used the same ones when saying the same things in English. Rose had watched them as well as listened. This morning, she had done the same thing with these two women. Without understanding all the words, she understood their con-

versation. There was also the occasional word in English: *pull-
over, bunk bed, linoleum*: each noun the center of a room filled
with people.

She suddenly remembered two lines from a poem by William
Carlos Williams.

> *Shut up! laughs the big she-Wop
> Wait till you have six like me.*

This handful of words had singled itself out in the middle of
a long poem she has since forgotten the rest of. He had been
her favorite poet in college, but these lines had frightened her.
They were grotesque, yet they had in them something as familiar
as the mothers and children crowding the bus stops in the south
Queens neighborhood she grew up in and left more than ten
years ago, when her marriage ended.

Rose sent a wave of herself toward the two women to see
what it would bring when it rolled back. Quiet children, the
oldest already teenagers, freshly done laundry, polished-wood ta-
bletops covered with lace. Bright sunlight outdoors; clean, ordered darkness inside. She wondered if either of them had ever
slept with a man other than her husband.

Rose was twenty-one when she got married. Her husband had
just been discharged from the service, and it seemed the next
logical step, the next sacrament, in the series of events she knew
to be her life. Five years later, when they separated and she
moved out on her own, she swam out of a familiar current, the
one, she imagines, that still carries these two women from each
moment to the next.

She thought of the simple, accepting way she had loved her
husband during the first years of their marriage. Each meal they
ate together told her who she was. Any disturbance of the steady
domestic pattern—the phone ringing, a television commercial,
a siren passing in the distance—was a reason to make love, a
space through which their desire would emerge. When that time
ended, the next one didn't begin. What would come next, in

the life of a marriage, she never knew. The person she was then is as unlike her present self as the two women she was now watching, so gracefully absorbed in their own lives.

They might not be sisters or cousins, these two women, but they had the profound and entirely unconscious linkage that can be formed only in childhood. They'd preserved a first sense of themselves and kept it wrapped around them like the flamboyant, gently civilian fabric of their homemade dresses. They would understand *her*, had they any reason to want to, only from inside that sense of their lives. From in *there*, inside the walled city of family, if she is anything at all, it is a road happily untaken.

As the train rolled into the Fifty-first Street station, Rose's stop, she realized the entire business was a pile of crap. She knew these two as well as she knew the crowd jammed into the next car. A bullshit meditation, a pious concoction like the novels she edits for a living. Too little coffee, too much thinking. A dream. Some small part of her remained awake, the part that knows what stop to get off at, while the rest of her had fallen asleep. It's dangerous to dream with your eyes open. Anything around you can enter without knocking.

The head waitress in the restaurant she worked in when she was married had sensible advice for days like this one: The whole thing'll be whale shit to the person you'll be tomorrow.

She's been in the bank more than ten minutes, and the line hasn't moved. And, oddly, none of the available-teller lights are flashing. Her eyes have been repeatedly drawn to the unusually tall woman standing at the front of the line. She carries a leather briefcase, wears a blue pinstripe business suit and a red silk scarf. This time of year she should be wearing an overcoat. Her short, neat hair is tinted a pale blond, and she is very beautiful. What first drew Rose's attention was her method of waiting, which was to stand perfectly still.

Rose then notices, behind her, an Asian man in a clean white apron and chef's hat. Behind him, a woman with two children, one in a stroller, the other, a small boy carrying a toy sailboat, holding her hand. Then, two middle-aged businessmen, also in pinstripes, a woman about Rose's age, in overalls, flannel shirt, and hard hat, behind her a soldier, and, after him and just before Rose, an elderly black woman in a simple blue dress and a wide, old-fashioned sunbonnet: the oddest collection of people she has ever seen, or could imagine seeing, on a lunch-hour teller's line in a midtown bank.

Any of them could be there, but not all at once. Still, anything is possible, and most important, the line *is* short. She slips her left heel over the back of her shoe and leans her weight to her right side. If the woman at the head of the line were the minute hand and she the hour hand, they would form two o'clock, the time her lunch hour will be over.

Yet she's been coming here for two years and doesn't recognize a single one of these people. She can no longer *not* acknowledge the full extent of the weirdness: although they are in a bank, none of them seem to be waiting on a *bank* line. All they're doing is *being there*, emanating their distinct identities like odd, soothing music. Each is an apparition of a self-contained life. Each life fitting the world it occupies like a glove. They must have been sent here by the angriest of gods, or the vilest of demons, to drive her so far out of her fucking mind she will never find her way back inside it.

Perhaps, while walking to the bank, she'd died but somehow hadn't noticed—the last in a brief, but densely packed series of events that took her from tired wife and coffee-shop waitress to Rosie Golightly, ex–English major, unattached cosmopolite, and assistant editor. A hit and run, a sudden heart attack, a slab of concrete falling from the roof of some building, and that's *all* folks. A big deal to the observer, but such a nonevent to the victim, she doesn't even notice until it's over. But that would be too easy. And that would mean that *this*, the Fifty-ninth Street branch of Chemical Bank, is purgatory.

She had fallen asleep. And had remained awake.

She slips under the cord and walks to the tellers' windows. Empty. Except for the people waiting on line, the whole place is empty.

She then notices someone walking across the concourse in her direction. He's wearing an NYU sweatshirt, jeans, and some kind of walkie-talkie in a holster at his waist.

She heads toward him. He looks annoyed.

"What the hell is going on?" Rose says.

"That's what I was going to ask *you*. Didn't you see the signs?"

Rose shakes her head. She then notices people entering at the far end of the bank, pushing canvas laundry carts filled with cables and wire, and tall standing lights on rolling bases. A glimmer of recognition tells her something is about to realize itself.

"They're at all the entrances," the guy tells her. He turns and points to each one as he speaks.

"Hey," Rose says. "You look like a flight attendant. You know, how they model the oxygen masks and point out the emergency exits?"

"The signs ask that you use the branch on Sixty-third Street, or the ATM machines in the lobby."

"Drop a check in an ATM machine, it takes an extra day to clear. As we speak, my landlord's greedy electronic hand is rummaging around inside my account"—she waves her check and deposit slip in front of him—"looking for this."

Rose watches him search for something to say, then come up with, "What is your problem?"

"I just got paid, and I'm already broke. That's a fairly big problem. On top of that I have to stand here and listen to some fool tell me I've done something wrong, but *not* what it is. Didn't you take English at college?" She points to his sweatshirt.

He looks down at himself, then at Rose. *"Yeah?"*

"Didn't they teach you to start with a topic sentence?"

He says nothing.

"In all this time," Rose says, "you still haven't told me what the hell's going on here."

"We're rehearsing a commercial."

Rose looks back at the line. It wasn't sleep. She was further away—more absent—than sleep.

"We're about to do the stills," he tells her. "When the equipment's set up, we'll shoot."

"A commercial . . ." Rose looks back at the people on line, still standing, still waiting. A woman, also wearing a walkie-talkie, has approached them. She motions with a clipboard and walks back and forth along the stretch of carpeted floor they stand on.

Rose exhales, audibly, using her voice to escort the breath out of her, then watches the body of her own breathed-out air rise and swell in front of her. She is standing in the middle of an enormous, unnaturally empty room, facing a nervous and angry stranger. The exact and sum total of what she is doing.

"*Maronna mia,*" she says. "You call this a commercial? It looks more like *The Invasion of the Body Snatchers.*" She laughs loudly, wildly, then stops.

He smiles. "Sorry you were inconvenienced. I don't know how you got past me." He raises his arm, hand open, drops it back to his side. "Didn't it feel weird . . . standing in an empty bank?"

"It didn't look like *they* felt weird. Tell me, do they talk or anything?"

"They'll just stand there. There'll be a voice-over, and music."

She points to his walkie-talkie. "Gimme," she says.

"What?"

"Just for a second. I'll give it back. Cross my heart."

When he hands it to her, she turns toward the people on line and says, into it, "Okay, Blondie, trade places with the chef. I want the kids in the front of the line. Size places. And you two executive types . . . out!" She slips the walkie-talkie back into his holster. "The folks at home'll never believe those guys ever stand on lines with the rest of us."

"You're funny," he says.

"You find that funny?"

"No," he says. ". . . You."

"Thank you."

"You're welcome."

"Funny's what you need in this commercial. These people are about to turn to stone."

He laughs, but begins to shift his weight back and forth.

Rose can see he's getting uncomfortable. "Well," she says. "Time to head back to the office. You know, I spent nearly half my lunch hour here. And I'll have to do it again tomorrow."

She's smiling the whole time. She can see he finds this confusing. He also seems relieved now that he knows she's leaving.

What she had loved about the poems of William Carlos Williams was how he could make her see a single thing so clearly she would actually stop seeing it—it would overwhelm itself with its own clarity, the way a word repeated over and over reaches, but then exceeds, its own meaning—and she would begin to see, instead, the world around it, even if he hadn't described it at all. There was relief in this, a world slightly newer than the old one, and more hers: the thing itself had brought it here, before disappearing.

"You read poetry?" Rose asks him.

"Yeah," he says.

"Ever read William Carlos Williams?"

"The guy with the wheelbarrow?"

"The same."

"You're a writer?" he asks.

"I edit books. I don't write them. I'm doing a novel right now about two lacemakers who rob banks on the side. What a movie it would make." She shakes her hand up and down, Italian style. "Wow." She takes a step back and looks at him. "Wow," she says again. "I just had the wildest idea. . . ."

He looks back at her.

"*You're* the guy who's going to film it."

"I'm just a production assistant."

"Not for long. You pitch this one to your bosses, you'll be producer on the next one. Guaranteed. Here's the gimmick. No ski masks or stockings for these two. They wear these incredible matching dresses, covered with red and green flowers. Ever hear anybody say about colors that they're loud? Well, these dresses are screamers, and you know what their outfits are saying?"

He shakes his head.

"Guess." Rose gives him a light punch on the shoulder.

He just stares back.

"They're saying, If you can't catch us in these, you couldn't catch a snowflake in a blizzard. No. That's not quite right."

"How about this?" he says, getting interested. "You couldn't find a lightbulb in a candle factory."

"Not bad, not bad," Rose says, "but not right. What we're looking for is something like, If you couldn't catch us in these, you couldn't find a scarecrow in a garden of cucumbers."

"Pearls in the pig slop," he says.

"Teeth in a hen's mouth," Rose says. "And that's not even the point. The point is, no one ever does catch them."

"How come?" he asks.

"They wear masks made of the most delicate lace in the world. It allows them to see everything that goes on around them without ever being recognized themselves. Plus, each job they pull, they're speaking another language. And it's never English. No one ever figures out who they are."

Rose starts to walk away.

"If they don't get caught," he shouts after her, "how does it end?"

"Like this," she says, walking toward the door, the street, the second half of her day.

Wednesday

Denise can see the upper branches of the sycamores against the darker tan and brown bricks of the housing project across the street. She's looking down at their reflection in the glass countertop at the Rite Aid drugstore and is surprised at how real they seem, and how clear.

The cashier has walked off to check the price of the small jar of Noxzema face cream Denise has just brought to the counter.

A starling drops into one of the trees.

Denise lifts her eyes, looks directly at the tree. Just as she finds the narrow branch on which it has landed, it lifts itself upward, hovers briefly, and flies off over the tops of the buildings. She then looks down again, at the reflection. Even after the image has traveled across the street, through the store window, into and back out of the countertop glass, it appears realer—the limbs are round, like thin arms, and closer to her than the brick wall—than the alarm clocks, hair dryers, calculators, and boxed pen and pencil sets on the shelves just beneath. It's more than a reflection; it is another, yet the same, thing. Like the words we speak when we are truthful in what we say: they are something other than what they describe, and they are the thing itself.

The cashier returns, punches one-ninety-nine on the register keys, slips the Noxzema into a plastic shopping bag that's much too large, and sets it on the counter. The electronic register computes the tax and displays two-fifteen. Denise adds a quarter to the two singles she's been holding in her hand.

She had come home from work and made herself supper. Then walked the two blocks to her sister Fran's apartment, picked up Fran's dark-blue pin-striped skirt, and packed it into her backpack, along with her own jogging shoes, bathing suit, and the clothes she will wear to work tomorrow.

She rolls the small jar inside the plastic bag until it wraps itself into a tube, then carefully presses it flat and wraps it around the jar like a bandage.

"I'm sorry," the cashier says. "We're all out of the smaller ones."

Denise hasn't looked directly at her the whole time, and when she lifts her eyes she finds the young woman watching her with a polite and anxious curiosity. "That's okay," Denise tells her. "It'll be perfect for packing my wet bathing suit."

"Oh," the woman says. "Where can you swim around here?"

"Nowhere I know of," Denise says.

She's on her way to the subway, from Brooklyn to Manhattan, for the second time today.

On Wednesdays, Fran has an early dinner with Ben, her boss, in the room he takes in the Vista Hotel, next to the World Trade Center. At four-thirty in the afternoon they lock up his small office on the Comex trading floor, take an elevator up to the Trade Center lobby, cross over to the Vista lobby, and then take another elevator up to their room.

Ben is a commodities trader. When one of his clients calls in an order, Fran takes it down and runs it out to him on the crowded trading floor. They have a great working relationship, Fran has told Denise, and he is teaching her the business. Commodities trading is a matter of knowing when the fruit is ripe. Do you pick it the first moment you see it, or wait until it's about to fall from the branch? Fran is his only employee. They're usually undressed and in bed moments after getting to the room. There's something exciting about this small, enclosed, domestic space so near to where they work. Then they take a shower, slip into hotel bathrobes, and usually, after eating a room-service dinner, they'll have sex again. The second time they do it more slowly, Fran has told Denise. He likes to be tender, at first, making sure to give her pleasure. Then he has her turn over onto her stomach, leans on her shoulder with his left hand, as if holding her down, and with his right hand makes himself come on her back. Afterwards, they lie beside each other, close their eyes for a few minutes, and pretend they can spend the night together. By 8:40 he's on the Path train that stops beneath the Trade Center, which takes him to the Hoboken terminal, where he catches the 9:05 commuter express to Saddle River, New Jersey.

Ben allows Fran to miss work sometimes and always calls her during the holidays and vacations he spends with his wife and children. He gave her an extra week's paid vacation last fall when she needed to visit her daughter, who lives with her ex-husband's mother in Florida. On Valentine's Day, he gave her a gold ankle bracelet. On her last birthday he took her to see *Cats* on Broadway. Sometimes he gives her money.

Fran is twenty-nine, has been working for Ben just over a year and sleeping with him for the last ten months. Denise is twenty-six. She works as a secretary in the registration office of the New School, where she is also taking night courses toward a master's in sociology.

On Wednesdays, after Ben leaves, Denise meets Fran in the room at the Vista and stays for the night. They jog on the indoor track, swim in the hotel pool, spend half an hour in the sauna. Sometimes they have a drink with Ringo, the bartender in the lounge, who is also an orchestra drummer. He has traveled with the road production of *A Chorus Line* and played the whole second year with the New York production of *Cats*, which was his favorite gig. That's why Fran asked Ben to take her to see it.

———————

Less than two hours ago, when she got off the train after work, the station was filled with people rushing toward home, clogging the exit turnstiles and stairways. Now she's the only person on the platform.

Taped onto the sheet of plywood covering the front of the closed newsstand is the front page of a tabloid newspaper with a decade-old photograph of Nicole Simpson, posed in a two-piece bathing suit, holding her infant daughter in her arms.

On one end of the subway car, a homeless man lies with his eyes closed, stretched out on a double seat, one hand down the front of his pants, the other inside the opened buttons of his shirt. She walks to the opposite end and sits across from a young girl, perhaps six or seven, and her father. On the floor in front of them, the spine of a yellow loose-leaf binder sticks out of the top of a red canvas tote bag. Her father, who periodically speaks to her in Spanish, sits with his right arm stretched across the top of the seat above where she sits. She is humming something and swinging both her legs, which don't quite reach the floor. Denise watches them and gradually distills the girl's voice from the sounds of the moving train. She's humming the march from *The Bridge on the River Kwai*. Other than the sleeping man, they are the only passengers.

Denise wonders how she will find her sister when she gets to the room. Will she have calmed down, or fallen asleep as she sometimes does. Or will she still be hysterical over not being able to find her face cream.

The subway stairs rise directly into the lobby of the World Trade Center. On this night, while she is crossing the lobby, walking toward the doors that lead to the Vista, Denise passes Ben. She knows he has seen her. They were less than twenty feet apart. He must have gone back to his office after he left Fran. Denise has met him before. One morning last month, he showed up at their room with coffee and fresh bagels. She knew Fran had asked him to do this. To show Denise he wasn't so bad. But tonight they don't acknowledge each other. If he's her sister's lover in secret, he is her acquaintance in secret, as well.

Fran peers through the crack allowed by the chain lock before she allows Denise into the room. She's wrapped in a bath towel. She's wearing face cream.

Denise sits on the bed, which has been remade.

Fran walks over to the full-length mirror on the inside of the bathroom door and begins to pull a brush through her long, dark hair. She does this with her full attention, as if to imply it was what she had been doing in the moments just before her sister knocked on the door.

There's a white plastic room-service tray next to Denise on the smooth, peach-colored bedspread. On it are silverware and napkins and a plate, the size of a record album, divided into pie-wedge compartments containing fruit and cheese and nuts, still under a tight Saran Wrap covering. There's a bottle, half full of red wine, on the floor beside the bed. Denise lifts it by the neck and takes a sip.

"You're wearing face cream," she says.

"Sorry. I get so nuts. . . . You know me."

The soapy sweet smell of bubble bath comes out of the bathroom. On the wall over the dresser is a framed reproduction of a Maxfield Parrish *Vogue* cover. A young woman, whose flesh has the quality of green marble, but pleasingly so, is leaning drowsily against a pillar beside a pool of water. The water is hard, clear, and still, and in it the reflection of the woman and the sky and clouds above her is as distinct and realized as its source.

Denise begins to unpack the clothes she brought in her bag. She hangs up Fran's skirt in the closet, then her own skirt and blouse.

"I saw him in the lobby," she says.

"Ben?"

Bubble bath, face cream, perfume, cigarette smoke. Denise thinks that these few motions, her unpacking and her sister combing her long hair, have stirred up all the smells Fran and

Ben had brought to the room and mixed them with the harder resident smells of polished wood and metal and carpet cleaner.

"Ben?" Fran asks again.

"What?" Denise turns, looks at her.

"Was it Ben you saw?"

"Oh yeah." She drifts back into the moment. "Yeah . . . No." She's smiling now. "It was Oliver North. That's who I saw."

"Really? You saw Ollie? Was he with Kukla and Fran?"

"Nope. He was flying solo. And besides, *Fran* was up in her room."

Fran turns toward Denise, who is smiling, then turns back and smiles at herself in the mirror. "Maybe we'll see him in the Nautilus room. I wonder what he looks like in gym shorts. I've only seen him in the uniform he disgraced and those campaigning-for-office ensembles."

"I'm not curious," Denise says. "I lost interest when he gave up the crew cut."

"You can depend on men in crew cuts."

Denise lifts the room-service tray, pokes a hole through the plastic wrap with her finger, and takes out a piece of cheese.

"How was he tonight?" she asks Fran.

"Ollie?"

Denise takes another sip from the wine bottle.

"It was fine," Fran says. "He was romantic." She's wiping her face with a cloth. "We had a glass of wine. He wanted to watch me take a bath."

"Is that *it?*"

"What do you think?"

"Was he in one of his my-wife-doesn't-understand-my-needs moods?"

Fran takes her handbag off the seat of the valet chair in front of the bed, pulls out an airline ticket folder, and hands it to Denise. "Mexico City," she says.

"You know it'll never happen."

"This time it will. In August. We'll have been together a year."

Last November, Ben had promised to take Fran to the Bahamas. Four days beforehand he canceled. On the day they were meant to leave, a VCR arrived, by messenger, at her apartment.

"Tell him," Denise says, "that this time, when he cancels again, you want another VCR. I'd love one with digital programming."

Fran slips the tickets back in her bag, walks into the closet, and comes out with a bathing suit and a towel. "Let's get ready," she says.

Denise walks into the bathroom and pulls shut the door. She watches herself undress in the mirror. She imagines her own eyes are Ben's, watching her sister bathe in the tub behind her, then looking straight ahead, at herself, standing naked in front of her own reflection, stepping slowly into her bathing suit, one leg at a time, pulling it up over herself. She thinks about the morning Ben showed up at the room with the coffee and bagels. That was when he told Denise that Fran—Francine he calls her— will be a great commodities trader. "And soon." He spoke with an absolute certainty.

Denise felt she had entered the narrow, personal beam of their communication. It pleased Fran and Ben, that moment together. It pleased her, too. A simple, almost engaging moment possessed of a kind of relief. He was human after all, and seemed grateful that Fran was in his life.

"The best years this market will ever have are over," he told Denise. "But don't get me wrong. There's still an abundant harvest out there if you work hard. In commodities trading you get rich young, retire early. You have to." He looked at Fran. "Francine can handle it, though. Of that I am sure."

Then he talked about his home in New Jersey. Enormous property taxes. Hardly any chlorine in the pool was enough to sting his son's too-sensitive eyes. His wife insisted he get a new awning over the patio. He was forty-two, but sometimes he felt like he was ninety-two. He spoke as if it would only please Denise and Fran to agree with each thing he said.

Talking about his family seemed all right, too. After all, it was no secret. But since that morning, Denise realized it wasn't that he was putting his cards on the table; he was simply speaking to Denise the way he speaks to Fran. As a coworker, as a buddy with whom one complains about the wife and taxes. He spoke as if these things represented the entirety of what he has on his mind.

Were they the things he and Fran always talk about? Is it possible that other people can be so much unlike her? Denise knows Ben's visit was a show. But there was more to it. That morning Denise could see and feel something tangible that connected this man and her sister. Something real that had grown in other, private moments. They are lovers who can be lovers and who can, as entirely, be buddies, who have coffee before the workday and sometimes dinner afterward.

In the sauna, Fran is explaining the ins and outs of commodities trading to Denise and a woman from Kansas City they met earlier at the pool. Her name is Sarah. She's a retired schoolteacher. She and her husband are in New York to celebrate their fortieth wedding anniversary. Earlier, they saw a matinee of *Cats*, then had dinner at Windows on the World. Her husband is asleep in their room.

"I bring the order out to him on the trading floor," Fran tells them. "It's just a piece of paper—a form, you know—but it can be gold, cattle, lumber, anything. It all goes on right downstairs, just beneath us."

Sarah looks down, lifts her foot, watches her wet footprint fade into the floorboard.

Denise is sitting at the other end of the wooden bench, her eyes closed, her head against the wall. A moment earlier, as her sister was talking, the image of the little girl on the subway filled her mind. Humming and swinging her legs, she and her father, their bodies simultaneously registering each bounce and shiver, each brief moment of smooth motion.

"What I don't understand," Sarah says, "is where the money comes from."

"Say the order is twenty thousand in gold," Fran says. "Right?"

"Right," Sarah says.

"Well, he sells or he buys, whatever the customer wants, at the best time to do so. Often it's seconds after they call. Makes lots of money for them. For him, too."

"He makes money," Sarah says, "but what else?"

Denise opens her eyes.

"What else does he have to make?" Fran says.

"Okay," Sarah says. She lifts her hands, palms together, then spreads them several inches apart, approximating the width of her face, as if to exactly measure the next thing she will say. "What I can't understand, and may *never* understand, is just what it is that makes a thing more or less valuable, when it never stops being the same thing. I just don't get it."

"You buy, you sell. What's there to get?" Fran says.

"There has to be more to it," Sarah says. "I'm talking value. And not the value of gold or radium or . . . I don't know . . . moon rocks, but ordinary things."

"I don't think I understand that, either," Denise says.

"Okay," Fran says, "*hogs*. They're ordinary enough. I bet you get to see a lot of hogs in Kansas," she says to Sarah.

"Not too many in Kansas *City*," Sarah says.

"Right," Fran says. She shakes her head, slightly annoyed. "Say three thousand hogs are sold four, maybe five times in one month. You follow?"

"We follow," Denise says.

"And each time they're sold, *some*body makes a profit. That's buying, and that's selling. All there is to it."

"You're still missing my point," Sarah says. "Now, these hogs haven't gotten any fatter nor had any more piglets than they would have if the first owner had never sold them. So how come they're worth more?"

"Worth more?" Fran looks at Denise, then at Sarah. "I don't get it."

"I don't, either," Sarah says. "That's why I asked."

"I mean, does it matter," Fran asks, "what they're worth?"

"It should," Sarah says.

"Well, there's something worth a million bucks to me right now," Denise says, wiping the sweat from her forehead, "if I had it to spend."

"What's that?" Sarah asks.

"A frozen daiquiri."

"Think we could get three for that price?" Sarah says.

"We'll put it on the expense account," Fran says.

"I like the way you do things in New York," Sarah says. "Speaking of the Big Apple, I was wondering . . . I hope I'm not being too inquisitive . . . but if you two live in New York, how come you're staying at the hotel?"

"I get a room sometimes," Fran says. "The business pays. We swim, we use the sauna."

"Yeah, the business," Denise says. "They cover it easy, with the millions they make selling all those pigs."

Sarah laughs.

"We were talking about hogs," Fran says, "not pigs." She stands up, wraps her towel around her shoulders.

"That's right," Sarah says, still laughing. She steps out and holds open the wooden door. "Same thing, I guess."

"Sounds different," Fran says.

"As far as I can tell," Denise says, "they're the same thing. They're cute when they're little and have tails like corkscrews, they get fat, they go to market, they stay home, they eat roast beef."

"Wolves try and break into their houses," Sarah says.

"People buy and sell them," Denise says, "four, maybe five times a month."

———

The three of them are the only customers at the bar. Ringo comments on how rosy they all look. "Just walked out of the sauna, am I right?" He's wearing a short red jacket, white shirt, and black tie. There's a diamond stud in the tragus of his left ear, and a small silver crucifix hanging from its lobe.

"Tell me if what these young ladies have told me is true," Sarah asks him. "Did you really perform with *A Chorus Line* when it came through Kansas City?"

"In the orchestra." He sets a blue frozen daiquiri in front of her.

"Then it's true."

Ringo smiles at Fran and Denise. They smile back.

"It is," he says.

"And you play the drums?"

"True again."

"It's so hard to believe, seeing you here as our bartender."

"What do *you* do?" Ringo asks her.

"Before I retired I was a schoolteacher. Grades six to eight."

"I'd never have guessed. Not from the way you sip a daiquiri, which is all I have to go by. I'd say you were a lawyer, maybe a golf pro."

Sarah laughs and shakes her head. Then she passes around a pack of Marlboro Lite 100s. They're in a hand-tooled leather case with a little pocket for a disposable lighter. Everyone takes one, Ringo too.

"No nonsmokers. A rare pleasure these days," he says, waving his unlit cigarette over the otherwise empty bar. "Just our own eight lungs and no others upon which to inflict any lethal damage." He pops open a Zippo lighter, leans over the bar, and lights everyone up.

"Look," he tells Sarah. "New York is filled with waiters, cab-drivers, bartenders, who are really performers." He leans close to her. "You saw *A Chorus Line*. . . ."

"That's right." She laughs. "Of *course* you're right."

Ringo stands upright, inhales deeply from his cigarette, and smiles at his three customers.

They all fall silent. Ringo leans his weight onto the counter behind the bar, the back of his vest nearly touching its reflection in the mirror that runs along the wall above the liquor bottles. Denise and Fran and Sarah sip their drinks and do not speak again until they've finished their cigarettes.

Sarah, who has kept a small, introspective smile on her face, says, "Ah," and sets her empty glass on the inside edge of the bar.

"One more?" Ringo asks her.

She thinks a moment, then says, "No, thanks. It wouldn't be much of an anniversary if I let my husband spend the whole night alone. Even if he is asleep." She takes her wallet out of her bag.

"No way," Fran says. "It's on me."

"On the business," Denise says.

"Happy anniversary," Fran adds.

Sarah thanks everyone. "You're all so nice," she says, then places a hand on Denise's shoulder and eases herself off the stool. "Good night." She smiles once more, at everyone, and walks off toward the elevators.

Denise says she's also about ready to head upstairs. There's work tomorrow, and class tomorrow night.

Fran says she'll stay for another.

"Well, if you're staying . . . ," Denise says. Ringo offers her a cigarette, and she takes it. "I guess one more won't hurt."

"It's like everybody in America . . . ," Ringo says to them both, nodding his head in the direction Sarah has just walked off in. "No, the world. Yeah, it's like everybody on the planet has to come here and stay at this hotel so they can climb to the top of the Trade Center and see if the real New York is the one they see on TV. You wouldn't believe half the shit I hear at this bar. Last night somebody asked me how I managed to survive the bombing. They thought the whole place went down. Both towers."

"People get the impression their lives are incomplete," Denise says, "compared to the lives they see every night on the tube. Places like this are where they come to find out if it's true."

"Hey, that's right," Ringo says. "You study this kind of stuff."

"Professor Denise," Fran says. "Now she's writing about cops."

"That was last semester," Denise says.

"Yeah? What did you say about cops?" Ringo asks.

"It was that weird course on groups, right?" Fran says.

Ringo smiles. "Like the Temptations and the Beatles?"

"No. Like people who share the same experience," Denise says. "Shared experience is a kind of language. Not one as simple as words. It kind of circulates between people, like electricity."

"I don't think I get it," Ringo says.

"That's okay," Fran says. "Nobody does."

"Our father was a policeman," Denise says.

"A sergeant," Fran says, saluting. "And *he* sure as hell wouldn't've gotten it. He had a hard time reading the Sunday comics without moving his lips."

"I wrote a paper about what police officers have in common," Denise says.

"What *do* they have in common?" Ringo asks.

"Just watch three cops. Not brothers, not friends, not even all men . . . Just watch them walking together down the street. You'll see what they have in common."

"What are you writing about now?" Fran asks. She takes a sip from her daiquiri.

"Pigs," Denise says. She pushes out her cigarette, then takes another from the pack Ringo had left sitting on the bar. "How come you couldn't explain why those pigs keep getting more and more expensive?"

"I can't explain a lot of things."

Ringo is watching, leaning into their conversation with a slowly waning smile left over from the last thing they were talking about.

"Three thousand pigs," Denise says, "and every week somebody sells them and some sucker buys them."

"I'm tired of this."

"Tired? You just got out of bed."

Ringo, as if on cue, pulls back from their conversation, turns, and busies himself at the bar.

"What is it?" Fran says. "The face cream? I'm sorry about the fucking face cream." She swallows the last of her drink, stands on the rung at the bottom of her stool, leans across the bar, and sets the empty glass into the shallow well on the inside edge of the bartop. Then pulls another cigarette from Ringo's pack, holds it between her fingers but doesn't light it.

"Why are you here?" she says to Denise.

"Because you need me to be here."

"You're here because your life's so goddamned boring you got nothing else to do." She slides off the stool.

Denise is standing just outside the open doors of the elevator, facing Fran, who stands just inside.

"What is it you want?" Fran says.

"Not a thing."

"Good night, then." Fran presses a button, and the doors begin to close.

Denise presses the Up button on the wall, and the doors slide open again.

"Why do you hate me?"

"I don't hate you," Denise says. "I hate the way you let him treat you."

"How sweet." Fran holds both hands over her heart. "You're so full of shit it's coming out of your ears."

"Don't tell me you're not unhappy."

"I'm not unhappy."

"Yeah, *right*. You're happy."

"I didn't say that."

"You haven't said a damn thing."

"Not that you'd understand."

"Nobody understands poor Fran. I've seen that episode. Get a new script."

"Not nobody. Just you."

"Next week's episode: *The Mystery of Mexico City.* Tune in and watch a romantic vacation for two magically turn into stereo equipment. I guess that one'll be over my head, too."

"He needs me."

"He needs to do to you what he can't do to his wife."

"That's right," Fran says. "And I like it." She walks out into the hall, reaches toward her sister's hand, still pressing the button, but then opens the lid of the ashtray mounted on the wall beneath it and lifts out the metal bowl. "Looks like there's a hell of a lot more smokers around here than Ringo thinks." She flips it over, spilling cigarette butts and crumpled gum wrappers at Denise's feet.

"Are you crazy?" Denise says.

Fran walks back into the elevator.

"Control yourself."

"That's your specialty," Fran says, "controlling yourself. I failed that subject, remember? Ask my daughter. Ask our esteemed parents."

The doors start to close again. Denise presses the button.

"You asked if I was unhappy. I have a twelve-year-old daughter I talk to on the phone once a week and see two weeks a year, more if I can't *control* myself, which is usually the case. I have the romantic attentions of a married man in odd moments during the workday and three hours every Wednesday. I have a sister who hasn't had a steady lover in years, unless she's keeping secrets, and who seems to get off on hearing about how I accommodate my boss in his quest for pleasure and then sniffing around the room afterwards, like a detective examining the scene of a crime. How could anyone who has so much be unhappy?"

Denise steps into the elevator. She stands facing Fran. She folds her arms.

"Tell me, Denise, do any of your Joe College boyfriends stay around long enough to assist in an orgasm or two? I wonder, girl. . . . Why *do* you have such a fast turnover rate?"

Denise looks up. The ceiling is a square sheet of flat, darkly radiant light, like sky, or paper, or water, or skin. "I don't know," she says. "You tell me."

"Maybe . . . unlike me . . . you're saving all your love for Mr. Right. But who could that be?"

Denise now notices a faintly darker mass, a vague round cloud above her that doesn't reach the sides or corners of the ceiling but hovers over the central space where people stand. She hears her sister's words, clearly, one after the other, but they're not connected to each other. The darker mass could be a product of staring too long into light; it could be the collected molecules of hair and skin and clothing, too light to descend along with the people they detached themselves from, so they just hovered, briefly, and then got stuck to the ceiling as it came down on them, like a swatter coming down on a fly.

"My guess is a retired cop. . . ." Her sister is saying these words.

I am who I am, Denise says back, but not out loud. *That's all.* She is still looking up. *I have always been who I am.*

"A retired cop," Fran says again.

"What?" She looks back at her now.

"And *he's* married, too."

Denise suddenly grabs the front of Fran's sweatshirt and throws her against the wall. "What do *you* know?"

"I know that being Daddy's little girl—a role no one plays as well as you do—isn't so different from my indulging Ben's wishes. And I know one more thing. That you insist I live my life the way you do."

"I could give a shit less how you live your life." Denise's voice is trembling. She folds her arms again. The doors slide closed, and she leans back against them.

With one hand on the safety rail, Fran leans toward her sister, to close the few inches of space Denise had added to the space between them by leaning back. With her free hand, she points. "Bullshit," she says.

Denise is crying.

"You thought the returns came from obeying. You were really pissed when I left you alone on the path of righteousness and began making headlines—'Pregnant seventeen-year-old drops out, marries thirty-year-old telephone installer, gets divorced before she's old enough to vote, loses custody of infant daughter. . . .' That really lit a fire under your obedient ass. To compete with that, you had to go for the gold. You had to outdo all those folks already toeing the line. And you did. In terms of deviating from the norm, as you sociologists like to say, you went a lot farther than me, just in the opposite direction. You went right through normal and out the other side. You hear that?"

"I hear you saying that you're out of control, always have been, and can even find excuses for it."

"Then you heard shit. I make no excuses, and I wasn't talking about me. The extent to which you denied yourself, and still do, has to hurt more than all my fuck-ups put together."

They're both crying now. Fran leans back into the wall. She lifts her arms and looks around the elevator, realizing that it hasn't moved.

Denise, still leaning against the doors, pushes the button to the fourth floor.

"Before Ben and I go to bed," Fran says, crying harder, "even during the day, *I'm* what he wants. He wants me so much it feels like there's more of me than just one person. I like being busy. I like the sound my shoes make on the floor. I even like the job." She exhales, wipes her eyes, then wipes her hand across the front of her sweatshirt. "But on Wednesday night, after he leaves . . . If I touch something—a chair, a hairbrush, a doorknob—it's like I'm not really touching it, because *nobody's* touching it. . . . It's all other people's stuff, the whole world is other people's stuff, and nothing seems truer than that."

The elevator stops. The doors suddenly open. Denise stumbles backward and finds herself standing between Sarah and a gray-haired man in a plaid sport jacket.

"Victor woke up," Sarah says.

Denise looks at Sarah as if she hasn't seen her in years.

Sarah looks at them both: Denise, now standing beside her, Fran leaning against the back wall of the elevator, her eyes swollen, her cheeks wet. "I was worried we'd get back to the bar and you two would've left already."

Victor smiles politely.

Sarah takes his arm. "Girls, I'd like you to meet Victor."

Fran steps out of the elevator and kisses him. "Congratulations," she says.

Denise begins to laugh. ". . . On your anniversary."

"Forty years," Fran says. "That's truly an accomplishment."

"Is there a theme for forty?" Denise asks. "Like silver for twenty-five, gold for fifty?"

"Ruby," Victor says. "In fact . . ." He reaches into the side pocket of his sport jacket, takes out a small box, opens the top, and presents it to Sarah.

In it is a small gold cat sitting on a bed of cotton. It has a ruby for an eye. A thin gold chain runs through a small hole in the top of its curved back.

Denise takes the box from his hand so Victor can lift it out and place it around Sarah's neck.

"It's beautiful," Sarah says.

"*Cats,*" Victor says.

"The musical," Sarah says. She holds it away from her neck, looking down at it.

"It *is* beautiful," Denise says.

"The price of gold is up this week," Fran says.

"How about rubies?" Sarah asks, still smiling down at the cat. Then she says, "We're going downstairs to have a nightcap. I thought I'd introduce Victor to Ringo." She turns to Victor. "He's that nice bartender who's also a drummer. The one who actually *played* in *Cats.*"

Victor leans toward Sarah. "I still can't understand how that's possible," he says. "Isn't he with the Beatles?"

Sarah smiles at Fran and Denise. "No, no, Victor," she says. "That's another Ringo."

Denise smiles and yawns at the same time. Something that she usually keeps in motion is slowing to a stop.

Fran takes a step toward their room, then asks, "What floor is this?"

"Five," Victor says.

She steps back into the elevator. "We're on four," she says. "We'll ride that far with you."

Everyone else gets on, and the doors slide closed.

The car begins to move upward.

"Uh oh," Sarah says. "There's someone else waiting for this elevator."

Denise opens her mouth to say something, but yawns instead, and while she is yawning forgets what she was going to say. She laughs, then says, "Maybe it's Oliver North."

"The real Oliver North," Victor says, "or just someone who calls himself that."

Denise yawns again.

Fran shudders, then begins to sob quietly. Sarah touches her arm, then looks at Denise.

The elevator stops at the sixth floor. The door opens.

"Nobody," Victor says.

Denise is furious at Fran for how she made her feel before, and for crying now, with them in here. She will draw attention and they will see *her*, too. And right now what they would see is too big to disguise, because it isn't just herself, it is also something else.

The doors close again.

She begins to hum the march from *The Bridge on the River Kwai*.

Victor, behind her, begins to hum, too. Then Sarah, who giggles as she hums, then Fran.

The elevator stops.

"*Fourth* floor," Victor says, in an elevator operator's voice. Then, to his wife, "I still don't get it."

"What?" Sarah asks.

"I don't get it, either," Denise says.

Fran yawns, lifting her hand to her mouth.

Victor holds the doors open. When Denise and Fran step out of the car, they smile but do not speak, as if this were a nightly ritual of family and words were not necessary.

"I'm an internist," Victor says, "but I don't call myself Dr. Kildare."

Sarah smiles at them both, standing on the carpeted floor, for the moment the doors remain open.

"Why does he call himself Ringo?"

"How should I know?" Sarah says.

The doors begin to slide toward each other.

"I still don't get it," Victor says.

The Eye

Andy and Jeff are visiting Mack, who has added three rooms to his house in Vermont since their last visit. Ginny, who'd been Mack's girlfriend, and Lee, her six-year-old son, were going to move in with him, but somehow, back in December, that stopped being something that was going to happen. It's the Saturday night of Memorial Day weekend.

The three of them sit around an old cable-spool table on the unfinished deck, watching the sun drop into the mountains. Andy and Jeff are brothers, and friends of Mack's from their old neighborhood in Brooklyn. They're drinking herbal tea.

Jeff recalls how much drinking they all used to do, and the drugs.

"Look at us now," he says. He lifts his mug to his nose, inhales the tea smell.

A tree swallow lifts itself off the wire that runs from the poles along the road up to Mack's house. All three of them watch it fly directly toward the setting sun, turn jerkily, flashing light from its breast, and shoot by overhead.

". . . The three of us sitting around drinking . . ." He looks down into his cup. "What do you call this stuff?"

"Mint Medley," Mack says.

"We've come a long way," Andy says.

"My wife used to buy the kind with the little bear on the box," Jeff says.

"Sleepy Time," Mack says.

"I prefer coffee," Andy says. "But this ain't too bad."

"The little bear was asleep in front of his fireplace," Jeff says. "I used to like looking at him when I was in the kitchen. He wore a nightshirt and a little red sleeping hat. I never drank it, though."

"I know that box," Mack says.

"I guess she still buys it," Jeff says.

"I could get used to this," Andy says. He holds up his cup.

"I could get used to Jack Daniel's," Jeff says.

"You're already used to Jack Daniel's," Andy says.

Mack had spent all of September with Ginny and Lee at their home in Florida. That was when they decided to live together. When Mack came back, he began expanding his house. During that time he and Ginny would speak on the phone two or three times a week. They'd always talk after eleven, because it was cheaper.

One night in November, Mack overheard a man's voice in the background.

Ginny told him it was Ted. "He's married and has four children. He's just staying with us until he and his wife get their shit together."

"But *who* is he?"

"Don't worry," she said.

"Doesn't he have anyplace else to go?"

"It's not like that. It's just what I'm saying."

"What are you saying?"

"He has nowhere else to go. Don't worry."

Even so, in their phone calls between that time and December, Mack felt Ginny pulling further and further away. They would speak about Lee, they would speak about Mack's progress on the house, but the more he pressed her to explain what was happening, the more evasive she became. Mack became certain that whatever was going on, it was bad, and worsening. The oddest thing was that although Ginny wouldn't say what it was, she was acting like it was something he already knew about.

One morning he called her before dawn. He wasn't sure why. Maybe he would talk to Lee, maybe it would affect things if he changed the pattern.

Ted answered.

"This is Virginia Salerno's residence," Mack said. "Am I right?"

"Yes . . ."

"Then what the fuck are *you* doing in it?"

"Who is this?"

"Why aren't you in your own house?"

No one said anything for maybe thirty seconds. Then Ginny got on.

"Who is this . . . Mack?"

He slammed down the receiver. He held it pressed into the body of the phone.

She called back later that week.

"I'm sorry," she said. "It's not Ted. He has nothing to do with it."

"To do with *what?*"

"In fact, he moved out."

"All I know is, the two of us were going to live together. Now everything's fucking *Twilight Zone.*"

"I'm sorry."

"For what? What the hell *is* going on?"

"I think it's because you said you didn't want to have a child. You know I wanted another child."

She hung up after she said that, and Mack didn't call her back.

It was like a wind had come out of nowhere, blown through both their lives, and completely changed everything.

Earlier, when Jeff and Andy first arrived and he was showing them the new work on the house, Mack told them his mistake was in thinking that anything in life was actually his. "Not like in owning it, like in understanding it. Nothing holds still long enough to be *ours* that way."

"When I was five," Andy said, "I was going to buy my mother a birthday card. I went to the store that used to be on the corner. I could read already. I picked one out and I remember the lady behind the counter saying it was nice when I gave her a dime for it. When I got home, you know what happened? It changed. I imagined it happened on the way home, in my hand. When I gave it to my mother, it said, 'Good Luck on Your New Apartment.' "

Mack smiled.

"I don't remember that," Jeff said.

"It happened," Andy told them. "Cross my heart."

Mack and Ginny didn't speak or write for months. Then, in April, Ginny called again. She was already crying when Mack picked up the phone.

She was pregnant. Over four months. It was Ted, but he really did move out in December. It wasn't like that. It wasn't meant to happen, and things were worse than they were before.

"His wife won't let him back in," she said. "I won't, either. Mack. . . . Everything has turned upside down. Everything is upside down."

She didn't apologize, nor did she ask for anything. She just wanted to talk. Mack has called her twice since then. Once, she was at the doctor, and he spoke with the baby-sitter and then with Lee. The other time, she was home, and they talked again.

Mack gets up, goes inside, and puts on more water for tea. Then Jeff gets up, walks a few yards from the house, and pisses. Andy leans back and stares up into the slowly darkening sky.

Jeff, who is divorced and the father of two young children, is a telephone installer. His ex-wife and children live on Long Island. He lives with his girlfriend in Hoboken. Andy teaches

English at the high school they all attended and is the only one of the three to still live in the neighborhood they grew up in.

When Mack comes back out, he tells Andy and Jeff that earlier today he took a walk over to see Jim Ryan, a retired fireman from Boston who lives down the road. They'd been neighbors for over a decade but hadn't met until three years ago. Mack, who is a recovered drug addict, works for the state as a rehabilitation counselor for substance abusers. Jim is a member of the volunteer fire brigade.

They met when a teenage client of Mack's, high on Dexedrine, set her father's van on fire, took off the emergency brake, and set it rolling down the driveway and out onto the main street of the town they lived in. Jim helped put out the fire. Mack was on the scene to convince the father not to press charges against his daughter, who was already on parole.

That morning, when Mack walked over to their house, Jim and his wife, Pat, were sitting on their front porch, drinking Michelob and watching the cowbirds eat the seed in the feeder they'd set beside the stream that runs across their property.

" 'You guys got the life,' I told them."

"Yeah, the life of *Ryan*," Jeff says.

"So then Pat tells me how each morning she picks up the floor mat they keep just inside the front door and hangs it over the porch railing. She does this because Danny Boy—that's their dog—sleeps on it, and now that it's warm again, he's begun to shed a lot."

"This is fascinating," Jeff says.

"Does she do this before or after she brushes her teeth?" Andy says.

"If the two of you had any imagination, you might've realized that the best part's coming. However, if you want to be assholes, we can talk about something else."

"Andy bought new shoes," Jeff says. "Let's talk about that."

"You want me to go on?"

"At least be a polite asshole," Andy says to Jeff. Then he says, "Mack, we're all ears."

Jeff waves a moth away from the lip of his mug. Then he leans toward Mack, cupping an ear with his hand.

"The other day Pat notices that the orioles are picking the hairs off it—the doormat, that is—to weave into their nests."

"Wow," Andy says. "That *is* interesting. No shit this time."

"She used to shake it out. Now she lets the birds do the work for her."

"I don't have anyone to clean my doormat at home," Jeff says.

"That's perfect symbiosis," Mack says.

"You don't have a doormat," Andy says.

"Perfect harmony," Mack says.

"Their life sounds so sweet, and so—I don't know—so fucking *still*. . . ." It's Andy who says this. "Like a painting."

"Maybe that's the secret," Jeff says. "Being able to sit still."

"They do a lot of *that*," Mack says. "Except for the occasional fire, Jim never goes anywhere. Pat doesn't, either. Once, maybe twice, a week, they go into town. To the supermarket and maybe the video store. That's it."

"That's something I'll probably never learn," Jeff says. "Sitting still. I'm the opposite of that little bear on the tea box, so peacefully asleep. There's nothing he wants outside of that dreamy little fucking room. And he knows—even in his sleep he knows—that if he ever actually woke up, it would all be there, unchanged. His wife and kids, the chair, the cat, the fireplace, his little fucking nightcap . . ."

They are all quiet for a while.

Andy puts his feet up on the table and leans back.

"Those shoes aren't new," Mack says to him.

Andy doesn't answer. They are all quiet again.

The last of the sun spreads a belt of copper light just over the mountain that faces Mack's house. The sky directly above is already pure night sky.

After a while Mack's dog climbs up onto the deck. She was a puppy when he moved up here a dozen years ago. She has been sleeping and lets out a soft yawn-cry. Her haunches roll as

she crosses the deck toward Jeff, whose lap she lays her head on
to be scratched.

"She owes me money," Mack says. "She hasn't offered to pay
it back. I haven't asked."

Andy leans further back into his chair and looks up. The sky
is filling with stars.

"Will you?" Jeff asks.

"I don't know."

"You've been thinking about it?" Andy says. "About asking her?"

"I haven't," Mack says, then stands up, stretches, looks into
one of the new, unfinished rooms. The dog lifts herself, walks
over, and stands next to him.

Jeff and Andy, still sitting, look through the window along
with Mack. The walls are covered with unpainted Sheetrock.
There are smears of spackling around the edges and dotted over
the nailheads.

"When you expect to finish?" Jeff asks.

"I've stopped for a while." Mack sits down again, drops his
arm off the side of the chair, scratches the dog.

"I just remembered something," Jeff says. "If you look at the
room where the bear's sleeping, you see something that doesn't
make sense. It always kind of bothered me."

"What bear?" Mack asks.

"On the tea box."

"What is it that doesn't make sense?"

"The room is lit with oil lamps. You know, the kind with
wicks and glass covers and smoke coming out the top. But next
to him, on this table, there's a radio. A big one. Round and
heavy-looking, like everything was back in the fifties."

"Kind of like, *Drink this tea and go back to the good old days*,"
Mack says.

"The late twentieth century is not the best place for a good
night's sleep," Andy says. "That's for sure."

"But what is it that bothers you?" Mack asks.

"If there's no electricity for lights," Jeff says, "how they going to plug in the radio?"

"He can't listen to it anyway," Mack says. "He's asleep."

"Hey," Andy says, looking up into the sky. "Aren't there supposed to be only *two* dippers?"

"What the hell is he talking about now?" Jeff says.

"The big one and the little one," Mack says. "Just two."

"Then what's that?" Andy points to a dipper-shaped group of stars just above the western horizon.

"Where?" Jeff says.

"There."

"A dipper," Mack says.

"Now look over there. Above it and a little to the left. That's definitely the little one. It's got the North Star in its cup." Andy then turns and leans back and points his finger straight up into the middle of the sky. "Now look at that one," he says. "Right over our heads. Tell me, what the hell is that?"

"The *Medium* Dipper," Mack says, without even looking.

"Seriously," Andy says. "What is it?"

They all look up.

"What do I look like?" Jeff says. "A fucking astronomer?"

"See," Andy says. "*This* is a lesson in what life is about."

"*Uh* oh," Jeff says.

"We accept things simply because they're there. Like the radios that can't be plugged in. Say you're walking through the woods and you come across an oriole nest hanging from a branch. Would it ever occur to you that the material it's made out of might have once been part of a dog?"

"Not in a million years," Mack says.

"What does that have to do with radios or electricity?" Jeff says.

"Andy's got a point."

"Anything on television?" Jeff asks.

"I mean, how often do you turn the C tap and it's the *hot* water that comes out?" Andy asks.

"Do I give a shit?" Jeff says.

"Come to think of it, a lot," Mack says.

"Do I give a shit?" Jeff says again.

"This is much better than TV," Andy says, still looking up.

"It's a good thing," Mack says. "I get terrible reception."

"You got any more of this Mint Medley?" Jeff asks. "It's making me mellow. Makes me more tolerant of this weird shit the two of you are getting into."

"I think it's Jeff with the bad reception," Andy says.

"I think I'll need that Mint Medley pretty soon."

"Go inside and watch television," Andy says.

"Can't," Mack says. "I only get one channel. And spring and summer, when the leaves are out, I don't even get that."

Mack yawns, slides his chair back, and puts his feet up on the table. He's wearing thick sweat socks, gathered at the ankles, and worn, unlaced work shoes. One of the laces snakes loosely across the tabletop.

He yawns again. Jeff responds with a deep, voicy yawn of his own, then says, "I'm starting to feel like that Sleepy Time Tea bear."

Andy, still leaning back and looking up, suddenly says,

"When the blackbird flew out of sight
It marked the edge
Of many circles."

"What?" Mack says.

"I thought no one was drinking tonight," Jeff says.

"It's a poem. By Wallace Stevens."

"What does it mean?" Mack asks.

"A lot of things. One of them is that where the periphery of your vision ends, someone else's starts."

Mack smiles. "I imagine the whole sky filled with the beams

of aircraft searchlights, but they're not moving at all, and each one comes right up to the edge of the next one."

"Fantastic," Andy says.

"When does the bell ring?" Jeff says.

"It's even more than that. It's like when the blackbird flies into a new circle, it's a different blackbird and a different sky."

"It is?" Mack asks.

"Cause it's someone else's circle."

"It's like the constellations, too," Jeff says. "Andy keeps finding dippers. . . . But the whole sky can be dippers. It depends on how you cut up the pie. Thousands of years ago, people saw hunters and bears. All kinds of shit."

"That's right," Andy says.

"I know it's right," Jeff says. "Now can we talk about something else?"

"Twenty years ago," Mack says, "all three of us started building our own separate circles."

"See what you started," Jeff says to Andy.

"No, seriously," Mack says. "Andy went to college, you went into the navy. And you know where *I* went . . . eighteen months split between Rikers and Ossining, where I shot even more dope than before I went in. Then detox, the two years in Phoenix House, followed by a leisurely, fun-filled half-decade of parole . . ."

Andy tucks his feet up on the seat of his chair. A car passes on the road below. The dog lifts her head and barks once.

The advancing night exerts a steady, gentle gravity on everything. In the distance, a persistent chain saw steadily clarifies itself amidst the general deceleration of activity.

Jeff smiles, then says, "Look at us now. Three reunited circles. Like the Ballantine beer logo, which reminds me of how pleased I would be to learn you had one in the refrigerator."

"You think we get what we truly want?" Mack asks Jeff.

"How so?"

"Well, when you talk about your ex-wife you're bitter as hell, but I think getting divorced *is* what you wanted."

"We do get what we want, but we only get one thing at a time."

"That's true," Andy says. "Jeff, you want what you had *and* what you got."

"Everybody does," Jeff says. "You don't stop wanting something just because you also want something else."

"I wonder if me and Ginny got what we actually wanted," Mack says.

"What *did* you want?" Jeff asks.

"At this point she's six months pregnant. She said the whole thing started when I said I didn't want a child."

"That's the part I never understood," Andy says. "Why didn't you want a child?"

"When I said it, I didn't mean it to end there. What I said just belonged to that moment. I thought she knew that, but how could she? She wasn't inside my head. I just couldn't think it all the way through yet. What I didn't know—not until all this shit happened—is that she heard something different or, like, *half* different from what I said."

Andy leans back, looks up again. Then Mack and Jeff look up, too. The sky is entirely motionless, uniformly blue-black, and filled from horizon to horizon with stars.

"You know something? I don't know *what* I said, because I don't know what she heard. And now it seems like years ago."

"What did you think she would hear?" Jeff asks.

"I'm forty-one, never married. I'm an ex-junkie with a bald spot the size of a monk's. . . . And suddenly I'm going to have a family. I was trying to believe *that* much. I couldn't begin to think about more. That's what I heard myself saying."

"What does she say about it?" Jeff asks.

"When we talk, we talk about these things, but it's like we're talking about other people. I don't know if I feel a thing. Or if she does."

"What do you think will happen?" Andy asks.

"Don't know. At this point *nothing* is what's happening. It's like making a phone call through the eye of a storm." He looks at Jeff, then Andy. "That make any sense?"

"Now you're talking about my life," Jeff says. "The eye of a storm. A whole lot of shit has happened, and that's over. And soon, and not far down the line, a whole lot more is coming."

"That's it," Mack says.

"Is *this* middle age?" Andy says.

"Be serious," Jeff says.

"I am serious."

"Whatever it is," Mack says, "the calm won't hold much longer. The wind'll pick up again. I know it."

The three of them listen to the tick-tick sound of the dog's nails on the wooden steps. A moment later she passes through the shaft of light that spills out of the window, falls across the deck and out onto the grass.

"There's something that blackbird poem and Pat Ryan's oriole nests have in common," Mack says.

The dog barks at something. By the sound, they can tell she is already quite far from the house.

"Birds," Jeff says. He leans his head back onto the top of his chair and looks up.

"No, more," Mack says. "They both have something to do with how, for people, for animals, too, a thing can be the *same* thing and an entirely different thing at the same time."

"I think I've heard enough of this shit," Jeff says. "Now be quiet and look up." He points into the sky. "I've discovered some new ones. *There.* That one's a bicycle, and next to it, a telephone. Do you see the one just over the handlebars . . . ? *There?* That one's a condom."

"The night sky is the most accurate reflection of life's mystery," Andy says.

"Who said that?" Jeff asks.

"I did."

"Hey, Mack, we're drinking Mint Medley with fucking Plato over here."

Then Mack says, "It's now clear to me that those ancient astronomers had this shit all wrong. See those three stars out there with the four other ones on top and a little to the left?"

He looks at Jeff and Andy. He watches them look at the sky. "What do they look like to you?"

"I don't know," Jeff says.

"A tree?" Andy says.

"Nope. Look closer."

"We can't *get* any closer," Jeff says.

"See those three on the bottom?" Mack traces them with his finger. "See how they are like eyes and a nose? And see how those little ones on top are like a flower?"

"Yeah," Andy says.

"Well?" Mack says.

"Well what?" Jeff says.

"It's Billie Holiday." Mack smiles.

"Well, I'll be," Andy says. "It is."

"If anybody deserves her own constellation," Jeff says, "she does."

"You can believe *that*," Mack says. He reaches out his arms and sings to the sky, "*I'm all for you, body and soul. . . .*"

Andy and Jeff join in. The dog barks again in the distance.

Then Andy says, "With all those extra dippers hanging around up there, you know the old system's not working anymore."

"Why don't we rechart the skies?" Mack says.

"Gemini and the Seven Sisters, combined, will henceforth be known as the Brooklyn Dodgers," Andy says.

"Look at that cluster over there," Jeff says. "Sophia Loren."

"I can't quite make her out," Andy says, squinting.

"Just connect the dots."

"Whew," Mack says.

"See those two?" Andy says. "That's Pat and Jim Ryan."

"I like that," Mack says.

"And that whole area there," Jeff says, pointing east. "That's for wild-card constellations. That patch of heaven is freestyle. Anything you see there *is* there. No questions asked."

"I like that, too," Mack says.

"Constellations for the new millennium," Jeff says.

"Let's have a toast," Andy says.

"To the future," Jeff says.

Mack lifts his cup.

"To the future," Andy says.

"Whew," Mack says.

The Funeral

1

Early September. A clear, hot Saturday morning. There are two funerals in St. Catherine's Corner of Holy Cross Cemetery. A line of cars, stopped and waiting, carrying members of the second funeral, snakes backward from the hearse and reaches nearly to the gates of the street entrance they'd passed through more than twenty minutes ago. Many of those waiting share the cars that have air-conditioning. Others sit in folding chairs under the trees that line the narrow, winding road.

Sonny, the nephew of the deceased, points out the window of the third car in the procession to a tall marble monument and says to his family, "They don't make em like that anymore. . . . Too expensive." He shares the back seat with his parents.

"You better believe it," his brother Julius says, turning from the driver's seat. Joseph and Lucia, their parents, remain silent. "You better believe it," Julius says again.

Joseph, slowly wringing his hands between his knees, nods to his sons. He is watching the cemetery workers lower a coffin into a grave not twenty feet from where his brother will lie. "They're so close," he says.

Lucia has been watching the same thing, and as her husband says this she remembers the check-cashing place they drove past on the last street before the cemetery, with Spanish and Chinese words painted on the window. It had been a shoe repair shop when they last lived in the neighborhood. The shoes she is wearing this morning had once been resoled there.

"They're so close," her husband says again. And this time, his saying it causes her to imagine a house being built. After the coffins are lowered today, and the ground is filled in, they will build a house, right on the spot where her husband's eyes are focused. If the house were as big as the one she and Joseph and their sons used to live in, her brother-in-law and this stranger might lie under the same room.

Connie, sitting next to Julius, her husband, opens her window and takes a breath of air. She looks out onto the cemetery grounds. With the window open she can see more clearly.

"I got the air conditioner on," Julius says.

"All right," she says, then inhales once more, deeply, and rolls up the window.

Sonny and Julius continue marveling at the old monument. "What do you think?" Julius asks. "By today's standards, I mean?"

"Five thousand, maybe."

"Easy," Julius says. He then reads aloud the name at its base. "Flaherty."

"Irish," his brother says.

Connie reaches over the seat and taps her mother-in-law on the knee. "You thirsty?" She had seen a vendor's cart, beside the gate, when they first pulled in. Lucia tells her she is, and smiles.

A small, three-wheel vehicle, its driver wearing Walkman earphones over a red bandanna, passes in front of their car and continues along a path intersected by the road.

"What's today?" Joseph asks from the middle of the back seat. "Saturday?"

Both his sons tell him yes, it's Saturday.

2

Wayne Newton is singing "Danke Schön" at the Desert Inn in Las Vegas. A harbor of tables fans out from the stage. Julius has just given Connie a new charm for her bracelet: a pair of gold dice, cast so that from every angle they read seven. They sit across from each other at a table they share with two other couples from Ozone Park. Both of them notice, but do not mention, that Wayne Newton's left eye seems to wander independently, unfocused, while his right eye remains anchored on the center table, which is where they sit. Today they have been married nineteen years.

Including the dice, there are six charms on Connie's bracelet: a gold XV for their fifteenth wedding anniversary, a New York Yankees symbol, two coin-shaped portraits—etched from photographs—of Lucy and Michael, their children, and a tiny replica of the space shuttle. Lucy, named for her grandmother, will graduate from high school next June. She will apply to Fordham, and her grades are excellent. After that, who knows? Maybe even law school. This is their hope for her. Michael has a collection of beer cans that covers the top of his dresser and both windowsills in his room. Julius promised to try and find an original classic Coors can on this trip. They both worry about Michael, who is twelve and has diabetes.

Julius has had four Scotches since they arrived. Connie is still nursing her first Seven & Seven.

"Just for our anniversary, he came back," Julius says to her, nodding toward Wayne Newton.

"He never leaves Branson anymore," Connie tells him. "I read an article that says he's even building his own theater there."

"The day they allow gambling," Julius says, "is the day we see him in Branson."

"It said something else in that same article," Connie says. "It really stuck with me." The couple on their right turn their attention from the stage and lean toward her.

She tells them and her husband that in the good years, before the bankruptcy, Wayne Newton had bought a racehorse named Last Exit for nine hundred and fifty thousand dollars.

Julius smiles at Connie, and then at the other two. "A horse," he says, then, still smiling and slowly shaking his head, returns his gaze to Wayne Newton.

A waitress comes by and he orders another Scotch. He looks to Connie, who shakes her head and places her hand, palm downward, over her glass. Julius has had sexual encounters with many women since they've been married and still does, although with less frequency than in the early years. Mostly, they are prostitutes, whom he doesn't sleep with. He pays them for the things they can do to him while sitting in his parked car.

He leans toward Connie and tells her that for some reason he has suddenly thought of Michael, sitting in his room, listening to his Boyz 2 Men tapes. *"In the middle of all his beer cans, listening to his Boyz 2 Men tapes. . . .* That's probably what he's doing right now."

Connie smiles. Julius settles back into his seat. Wayne Newton is building up energy as he begins the last choruses of "Danke Schön." It occurs to Julius that he must sing it every night of every day of the year, yet he doesn't seem tired of it.

That afternoon, while he was downstairs at the blackjack table, their daughter called from New York, and Connie answered. Just after sunrise that morning, Julius's uncle Anthony had died. Although he was ninety-one, Connie knew her husband would be surprised. He was the oldest of her father-in-law's brothers and sisters, and the first to die. There have been few periods of Julius's life that haven't, somehow, included the presence of his uncle Anthony. She called the airline and moved up their return-flight reservations. Tomorrow they will go home. Even so, she chose not to tell him until later tonight, in their room. She didn't want to ruin their anniversary dinner.

Wayne Newton now sings each chorus in a higher pitch. Each time, the energy builds and the beat quickens. The other couples at their table are rocking and clapping and tapping their feet.

Connie keeps the beat with her swizzle stick. Julius slugs down the last of his drink. He leans toward Connie again, nearly touching his forehead to her lips, and tells her: "*This*"—he smiles—"*This* is what I call music."

3

It's seven-thirty, and Sonny is lying on the living room floor watching the commercial that comes on before *Family Feud* and laughing to himself. It's a public service announcement: Miss Universe has just asked everyone to "Buckle up." He can't tell what kind of accent she has. First he thought it was French, then Spanish. She sits in a bucket seat, headrest and all, that's not actually *in* a car, it's out in the middle of a room someplace, where you can't see anything around it. "Don't become a Labor Day Weekend death statistic," she says, then buckles her seat belt so that it crosses her Miss Universe sash like the ammo belts of a Mexican bandido. That's the best part. She did it last night, too.

You could see it as the commercial before *Family Feud*, or you could see it as the commercial after M*A*S*H. Sonny watches both. His mother only likes *Family Feud*. She finds M*A*S*H too crowded and too fast. All these people, and often new ones that come and go from one night to the next. So much happening. For his father it matters less. He's usually asleep before the first commercial, while Lucia, sitting next to him on the couch, answers the questions out loud. Although she's eighty-one, her answers are more often right than wrong. "You have to know how people think," she always tells her sons.

Sonny, lying with his hands behind his head, hears through the floor that the family downstairs have their TV turned to the same station. Except for the two years he served in Korea, he has lived with his parents his whole life. After Julius, his younger brother, got married, they left their home in Flatbush and moved here, to Ozone Park. They have two bedrooms, all they need, and the neighborhood is quiet. Julius owns a home just four blocks away. Sonny himself has never been married and, since they moved to this apartment, has rarely thought of it. On his next birthday, he'll be fifty-nine years old. He lays his head sideways in the crook of his elbow with his ear against the carpet. He can watch the screen in front of him and listen to the sound as it reverberates through the floorboards. The words are muffled, yet richer, as if each voice were several voices at once.

He hears, faintly, his mother's voice from the couch behind him. She can't be answering the questions yet. They're only at the part where the host introduces the families. Lucia once asked him if he liked M*A*S*H because it reminded him of his time in Korea, but he said no. In Korea, or anywhere else he has been, people never talked so much. The Hestor family give the host a scorpion preserved in amber. "It's a paperweight," the mother tells him. The Hestors' teenage daughter has half her head shaved to a crew cut. The other half is done in tight blond braids, all wrapped together. Sonny can see she doesn't want to be there. She doesn't respond or smile, just holds herself in an angry-sleepy silence between her mother and her younger brother. Her lipstick is so dark that on the TV screen it looks black. Sonny's anxious to hear her speak, but he knows she won't until she is asked something. "The Hestors are from New Mexico," the host says, "where you never get bothered by ants when you have a picnic." He holds the paperweight up for the camera. The scorpion looks like a thin, dark finger inside the glass. "That's because these babies show up."

Lucia nudges Sonny with her toe. "Can't you hear?"

"What?"

"Listen."

He sits up. From outside he hears the jingle of a Mister Softee truck.

"I want chocolate," Lucia says. "Joseph?" She turns to her husband.

He waves his hand and shakes his head no.

Sonny goes to his room and takes a five out of his wallet. Next to the dresser is his mother's wastepaper basket. Not a garbage pail, and not his; a wastepaper basket. His mother's wastepaper basket. That's how he sees it. It somehow ended up in his room. He never throws anything in it. It just sits there, uselessly, next to his dresser.

Last Easter, all the old women in the parish got one. Grade school students made them, and other old women, from the Rosary Society, brought them around. It's made of three Styrofoam egg cartons—a yellow, a pink, and a green one—that stand upright and open and are somehow attached to form a tubular circle. A small white trash bag hangs in the center. It's barely an object. An old-lady thing. If you put it outside, it would be destroyed by the first wind or rain that came along. His mother is an old lady, and her wastepaper basket is an old-lady thing.

Out front, he stops the driver before he starts down the street. He gets a small chocolate, no sprinkles, for his mother, and a large vanilla for himself.

A few years ago, his niece Lucy and some of her friends got in trouble when a neighbor saw them reach through the open windows of a Mister Softee truck, just as it was pulling out, and turn on the custard machines. Sonny imagines the truck, half an hour later, rounding a corner with tons of Mister Softee squeezing out the windows, vanilla on one side, chocolate on the other. He and Julius laugh about this whenever one of them brings it up. First, giggling, Sonny will say, "Still, you can't let kids get away with things like that." Then Julius will add, "They have to learn right from wrong." At this point they both fall into hysterical laughter, while Joseph and Lucia look on, smiling and wondering how these two can laugh so hard, over and over, at the same thing.

4

Connie, her back against the passenger seat, squeezes open a container of Sunkist orange drink, slips in a straw, and hands it to Lucia, who sits directly behind her. Lucia first offers it to

Joseph, who takes a big sip, exhales, and hands it back. Connie gives one to Julius and hands another back to her brother-in-law.

"I bet he's makin out all right," Sonny says, pointing to the orange-drink container but meaning the vendor, whose cart is just outside the cemetery gate on Albany Avenue. "You better believe it. On a hot day like this?"

Julius lights a cigarette, then nods toward the row of cars now moving slowly toward the exit on the opposite side of the cemetery. "Well," he says. "They're done." He takes a drag from his cigarette. "It's funny. We don't know any of them and they don't know us, but we're all here for the same thing. It's like havin something in common."

"If you're going to smoke," Connie tells him, "I'll have to open the window. It'll get hot."

"One of these days," Sonny says, "we'll all be here for the same thing."

Julius smiles, opens his window, flicks out the cigarette, and closes it again.

The people who left their cars are now getting into them.

"It's Saturday," Joseph says, "right?"

"Yeah," Julius says.

"We already told you," Sonny says. "Remember?"

Joseph watches two workers remove the cord and stanchions that had blocked the path of the hearse and the cars that followed. "*Maron*," he says. "Saturday," he says again, slowly shaking his open hand. "I bet they're makin some fuckin overtime."

Lucia shakes her head. She's angry. "Is that what you think about at a time like this?"

Sonny and Julius start to laugh.

Connie smiles. "Mom," she says to Lucia. She reaches toward her and exchanges a napkin for the empty orange-drink container. "Remember who else is buried in St. Catherine's Corner? We talked about it this morning."

"I don't know. That baseball player or something."

"Gil Hodges," Sonny says. "Brooklyn Dodgers."

The car ahead of theirs begins to move. Julius, his palms hung loosely over the top of the wheel, lifts his foot off the brake, and allows the car to slowly carry them forward.

"What do I care?" Lucia says, wadding up the napkin in her hand.

"Hey, we're movin," Joseph says.

Real Dreams

The language of the Dream = Night is)(that
of Waking = Day. It is a language of Images
and Sensations, the various dialects of which
are far less different from each other, than
the various <Day> Languages of Nations.
Samuel Taylor Coleridge

As I opened my mouth to offer some excuse,
I woke up.
Yasunari Kawabata

1
Neighbors

When it starts, you and I are lying beside each other on my
bed, talking. We've never done this before.

Suddenly a small dog, a white one with brown spots, emerges
from your midsection. It doesn't come from inside you. It had
been a part of you like a puzzle piece that for reasons of its own
has decided to detach itself. Now it stands beside us on the bed.

"I've seen this dog before," I tell you. I feel tears forming in
my eyes. "I'm not sure where, but I know I've seen it. I didn't
know it came from you."

"Fred . . ." You call the dog. He comes closer, and we both
scratch his head. Then he jumps off the bed. "Now you know
where he comes from," you tell me.

I'm deeply moved. We lie back, talking about the dog, talking
about each other. Both of us speak a pleasing and casual language the other totally understands. We are next-door neighbors
but have never felt this close.

I tell you I've come pretty close to making a dog, like Fred, come out of me, but at the last minute I get really frightened and clench up like a fist. "It's all over after that."

"Are you kidding?" you say. "It's so easy."

"For you maybe."

"I don't have much to do with it. I don't even know when it's going to happen. And that's how it's been since I was a little girl."

There are now tears running down my cheeks, and you're smiling.

"That you can do this," I say, ". . . that this could actually happen, might prove the existence of God."

"Don't make such a big deal out of it," you tell me.

Fred has been wandering around the room. He gets up on his hind legs and looks out the window.

"Fred." I try to get his attention.

"There's nothing I can do but lie here until he comes back," you say.

That makes me sad, so I call Fred again, and this time he looks back at us but then turns and continues looking out the window.

"He's just like other dogs," you say. "He won't come back until he's good and ready."

2
Love

It happens on television. I'm a detective in a police drama
and you come down to the station because you're having trouble
with the law. I'm on my way out the door when you get there,
but I stop and walk you back to my desk. I sling my sport jacket
over the back of my chair and invite you to sit down. I'm wearing a shoulder holster. I ask if you'd like some coffee.

· It's later the same day. We have just made love in the back
seat of your car. Time has been passing and we've been lying
together, trembling yet calm, and happy.

Suddenly we hear gunfire. The world outside the car is filled
with it. I sit up and look out the window. Dozens of men, wearing suits and ties, are running around the street, hiding behind
cars and streetlamps, firing at each other.
"Get down," I tell you.
We huddle into the back seat.
I look up and see this guy staring at us through the front
windshield. I reach for my gun, but it's too late. He fires. The
bullet goes through the glass, without actually breaking it, and
hits me in the arm. He runs off.
"Look," I say. "Let some of this blood go on you. Our only
chance is to play dead. These guys don't want any witnesses,
and they mean business."
I smear blood over the front of your blouse. It looks pretty
convincing.
Then I look up and there's another guy looking through the
windshield. Standing next to him is the guy who shot me in the
arm. I can see by the look in his eyes that he believes you're
dead but can see that I'm only wounded.

He fires through the windshield. This time I get it in the stomach. Not in the middle, but near the side, so I think I'll be okay. I'm conscious. I feel no pain other than the sense of there being a hole in me. The bullet must have missed the vital organs.

But he fires again. And I'm hit in the stomach again. This time nearer the center. I'm worried. I'm still alive, still com- pletely awake. How . . . ? Still, all I felt was the bullet entering and the new hole. My shirt is now entirely soaked with blood. The guys go back to the fighting.

I figure that if I get to a hospital in time, I'll be all right.

Then the back door swings open. One of them pokes me in the ribs with a rifle butt. They're making sure I'm dead. I'm worried that now they'll see that you're still alive, but they don't. I'm holding my breath and am also worried that if they're not done quickly, I'll gasp for air. Of course they'd notice, and this time they'd do the job right.

But they leave. They slam the door. I breathe.

Outside, the fighting stops.

There is a silence and we're both so relieved. It's all over and we're still alive.

3
PJ

I was leaving the building one morning and ran into PJ, the super, who was plastering up a hole in the wall beside the door of his first-floor apartment. I asked him what happened. He told me that last night, while he was in the bodega on First Avenue, there was a couple ahead of him on line, and each of them was carrying a newborn twin in a chest papoose. They were so small. They were the youngest identical twins he had ever seen. The lady behind the counter was all smiles, and so was everybody else waiting on line to pay for their groceries, but nobody noticed, except for PJ, what the couple had bought: two *TV Guides* and nothing else. I was the first person he'd seen since it happened. The first he'd told about it. "Do you believe it? And nobody else noticed. I *see* things. . . . You know what I mean?"

What he didn't tell me was that when he got home he discovered that he'd locked his keys in the apartment, so he got a crowbar from the basement and gouged a hole through the wall beside the doorknob.

PJ never did anything but realign the row of trash cans in front of the building after the garbage was picked up. He wasn't any good at fixing things, and since he was prone to sudden fits of rage, most people were afraid to ask him. He moved in in 1973, when he got out of the service, and moved out in 1978.

One night, for no reason anyone knew of, he dragged all the cans into the courtyard and jumped on them until they were as flat as sheet metal. The woman whom I lived with then, and whom I loved very much, awoke and suddenly sat up in bed. When she realized what all the noise was about, she lay back down, relieved that it was only PJ, a familiar violence, and nothing worse. Before she fell back to sleep, she whispered, in half-conscious and gently misemployed language, "PJ's on the war*page* again."

One day he was playing Hit the Penny with the nine-year-old son of the guy who owned the candy store on the corner. He thought the kid was cheating and started yelling so loud he frightened him. His father came out of the store and told PJ to leave. PJ then picked up the father by the belt and the neck of his shirt, carried him into the store, and threw him onto the glass counter, which shattered from the weight. The man was unconscious and cut up pretty badly when the police got there.

Two days later, PJ was out on bail, but in less than a week he got into another fight and was beaten up so badly they kept him in the hospital for two days. "There was eight of them," he said, when I saw him soon afterwards. There were bandages over the tops of both his black-and-blue eyes.

Then he disappeared. My downstairs neighbor said he'd gone to California to avoid going to jail for assaulting the candy store man. She also said he could never go back to Maine, where he grew up, because he was in a lot of trouble up there, too.

Last July—it's now many years later—I was walking home. The sun had just set and the sky was gray and orange. The temperature was in the nineties, and the air felt like damp fur. From down the block, I could see there was some kind of commotion in front of my building. When I got there, some of the neighbors, two policemen, and the landlord and his son were all standing around.

"PJ came back," the landlord said. "He wouldn't leave. They had to come and take him away."

"Do you believe it?" his son said. "He was so drunk he forgot he moved out over ten years ago."

Here is where the dream starts.

I'm walking down the street. The sun has just set, and the sky is gray and orange. The air is damp and hot like wet fur. I see from a distance that there's something going on in front of my building. A small crowd has gathered there, and I notice the landlord and his son among them. They're laughing, and when they see me approaching, they laugh even harder. They're glad I'm here. They're sure that when I learn what's going on, I'll start laughing, too.

Then I see PJ, sitting on the garbage cans. Two cops are holding his arms. He's crying violently, the way a small child cries, his mouth tearing a hole in his face.

When he sees me, he calms down. His eyes brighten and focus, as if now that I'm here, I can help him settle something and bring relief. He smiles as if a totally new kind of moment has just begun.

"How you doing?" he says.

"I'm okay," I tell him.

"They don't believe me." He shakes his head. Then he tries to stand, but the policemen hold him down. "Tell these assholes, will you? Just tell them. They don't believe I still live here."

How Different My Living Body Is

I awoke knowing I'd had a dream like this before, one in which words spoken, a certain kind of words, accompany me into wakefulness, the way the stalk of an aquatic plant rises above the water's surface.

The first dream I had just months after my father died. All I woke with were these words: *He'd been in two or three world wars but he poured up unkidding.* I had been in the presence of other people—I remember them only as a shadowed mass—and they spoke the words to me. I think there were three voices, and they all said it. *He'd been in two or three world wars but he poured up unkidding.* This, I thought, was the language dead people spoke. It used the same vocabulary as living language but to mean different, or partially different, things. The dead are unlike us, but not entirely unlike us. If you could actually locate the few instances in which the words meant the same things, you might also be mapping the places where their reality intersects with ours.

He'd been in two or three world wars but he poured up unkidding. They were saying this about my father. It was something they very much wanted me to know. He'd worked hard, my father: before the war, when he was a teenager and a young man, and afterwards, when he came back and started a family. Work was all he ever did. But this was only the first part of what they wanted me to know, the part I knew already. I couldn't understand the rest, and I wanted to, because I knew it was a good thing.

The only words left behind by *this* dream, the one I woke from earlier today and mean to tell you about, is the name of one of the people in it. *Prince Denverscreen.* I think this is a dead person's name. Although the people in this dream were different, the name was born in the language spoken by the people in the first dream. It's not a name like Charles Wachtel, which is the kind of name living people have.

Prince Denverscreen is one of three doctors examining me. I'm a woman in this dream. I'm lying on a clean, polished wood platform, raised about three feet off the ground. On the platform with me are two stone-like objects, the size and shape of human torsos. They both widen at the top, in the form of armless shoulders. I'm lying on my back, with my hands at my sides. The doctors are wearing nineteenth-century waistcoats. At least two of them are wearing pince-nez. They bend over me, conducting their examination, talking only among themselves. From the moment I find myself in this dream, I'm frightened.

The two objects on the platform appear to be made of a soft, dry, gray mineral. They have thin green veins running through them. I ask them if they would please tell me what is happening. Prince Denverscreen smiles and tells me I wouldn't understand.

I gather from the things they say to each other that the objects on the platform are the petrified remains of people who have died violently, and that they're over a century old. What they're doing is examining me to see how alike and how unlike my living body is from these long-dead ones.

I tell myself that what I must do, until this is all over, is spread out my fear. Unclench myself and let it drift from my torso into my arms and legs. If the fear's not all collected in any one place, it won't be so bad, it won't be all there is. If I can spread it, it will thin to a steady ache.

I have no memory of arriving here, or what my life was like before this moment. But I know this isn't the first time I've survived fear.

5
Animals

There are a lot of us, we have all just woken up, and we are on a new planet. At first I hope to recognize someone I knew back on Earth—I know all life there is over and this is the next place we are meant to be—but I don't know anyone here.

The soil is the color of dark sand, and there are round-topped mountains, vaguely at a distance. I don't know how many of us there are. I cannot remember any trees. We live in tents and have axes, hammers, bows and arrows. These and our other possessions are brightly colored—red, yellow, blue—and of extremely light weight. Clothing, too. We are all races, like *Star Trek*, yet unlike *Star Trek*, we are all humans.

There are animals on this planet and, among them, creatures that are a mixture of cats and apes. They hate us, and when they can, they attack us. They're as tall as we are, and when they stand erect, facing us, anger shows in their eyes. Their anger frightens me.

At first we plan to kill them. We get bows and arrows ready. We also have spears. Then we decide we won't protect ourselves the way we did on Earth: that is, to kill enemies simply because we can. We often think things at the same time (though not always, it seems) and can act in accordance with our simultaneous and collective thoughts without having to speak them. I think we'd had this ability since we arrived.

We have rope, so we decide to make lassos and catch them when they attack. Then we'll bring them to another, uninhabited part of the planet and let them go. We look forward to the day when we will have moved all of them to this other place. After that, we can all live in peace.

Time has passed, and we have relocated nearly all of them. A single, new thought occurs to us all: Maybe we should have

134

tried talking to them. We'd never tried this with Earth animals.

Let's try now, we decide, with the ones we have left.

As it turns out, we can talk to each other. We can't think together, as us humans do, but are able to speak, and can do so in the same language. However, by this time there are only two of the cat/apes remaining among us, and they are the oldest ones. That's why these two never attacked us.

We all go to see them, to hear what they have to say. We find them sitting together on a bench beneath a striped canopy. They tell us that all the other cat/apes, the ones we brought to the other place, are dead by now. They can only survive here. Also, that they, too, will die soon, since they are so old.

We fucked up again, one of us says aloud. Hey, this isn't funny, another one of us says. I wasn't *being* funny, the first one says.

Then, suddenly—faster than awareness—everything changes. We have all turned into blue skeletons. It happens entirely without physical sensation. We can see through each other's bodies, through the hollows between the bones.

We will not be on this planet much longer. Our time here was meant to be much shorter than our time on Earth. It then occurs to us all that we will arrive in the next place the same way we arrived here: by waking up. However, this next time, we will be very different from what we are now, or have ever been. These are the last thoughts we will have as humans.

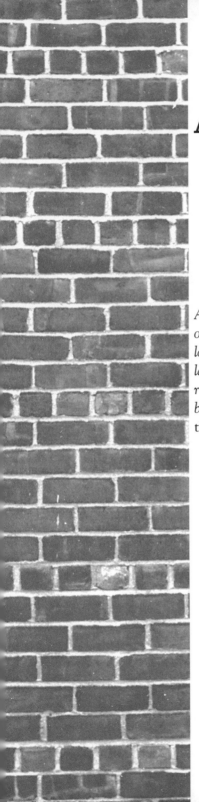

A Joke

And now I thought: till now I had only heard, seen, moved—followed up and down where I was led or dragged—watched event rushed on event, disclosure open beyond disclosure: but now, I thought.

—CHARLOTTE BRONTË

Prologue:
The Two Farmers
and the Woman from the City

Late one afternoon, A & B, two farmers (often they are brothers), notice that a car has come to a stop on the road alongside their field. The driver, C, is a woman from a far-off city whose car has broken down (or she has gotten lost or run out of gas). It's late in the day, and there's no way to remedy her situation until morning, so the two farmers invite her to stay the night.

As it turns out, A and B have only one bed, in which they both sleep: thus the woman, who has accepted their offer, must share it with them.

In the middle of the night she rolls to one side—she is lying between them—wakes A, and asks if he'd like to do it. He's never done it before but readily agrees. Before he enters her she slips a condom over his penis and tells him, *If you don't wear this, I'll have a baby.* After they have finished, he rolls onto his back and falls asleep. Later in the night she wakes B and asks him if he'd like to do it. He also agrees, so she slips a condom onto him and tells him the same thing she had told A.

The next morning the two farmers fix the woman's car and see her on her way.

Sometime later (in some versions that same morning, in others as much as a year later), A asks B, *Do you care if that woman has a baby?*

No, B answers.

I don't, either, A says.

That being the case, A tells his brother, *let's take these damn things off.*

1

Bob, squatting inside the culvert that passes under the road, calls out to his brother, Al, to reach in and hand him the chain saw. A maple branch, with a whole tree's worth of thinner off-shoots and wet dead leaves, has gotten stuck in the middle. He can't even see through it to the other side. The culvert, a corrugated sheet-metal tube three feet in diameter, collects the runoff from the hillside across the road and feeds it into the irrigation ditch that cuts through their hayfield. The thaw waters and spring rains were strong enough to carry the branch midway through the passage, but not strong enough to float it out the other side. So it just lay there, soaking up water and swelling until the thinner limbs spread out the way a sleepy man spreads his arms when he yawns. The only way to get it out will be to cut off the smaller branches.

Al hasn't answered, so Bob calls him again. This time just his name. No answer again. Bob squats lower, gathers himself into a tuck, and turns his body, in small side steps, toward the opening he crawled into. He's surprised by the clear, radiant circle of green grass and wet soil. It's like holding a drinking straw up close to your eye; it's like being inside the barrel of a cannon.

It had drizzled on and off during the night, and when the sun rose this morning it disappeared above a ceiling of gray cloud. When Bob sticks his head outside, he finds the sky clear from horizon to horizon: a light, wet blue.

This is April, he thinks. This is what we wait the year for. He stands outside now. His brother Al is nowhere in sight.

The saw, along with a rake and shovel, are lying on the bank of the outfeed. He hears Al's voice at a distance, calling to someone.

He climbs up the shoulder and sees Al walking toward a light-green car, a compact, stopped in the middle of the road, maybe a hundred yards from the culvert, where the hill that climbs the two miles up to the highway levels out. Bob wipes the sweat off his forehead, then pulls the brim of his hat lower so he can see more clearly. There's a woman standing at the driver's side, beside the open door. Her arms are crossed. Just as Al arrives at the car, Bob slips through the barbed-wire fence and starts to walk toward them. He notices that his shirtsleeves and his pants, below the knees, are caked with wet, black mud.

Claire is leaning against the front fender of her Subaru. Both the hatchback and the hood are open. The three of them are smoking her long, thin, dark cigarettes. She has three earrings in one ear, all of them silver hoops, and a small aquamarine stud in the other. Al had turned the key, but the engine was stone cold. Bob looked around under the hood but couldn't find anything wrong. Claire searched the glove compartment and then the trunk for the car's manual but couldn't find it.

"This has happened before," she tells Al and Bob. "Maybe two months ago. I was driving down the street I live on. I switched on the directionals, just before turning into the driveway, and it just stopped."

"What happened then?" Al asked her.

"I was home already, so it was easier. My mechanic looked under the hood like you just did. . . ." She nods at Bob. "Then he reached under the dashboard and pulled out this little glass thing—like maybe the size of a Tylenol capsule—and says to me, 'Here's your problem, Claire.' "

Al smiles at Bob and then at Claire. "A fuse," he says.

"*That's* what he said," Claire tells him. "I remember now. He put a new one in and it's been like nothing wrong ever happened."

"Until now," Bob says.

"I bet that's the case again," Al says. "Blown fuse."

Claire shakes her head and smiles. "My mechanic told me to bring it back to the dealer and have the electrical system checked out. I wish I'd taken his advice."

Bob tells her he'll just have a look at the fuses.

"You better let me do that," Al says. "You don't want to get mud on the lady's upholstery."

He then lies down across the front seats, while Claire and Bob, standing just outside the car, lean in and watch him. Claire tells him to look right in the middle, underneath the radio.

Bob notices that Claire is wearing a man's sport coat over an open flannel shirt over something tight and black that could be a bathing suit. She's also wearing red high-top sneakers. He's careful not to get any mud on her.

"I found it," Al says. He slides further under the dashboard. His head and neck are now completely hidden. His shirt has ridden up, and his stomach and the waistband of his white undershorts are visible. Bob feels embarrassed, knowing Claire sees this, too.

When Al slides back out, his face is red from exertion. "I found it," he says again. He holds the small fuse between his thumb and forefinger. He sits on the edge of the driver's seat, with his feet set on the ground.

The sides of the glass fuse are a dark, sooty gray. "All the others are clear," he says. He then hands Claire a silver Zippo lighter and smiles as if suddenly having it in his hand was the last part of a magic trick. "Thought you might be looking for this. It was under the driver's seat."

She looks down at it, resting in her open hand, as if its being there were truly an act of magic and Al had produced it out of thin air.

Al and Bob stare at it, too. It has a small artillery cannon and the words *Fort Sill, Oklahoma* etched into its side.

"My mechanic also told me to keep extra fuses in the car," Claire says. "Next time I *will* take his advice." She opens the lighter and flicks it. The flint sparks, but it doesn't light. She slips it into her coat pocket.

"Why don't I walk back and get the car," Bob says to Al. "I'll drive up to Mike's and see if he carries them."

Al hands Bob the burnt fuse.

"Who's Mike?" Claire asks.

Bob smiles and looks at Al. "Only the proprietor of Mike's All-In-One."

Both brothers look at Claire.

Bob, still smiling, but shyly now, says, "Gas, parts, video tapes, lottery tickets, bait, tackle, ammo, groceries, and liquor."

"Mike's is also the post office," Al says.

"You name it," Bob says, "he's got it."

2

Al and Claire are sitting on kitchen chairs on the front porch. A two-liter bottle of Diet Pepsi sits on the floor between them. After he pours their glasses full, Al looks at the inside of the cap, shrugs, smiles, and holds it out to Claire so she can look inside it.

"What does it say?" she asks.

He holds it closer, and she reads the words *Sorry. Thanks for playing. Try again.* She takes a sip from her glass.

"Last year Bob got one that said, *Congratulations. You've won five cases of Pepsi.* We used them up in two months. We drink a lot of this stuff." They are quiet for a while. Then he says, "This is the first day it's been warm enough to sit out-of-doors."

"The day is beautiful," Claire says. "Not hot, not cold."

"Everything feels wet this time of year," Al tells her. "Like the air itself were thawing out." He pours a half-inch of soda into her glass, filling it to the top again.

"You on a diet?" Claire asks him. "Most men don't drink the diet stuff."

"Nah. I just find the regular too sweet. Bob likes it, though."

"I drink the diet stuff cause anything with sugar in it goes right to my hips."

Al smiles at this but doesn't look her way. He tries to imagine her hips. He hasn't yet looked closely at her, and the general impression he has of her shape is that she is plump and about as short as their mother, who had been a short woman. How odd, he thinks. Here he is, looking out into a valley carpeted with a hayfield, while trying to imagine the appearance of a woman sitting right next to him.

"Can I try the phone again?" Claire asks.

"Help yourself."

She comes out a second later. When the wood-framed screen door swings closed, it whacks the jamb loudly. She turns, looks at it for a moment, then says to Al, "Still busy."

On the way in and back out, he wasn't able to look at her in a way that wouldn't have seemed impolite. He did notice, before, when he poured her soda, that some of the hairs in front, falling down the sides of her face, were already gray, while the rest of her hair was still a light brown. He likes the way she wears it. Short on the sides and long in the back.

Claire started to sit down again, when she first came out, but then decided not to. Instead, she's been walking back and forth across the porch.

Al picks up her glass of soda and hands it to her.

"Thanks," she says, then walks over to the porch rail, leans her weight against it, facing him. "My sister's never home this time of day, so it must be my mother, yakking up a storm. Problem is, they're expecting me for dinner, and it's over two hundred miles from here." She pulls the half-full soft pack of her long cigarettes from the pocket of her sport coat. She shakes one out, lights it. It's as thin as a drinking straw, the color of a twig. "I told them to get call waiting, but it's like two bucks more each month." She sucks in deeply, then lets the smoke drain in slow, thick curls from her nostrils and mouth. "There's nothing my mother hates to do more than part with a dollar."

She falls quiet and looks, for a moment, toward Al. Her eyes are not really focused on him. He knows she sees what she is thinking more than she sees him. He looks back at her face, her open jacket, the flannel shirt, the shiny black elastic fabric underneath.

"I know what I'll do," she says. "I'll call Marie. She's my roommate. . . ." She looks down at her sneakers. Al follows her line of sight to the toes, pointed slightly inward, like a teenager's. "Can I use it once more?"

"Help yourself," Al says. "You don't even have to ask."

She walks inside again. But a minute later she's back on the porch. She sits down.

"I can't believe it," she says. "*Our* phone's busy, too. Only we *do* have call waiting. Know what that means?"

They both notice the car appear at the top of the hill, then turn downward, descending toward them. The slope of the hill is so sharp, just after the crest, they can see the whole car from the top: hood, roof, and trunk. It's like watching a squirrel climb headfirst down the trunk of a tree.

"Know what *that* means? It means someone else called the second before I did, and she had the first person she was talking to on hold. Probably Bob—*hey*, same name as your brother—her boyfriend. They can gab for hours. I'm talking three, four at a time. I think they prefer the telephone to being together. Here's the kicker—he lives like two miles away."

The car is on the flat stretch, where Claire's car is, a few thousand yards from the house. Bob's outline is now clear, behind the windshield.

So she knows another Bob, Al thinks. He hopes she also knows another Al. "Maybe one of the callers was your mother," he says to Claire. "Maybe that's why they were both busy."

"You could be right," Claire says. She smiles, one side of her mouth higher than the other, and nods slowly.

She turns when they hear the tires whisk the gravel at the side of the road, and they watch Bob pull the car up to the front of the house.

"My mother's got this habit of calling when she knows I'm not at home," Claire says to Al. "That way she can pump Marie on what I've been up to."

3

Bob sits on the porch rail facing Al and Claire, both hands extended toward them, open, palms up. In the left hand is the burnt fuse. In the right hand, nothing.

"Mike don't keep these in stock," he tells them. "Best he can do is first thing in the morning. That's when his supplier comes."

Sometime while he was gone, he'd managed to brush off most of the mud from his pant legs and sleeves. Al wonders if Claire can see that Bob is two years younger than he is.

"That is, if you wanted to wait till then. He can call up the supplier and have them on the morning truck. You can also rent a car—Mike's got a Camry he rents to people—and drive over to the dealer in Bluesville. That's a hundred twenty-eight miles. Or you can rent the Camry, drive where you're going, and pick up your car on your way back." He smiles and shakes his head, shoves his empty hand into his pants pocket. "Assuming you're on your way to *and* from somewhere, and you expect to pass this way on your return trip."

Al leans forward and raises his finger, as if he were going to add something, but then he settles back and looks at Claire as if *he* had said the things his brother just told her.

"Well," Claire says. "To rent a car, spend that kind of money, drive to Bluesville and back, then drive another two hundred miles . . ."

"We're talking close to five hundred," Al says.

"Is there a cheap motel near here?" Claire asks them. "Staying over might be the best thing."

"Used to be a Howard Johnson's," Bob says, "just five miles beyond Mike's, but they went out of business, what, six years ago?"

"More like eight," Al says.

"What am I going to do?" Claire asks. "Can I use the phone again?"

"Help yourself," Al says.

"What *are* you going to do?" Bob asks.

"I don't know. But I better decide before I call my mother."

"*Oh,*" Bob says. "I almost forgot." He reaches into his back pocket and pulls out a small paper bag. "Lighter fluid," he says.

"Thanks," Claire says. "But I don't need it. Really."

Bob, disappointed, quickly slips the small bag back into his pocket.

Claire holds up a red disposable lighter, shaped like a lipstick dispenser, and lights it. "That other one's not mine. These fit my hand better." She lifts her thumb and the flame goes out. She lights it again.

Al notices that underneath the gray hairs that fall alongside her temple and the back edge of her cheek is a scattering of delicate brown hairs, close against the skin. Not like sideburns, but longer, and much thinner. He imagines she's about his age, thirty-six.

Claire looks at Al, then at Bob. She's smiling. They both see it's a sad smile. "You see, my plan is to leave the car at my mother's. Day after tomorrow, I'm flying to Germany. I'm going to meet the man I used to be married to."

"Oh my," Al says.

Bob senses she is talking more directly to Al than to him, even though it was he who first asked her what she was going to do. Perhaps this got started during the half hour he spent driving to and from Mike's.

"He's a lieutenant in the army. They got him stationed in Düsseldorf. We've been talking on the phone lately and writing letters. We're thinking of giving it another try."

Bob smiles warmly, interested. He wants her to see it's important to him, what she's saying. *And why not?* he thinks to himself. *It is.*

"We'll get a chance to see what happens once we're together," Claire says. "We haven't been in the same room, or even on the same continent, in almost two years. Things can change a lot in that much time."

Al pours more soda into her glass.

"I haven't the slightest idea when I'll be back," she says. "Could be a few days, could even be a few years." She sips her Diet Pepsi.

"I got some of the regular in the fridge if you prefer it," Bob says.

She takes out her cigarette pack, looks down at it, and then slips it back into her pocket. "Can I use the phone now?" she asks.

"Help yourself," Al says. "You don't have to keep asking."

When Claire steps back outside, she has in her arms a two-liter bottle of regular Pepsi and three cans of Budweiser. She uses her foot to prevent the screen door from slamming shut. "I hate loud noises," she says. She crosses the porch and returns to the chair she'd been sitting in. "Guess what?" she says to Al.

Al smiles at her.

Bob watches him closely, to see what he guesses.

"I don't know . . . ," Al says.

"What?" Bob says, to them both.

Claire gets up, gives a cigarette to Al, one to Bob, and sits again. "My mother *was* talking to Marie," she says. "You called it, Al."

She stands up again, lights Bob's cigarette, then Al's, then her own. "I told her not to expect me for dinner. That's all I could tell her for sure." She picks up one of the beers and pops the ring top. She stretches her legs out in front of her and crosses her feet at the ankle. "Next, I got this car problem to solve."

"Why not stay here?" Bob asks her.

Al shoots him a look like he'd just said something terribly wrong.

Claire notices this. "Well," she says. "I wouldn't want to stay if I'd be intruding."

Al, seeing she'd actually consider it, unclenches his face and smiles. "An intrusion?" he says. "*Hardly.*"

"We could pick up the new fuse first thing in the morning," Bob says.

Then Al says, "We'd consider it an honor."

Claire walks to the small place between the two chairs where the drinks are sitting on the crossboards and picks up the two beers. She pops the top of one and hands it to Al, the other to Bob. She then touches her can to each of theirs.

"Then it's settled," she says.

They all drink.

"In exchange for your hospitality," she tells them, "*I'm* cooking dinner."

4

Along with their meal—Claire had made a meat loaf, string beans, and mashed potatoes—they drank from a large bottle of red wine, Valpolicello, that she'd had in her car. Both brothers enjoyed their supper a great deal.

After they clear the table and pour coffee, she passes around her cigarettes, and they each light up.

Al tells Claire that this is the only kind of meat Bob will eat. "Hamburgers and meat loaf, that's it. He won't even touch steak or lamb chops."

"Why not?" Claire asks.

"He calls it grrr-meat," Al answers for his brother.

"Grrr-meat?" After Claire asks this, she keeps her eyes on Bob, waiting for him to answer for himself.

"When we were kids, Al used to think that because he liked steak, chops, stuff like that . . ." Bob suddenly grimaces. "He even liked the gristle. . . ."

"I did not," Al says.

"He did too. He used to think it made him special—he still does—like a lion or something."

Al smiles at Claire, then at Bob. "Oh, *come on.*"

Bob looks down at his coffee, and his hand holding Claire's slender dark cigarette. "Well, that's how it seemed," he says. He looks at Al, then at Claire. "I eat what I like. I don't eat what I don't like. Period."

"Read her the essay," Al says.

"The essay?" Claire asks.

"I wrote an essay in high school. About meat."

"The teacher loved it," Al says. "She told him he should become a writer."

"Please read it," Claire says.

"Come on, Bob," Al says. Then, to Claire, he says, "It's great."

Bob walks through the living room into the bedroom, and

shuts the door. When he comes out, he has with him some sheets of loose-leaf paper with handwriting on them.

"Hurray!" Claire says. "What's it called?"

" 'Meat,' " Bob says.

"Hurray!" Claire says again.

Bob stands and faces them. "*Meat*," he says, beginning the essay with its title. He brings his hand to his mouth and clears his throat before starting to read.

"*I can sometimes imagine chasing a rabbit or a chicken or a duck, catching it in my jaws, sinking my teeth into its flesh, and enjoying a rich, warm, satisfying feeling that begins in my mouth, then spreads through my whole body, the way heat from a woodstove fills a room. . . .*"

"Wow," Claire says.

Al smiles at her, "What did I tell you?" he says.

"Please go on," Claire says.

"*In the moment I bite into it, there is no hair, no feathers, no gristle, and no bone. The flesh, firm and soft at the same time, is like bread. But it's more satisfying than bread, because it also feels familiar, like I'm biting into my own arm, but without feeling a thing. It's the kind of pleasure Elmer Fudd would have if he ever sunk his teeth into Bugs Bunny. Or the daydreams hunters always have when they're trying to catch Daffy Duck. There is usually two of them. They're big and they have beards and they're sitting at a table, with a knife in one hand and a fork in the other. This isn't really what they're doing, it's the daydream they have. And on the table, in a pot or on a tray, exactly as he was when he was alive, is Daffy, except he doesn't mind that they're going to eat him. In fact, he seems to agree that this is exactly what he's supposed to do, be their supper, and enjoy it, too. And part of that, of being their meal, is to not have grrr-flesh, to not be leathery, or bony, or stringy, but to yield to their teeth.*"

Bob sets the paper on his lap. "That's it," he says.

"Bravo," Claire says. She claps, and Al joins her. "Your teacher was right. You *should* be a writer."

"He never wrote anything else," Al says. "He just wrote that because my father used to make fun of him."

"For not eating grrr-meat?" Claire asks.

"That's right," Bob says. "And *you* did, too," he says to Al. "You still do."

"Not anymore," Al says. He looks at Claire, then at his brother. "And I'm sorry for it."

"I imagine that was a long time ago," Claire says.

"It was," Al says. "But Bob doesn't forget things so easily."

"When we were kids, we went on a school trip to the aquarium in Redville, and Al, just from watching the golden carp swimming in the tank, got hungry."

"He called me a cannibal," Al says. "Do you believe it?"

"And that night Al told our father, may he rest in peace, what I'd said, and just to taunt me the both of them chewed their steak extra loud and growled when they tore the meat from the bones."

"See what I mean?" Al says to Claire. "He never forgets a thing."

"Speaking of forgetting," Claire says, "I didn't hear anyone thank me for the delicious meal I cooked for you two guys."

After coffee, Bob brings a kitchen chair into the living room and sets it between the two recliners that face the TV. He insists Claire allow him to sit in it so she can enjoy one of the recliners.

They watch a documentary on manatees. The narrator, in a French accent, says that manatees might actually have been what sailors, for centuries, had thought of as mermaids. They float on their backs when they nurse their young and look a lot like human mothers.

"But they don't have any hair," Al says. "Mermaids have to have long hair."

"You're right," Claire says. "I don't buy it."

"Me neither," Bob says.

On the screen there is a cut to what look like real mermaids. It's an underwater ballet, a tourist attraction in Florida called Weeki-Wachee Springs. Young women dressed as fish from the waist down are doing a floating dance number to a familiar, electric, funky song.

"Hey," Bob says. "Isn't that the theme from the movie *Shaft?*"

"You have a great memory," Claire says. "That must've been like twenty years ago."

"I don't know where he gets it," Al says. "Sometimes I forget what day of the week it is."

Claire has brought the bottle of wine into the living room. She refills their glasses.

The documentary cuts to a team of divers trying to rescue a manatee that had gotten trapped in a wide sewer pipe somewhere else in Florida. The narrator speaks of how often these creatures have lost their lives because of human encroachment on their underwater world.

"Imagine if one of them got stuck in *our* culvert," Bob says. Then he says, "For*get* about it."

"You saw how long *their* hair was," Al says, referring back to the underwater dancers.

"*That's* how a mermaid should look," Claire says.

"Did you see those hoses?" Bob asks. "The green ones hanging all over like vines? That's how they breathe."

"Oh, *really?*" Al says. He reaches over and punches his brother's upper arm. "I thought they were *real* mermaids."

After the documentary they watch the news. As is their custom, after the feature stories Bob presses the remote and switches to the second half of *Cheers*.

"The weather they give is for Bluesville," Al says. "Our valley seems to have its own private climate. Neither of us care much for sports."

"Besides," Bob says, "the *Cheers* episodes they run at eleven o'clock are reruns. So we always know what happened in the first half."

Claire slips her feet out of her sneakers, which clunk one at a time when they fall from the footrest of the recliner to the wooden floor.

As they watch, the three of them sip away the rest of the wine.

Al picks up the empty bottle, brings it into the kitchen, and comes out with three beers. "There's plenty where this came from. I put another two sixes into the fridge."

During a commercial break, there is a coming attraction for an episode of *Star Trek: The Next Generation*. The captain and crew are on the bridge. The face of an angry, barbaric-looking alien fills the communicator screen of the *Enterprise*, then the TV screen itself.

"Who's the one in the high-tech wraparound glasses?" Claire asks.

"Lieutenant Commander Geordi," Al tells her.

Claire salutes. "A lieutenant. Like my husband."

"Lieutenant *Commander*," Al says.

"Wasn't he also in *Roots*?" she asks. She shakes a cigarette out of her pack, then two more. She hands one to Bob, one to Al.

"You got a good memory yourself," Al says.

"He played Kunte Kinte," Bob says. "My favorite character."

"What does he wear those weird glasses for?" Claire asks.

"You don't know?" Al says. *"You don't know?"*

Bob notices that his brother is speaking much louder than he has to.

"With those he can see *you*," Al says. "All three of us. He can look right through the screen. Right into this room."

Claire looks at Al and smiles. She then looks back at the TV screen and waves. "Hi," she says. "Hi, Lieutenant Commander . . . What's his name?"

"Geordi," Al says.

"Hi, Lieutenant Commander Geordi."

5

After *Cheers*, they watch *The Honeymooners*. After that, Claire sets the recliner straight up, sets her feet on the floor, lifts her hand to her mouth, and yawns deeply.

"Whenever you're ready," Bob says. "We put clean sheets on the bed for you." He points to the bedroom door, at the end of the living room opposite the kitchen.

Claire stands, yawns again, walks to the bedroom door, and opens it.

Al gets up, walks quickly past her into the dark room, pulls the cord hanging from the light on the ceiling right over the bed. "I didn't think you'd find it in the dark," he tells her, then walks back out into the living room.

Claire looks at the king-size bed. On each side of it is a single chair, and under each chair is a pair of bedroom slippers. She stands half in, half out of the doorway. "But this is your room," she says.

Neither brother answers her.

"Where will you two sleep?" she asks.

"In here," Al says.

"In those recliners?"

"We'll be fine," Bob says. "Al usually falls asleep out here anyway. He rarely makes it through *The Honeymooners*. Sometimes he spends the whole night in his chair."

"No way," Claire says.

"You're our guest," Bob says.

"Then let me sleep where *I* want to. In one of those recliners."

"We made the bed," Al says. "For you."

"No way," Claire says again. "I'll just stay up all night." She walks into the kitchen and comes out with another beer. She sits down on the kitchen chair between the recliners.

Al and Bob look at each other. Bob then lifts up his beer

can, now empty, shakes it, and nods toward Al. Al nods back. Bob goes into the kitchen and comes out with two more.

"This is ridiculous," Al says. "You're our guest."

"And I can't thank you enough for the hospitality you've already shown me."

"You can't stay up all night," Bob tells Claire. He sits beside her in one of the recliners. "You've got a long drive tomorrow."

Al sits in the other.

Claire laughs, then says, "Is this how you'd both be—Al, you in that chair, and you, Bob, in that one—if I wasn't here."

"Actually," Bob says, "it's the opposite. I always sit in the one Al's in. Your presence kind of mixed things up."

"Delightfully," Al adds.

"Then switch," Claire says.

"Switch?" Bob says.

"Get back into your own chairs."

The two brothers lean their recliners to their upright positions, step out of them, and change places.

"That's better," Claire says. "I want to feel my presence causes you the least possible disturbance."

In order to demonstrate how comfortable and how untroubled they are, having her in their home, both brothers, in perfect synchronicity, tilt their recliners all the way back.

6

"No," Claire says to Bob, who will not lie still. "Stay put. There's plenty of room. Lean back and put *both* feet up." She's lying between the two brothers, demonstrating that there's enough room for all three of them on the bed. They're all fully clothed, lying on top of the bedspread. "No one here's going to sleep in a chair."

Al, on Claire's right side, lies on his back, his head turned toward her, his arms stiff at his sides.

Bob, on her left, his head now on the pillow, both feet, in slippers, on the bed, stares up into the rectangular light fixture. He suddenly realizes that in his thirty-four years of life, each night of which he has slept in this room, it has never before occurred to him that the sides and angled corners of the glass fixture are exactly catty-corner to the wall. Without even knowing it, or remembering it, he has always found this soothing: the perpetually discordant symmetry, how the bright, milky glass perfectly opposes the angles of the ceiling's edges. If you look, first, at *it* and let the ceiling recede, it grows brighter. Like a white diamond in the heart of an ace, like the sun through clean Tupperware, like a window looking into a blast furnace.

"See?" Claire says. "We're all comfy."

Neither brother speaks.

Al, also gazing up into the ceiling light, suddenly thinks of the electric bill. He wrote the check yesterday, but earlier he noticed it was still on the table. It's Bob's job to seal it and put on the stamp.

Claire sits up. She then climbs lightly off the front of the bed, so as not to disturb Al and Bob, and walks out of the room. They hear water running in the bathroom sink, and the toilet flush.

"You didn't put the stamp on the electric bill," Al says.

"Put the what on the what?" Claire says, walking back into the room. She's holding three beers in her hands. She's wearing a T-shirt so long it comes down to her knees, and long blue socks that reach to a point higher than its hem.

"The stamp, on the electric bill," Al says.

She stands right in front of the bed. Across the front of her T-shirt is a photo image of Julio Iglesias and the word *Pisces*.

"I have to do that part," Bob says to Claire.

"You guys sure believe in the division of labor."

"It's not that," Bob says, "it's my brother's chemistry. There's something weird about it."

"What do you mean?" Claire asks.

"Every time I lick a stamp," Al says, "it falls off."

"Wow," Claire says.

"I can't even seal an envelope."

Claire fits herself into the space between the two brothers. They both sit up, lean their backs against the headboard, and take the beers she hands them. She smells of skin cream. Both brothers recall the scent from the scratch-and-sniff advertisements in magazines, but neither mentions it. The odor is sweeter, and much softer, when it comes off skin. Her socks are the color of seawater in a Florida postcard.

"It kind of feels like we're *your* guests," Bob says.

"Thanks for having us over," Al says.

All three of them laugh.

"You can use a wet sponge," Claire says to Al.

"A sponge?"

"For the stamps. A lot of people do."

"That's so simple," Al says, "it's positively brilliant."

"Why didn't we think of that?" Bob says. "Henceforth you can stop relying on me to lick the stamps."

"To self-reliance," Claire says, holding her can of Budweiser out for a toast.

Claire yawns, stretches out her arms, rolls her pillow into a ball, and slips under the blankets. The light is still on. Al and Bob are still lying on top of the bedspread, and their weight molds the blankets snugly around her body. In the mummy-like tightness, her body narrows slightly, above her round hips, and widens again at her shoulders. Her face, with her eyes closed, looks older than it did when she was awake. Both brothers find her fascinating. None of the ordinary things—washing dishes, hoeing the vegetable garden, bringing in their tools from the field—have seemed important since she got here. She has a pleasant, light, TV-teenage way about her. She calls her mother and sister *Guys*; when she asked Al and Bob about their parents, she referred to them as *your mom and dad*, like she knew them, instead of mother and father. She even *walks* young.

While she was preparing dinner, Bob told her about how their mother had been taken by cancer after fighting it bravely for ten years. Three operations, and never once did she complain. Even when the only way she could get from her bed to the living room, or back again, was to be carried by her husband or one of her sons; even after that, when it hurt her too much to be moved at all. And then three months to the day after she died, their father slid off the icy highway and plowed into a forked birch tree. The impact probably knocked him unconscious. When the state police found his frozen body, his head was face-down on the backs of his hands, still clutched to the wheel. The windshield was shattered, and the dashboard was covered with snow. It's been fifteen years since.

He told her how Al wanted to get rid of everything they'd owned, right away. Before a year had passed, he'd given it all, even their parents' bed, to the Methodist church in Redville.

Al explained it to Claire the way he explained it to Bob, countless times. "You have to live in the present. Otherwise the past won't stay in the past, which is where it belongs."

"She's awfully nice," Al whispers to Bob. Neither of them has stopped being conscious of the smell of her skin cream.

After the two brothers go to the bathroom—first Al, then Bob—they walk quietly back into the room, sit on the chairs on their respective sides of the bed, take off their slippers, set them on the floor, and look at their sleeping guest. She is nearly absent in her deep sleep: her body unmoving except for the small rise of her soft torso with each inhalation, the slight filling of her cheeks each time she exhales.

"Well," Al says, "I'm ready." He gets up and pulls the cord that turns out the light.

Bob hears the muted clink of his brother's belt buckle against the wood of the chair, then the sound of his feet sliding down the sheet. Bob then slips out of his own shirt and pants and climbs into his side of the bed.

The two brothers, acting together, pull the blanket up to their chins. They then turn their bodies away from each other, away from Claire, close their eyes, and wait for sleep.

7

Bob has opened his eyes. Hours must have gone by—he knows this by how deeply asleep he was, by how far away he seemed to have been when he was called to wakefulness—but he can't tell how many: It's a moonless night, and the room is the same pitch black it was when his brother turned off the light. It wasn't the phone or the alarm clock, the only things other than the sun that ever wake him. There are fingers tapping him—Claire's—lightly, on the shoulder.

He lifts his head. She reaches further around him and taps him on the chest. He rolls onto his back and finds her face close to his.

"Hey," she says, quietly. He can't see her, but he can smell her breath: sweet, like beer and like toothpaste, mixed together with her own warm smell. She is so close he tastes it, too.

She takes his hand. "I've never slept with two men before," she whispers, then laughs a soft, breathy, fast laugh.

Bob cannot speak. Claire holds his hand tightly and rubs her thumb across his forefinger and knuckle.

She then presses her lips against his, kisses him, and he kisses her back. He doesn't taste her breath when their mouths are together, only when she lifts her face above his again and kisses his cheek, his earlobe, and the inside of his ear. Then she whispers, "Wait."

She crosses her arms, reaches downward, and pulls her long T-shirt over her head. He can feel she hasn't taken it all the way off. She has gathered up the front, like a hoisted sail, and laid it behind her neck, with her arms still in the short sleeves.

She sets both his hands on her bared breasts. They know just how to move, and he lets them. He kisses her, on his own. Small kisses on her cheeks and lips and forehead. Her hair, too.

Claire then takes his penis, which is already poking through the fly of his boxer shorts, into her hand. There's a sudden shock, like the moment you see a bird fly out of nowhere into your windshield, and his pelvis, without his wanting it to, jerks back. He's embarrassed at how he trembles, as if two hands have taken hold of the sides of his hips and are shaking him. Their kissing, which continues, is what holds them together.

Then Bob feels his penis swell, though it was hard before she touched him, and sort of leap, on its own, as if it were trying to move more deeply into her hand. He can't understand why it feels so different to have another person touching him. He can hardly hold himself still, or keep himself from making noise and waking his brother.

It's so different when the hand that touches you is someone else's. When it doesn't feel on the inside what *your* hand feels on the inside when you touch yourself: when you don't even know what the hand feels, and don't know what *you* will feel till the moment the hand first touches you. Could it be that way each time? Claire moves her hand back and forth, like he does when he strokes himself, and over the top and around, which he's never done with his own hand. Someone else's hand does what *it* wants to do. That's part of what makes it so different.

They're now kissing with their tongues inside each other's mouths. Bob likes this, but it feels funny when she arches her tongue and touches the inside of his front teeth.

Claire places his hand against her underpants. Her vagina, at first touch, feels warm and damp, like a small, soft head under a thin scarf. He holds his hand with the fingertips downward now, but he rubs with the same motion he first used to rub her breasts.

While he's doing this, she slips her underpants out from under his hand. Her hair is deep and curly, and he separates his fingers so he can reach through it to the skin underneath. He finds the top of the labia. It first feels like the place between fingers, at the bottom, where they grow out of the hand. The difference is that it's wet between the sides, and much softer, and it gets wetter and smoother as he parts them with his fingertips. He loves the feel of it, touching her, the way his hand moves, that he's not afraid, and that he knows how to do it. With the other hand he's still slowly rubbing her breasts. He moves from one to the other and back again.

He wants to speak aloud. He wants to ask Claire why he loves this so much. Why is it so different from touching an arm or a hand or a knee?

"Let's go all the way," Claire whispers.

"Where?" Bob whispers back.

"Inside me. Want to come inside me?"

"Yeah," he says. "Yeah, I want to come inside you."

"Ssssshhhhh . . ." She is laughing. Not with her voice, but with fast breaths.

Tugging at both sides of his boxer shorts, she slowly lowers them to a point just below his knees, then reaches downward through the waistband, and helps him slip his left leg out. He feels embarrassed, yet is also aware that Claire's body, turned toward him, has formed a wall between him and Al and created a separate area, *their* side.

She then takes something out of one of her socks. "Here," she says. "Put this on."

He feels something plastic and unpleasant against his belly. It has a sharp edge, like those little takeout packets of ketchup. "Well?" she says.

"Put *this* on?"

She takes his hand and brings it to her other hand, holding the wrapped condom.

He now realizes what it is. He knows it's important for safe sex. He's seen the advisories on television, and there's an AIDS poster at the Greenville Clinic, where he and his brother get checkups. So much of what he's known only from a distance, from TV, and from imagining is becoming real all at once. He has only the vaguest idea of how to actually use a condom.

"Ever done this before?" Claire asks him.

He doesn't answer.

"No?" she says. Then she kisses him. Deeply and warmly, just on the lips. He can feel, pressed between their two faces, tears coming from her eyes.

"You have to wear this so I don't have a baby." She opens the packet, partially unrolls the condom, and slips it over the head of his penis. "Okay?" She then roll-slips it a little further, like a sock. He reaches down and feels some of it drooping off the end. "This okay?" she asks.

Bob has always thought a condom would feel like a sandwich bag, but it's softer, oily and tighter. Once on, it's clear to him how it works. He pulls it a little further onto himself, to be sure. It gets tighter. Almost too tight. He imagines his penis is a creature that needs, on its own, to breathe. For a second this frightens him. It's as if his whole body were inside it.

She begins to rub him again. Over the condom and on the bottom of the shaft of his penis, where it's still uncovered. He grows even harder and bigger. He's worried it will break, but it stretches. Even so, it feels too tight.

Slowly, and without making a sound, she climbs over him and sets her knees, spread apart, on each side of his hips.

Bob suddenly thinks of his brother. Will he wake? But as quickly as the thought forms, it seems to melt. It's as if Al, whom he cannot see, were nowhere in the room.

Claire reaches one hand behind her and rubs his balls and stomach and the whole bottom of his body. Bob feels happy: oddly small, and calm, and very happy. What the two of them are doing, now, is all there is in this whole night.

Claire moves her hips, slowly, as if her vagina were a paint-brush and she were painting the underside of his penis, pressed flat against his stomach. On their own, his hands slide upward, move further apart at the round outcurve of her hips, and nearer to each other at her waist. He slides them down again, up again. Her hips and torso rise and fall, a little more each time, with the movement of his hands.

On one of the cycles of upward movement, she lifts her

weight entirely off him and his penis springs upward. When she lowers herself again, he is inside her.

Uncounted hours nearer morning—Bob, lying on his side, facing away from Claire, is sound asleep—Claire leans onto her right side and taps Al lightly between the shoulder blades. He first tries to press his head deeper into his pillow, then lifts it, rolls part of the way toward her, and says, "What?"

She kisses him, and in the dark she partly misses his lips and kisses his nose and lightly stubbled upper lip.

"What?" he says again, quieter, and in a less upcurving, less interrogative tone of voice.

"I've never slept with two men before," she says softly. She kisses him again.

She then pulls her body, head to toe, nearer his. Al turns the rest of the way toward her, slides his arms around her lower back, clasps his own forearms, and hugs her tightly.

"Go easy," she whispers. "I'm not a tube of toothpaste."

He opens his embrace, leaving his left hand under her waist and resting his right on the top of her hip. Unlike his brother, Al sleeps in a long-sleeve shirt, as well as his undershorts. Claire unbuttons the front and rubs his chest.

He begins sliding the palm of his hand up and down the curve of her hip. Then down her thigh to the side of her knee, up again to the valley of her waist and to her rib cage and above. Each long upward stroke of his hand brings her T-shirt up a little higher, and on each downward stroke he finds more of the skin of her thigh, then her hip.

Claire parts the two wings of his shirtfront.

Al slips his hand under the hem of her T-shirt.

She lifts her hip so that, using his left hand, as well as his right, he can lift the front all the way up to her neck, making the entire front of her body available to him.

As she did earlier, with Bob, she rolls the fabric and pulls it behind her head so it doesn't slip down between them. She then slides his boxer shorts down, but not off, and helps him lift one of his legs free.

When they are settled again, they begin to kiss. On his own, Al begins to rub her breasts, one in each hand, in a circular motion. He feels her pubic hair, like the back of a hand in a wool mitten, pushing against his penis. As it stiffens, it climbs upward, to a place above her hair, and his, and he feels its head pressed between the smooth skin of their bellies.

She takes his hand from one of her breasts, pulls her hips back, and sets the tips of his fingers at her vagina. He quickly finds the wet entrance and pushes one of his fingers inside. As he does this, he lowers himself a bit and begins to kiss her nipple, then to suck on it. He then tries to push his forefinger inside her along with his middle finger.

"Wait," she says. She places her hand over his. "You must go gentler there." She takes the tip of one of his fingers and begins to move it slowly, upward and downward, just inside the soft, open labia. She widens the circuit a bit, into an oval path, a shape like a candle's flame, like the narrow, complete circles that sometimes form in the grain of wood. And Al follows her movement and lets her direct his hand.

As she does this she begins stroking his penis. She rubs him gently, moving her hand from the head, down to the base, and back up to the head again, at the same speed and to the same rhythm as the movements of her other hand, guiding his fingers along the lips of her vagina, up to her clitoris, and down along the lips again.

With his free hand he cups her hand, closed around his penis, inside his, as she has done to him, and guides her. She wasn't squeezing as tightly as she could have, and it feels better when she moves her hand mostly nearer the top.

Claire exhales three syllables of quiet, acknowledging laughter.

In this way, Al thinks to himself, they are both touching themselves, but with the other person's hand.

They do this for a while. Then Al asks, "Can I?"

"Come inside?" Claire whispers.

"Can I?"

She reaches both hands downward and for a minute presses her head against his chest. She pulls the fabric of one of her socks away from her calf; with the other hand she slips something out of it. "But you'll have to put this on first."

This time, instead of asking, she opens the packet and begins to roll the condom onto him. Al doesn't like the feeling. It's too constricting. A moment before, his penis was hard and throbbing, but now, inside the tight condom, it's softening and beginning to droop.

Claire rubs her hand over his penis, outside the condom, in the same motion—tightly and mostly near the top—that he had shown her with his own hand.

"Wait," he whispers. He rolls the condom back up a bit from the base of the shaft. It had trapped some of his hairs there and was pulling them as his penis grew hard again. "Okay," he says, and she continues moving her hand.

"It feels like an astronaut," he says, "in its own little space suit."

Claire laughs again, quietly. "I wish you didn't have to wear it," she says. "But if you didn't, I might have a baby."

When he is fully hard again, she turns away from him and onto her back, then lifts her leg, the one nearest his side. This enables him to enter her from the side, and partially from behind, without their having to turn farther over.

Al is surprised that his penis can find its way into her through all the soft, vague technology of her body. He begins moving quickly once he feels himself solidly inside her vagina. Claire lifts her head briefly. Al moves his head against hers. "Where you going?" she whispers, upward, into his ear. "To a fire?"

When he slows down, and their bodies fall into a regular rhythm, she takes his right hand off her hip and places his finger, lightly, on her clitoris. She then begins to move it, just as she had earlier.

When he woke up yesterday morning, he was a man who'd never made love to a woman. This is all so sudden, and so amazing. He cannot begin to describe, in the language he uses to talk to himself, the things he is feeling.

He had thought sex would be something he, the man, did *to* the woman. It's not that at all. He could never have imagined this, that his body and someone else's body could become a single, interlocked machine. Her thigh rises and her hips press back, as he lifts himself and presses forward. On the downward part of its small orbit, his fingertip—*his*, and hers, too—can feel his penis, under the smooth, wet skin of the condom, moving in and out of her, in and out of her. Amazing.

8

Al and Bob awake at sunrise and find that Claire is no longer lying between them in bed. They hear the shower running in the bathroom. From outside, they hear the morning fill with birdsong, while inside, the pale light grows denser, slides slowly down the walls toward the floor, and finds every object in the room. The shower stops. Claire pads from the bathroom across the living room and into the kitchen. They hear the chug and screech the kitchen sink tap makes on its first opening of the day. Then water falling against the bottom of a metal pot.

The two brothers—each lying on his side, back to the other, each holding himself to his opposite edge of the mattress—neither stir nor speak.

In a moment Claire is standing in the bedroom doorway. She yawns, smiles at Al and Bob, lifts her fisted hand to her mouth, and yawns again. Her hair, wet and straight, falls to the ridge of her chin at the sides. Al sits up, then sets his bare feet on the floor. Claire turns, slips back into the living room. They hear the sound of her dragging a chair across the floor, into the kitchen, and up to the table.

Al, sitting next to Bob and across from Claire, asks, "You think Mike's got that fuse by now?"

Bob knows Al knows he does. Since Claire's been in their presence, both brothers have been discussing aloud the things they know of as certainties and would thus, ordinarily, not even speak of. "I'd be sure of it," Bob says. "The truck's usually there and gone by dawn." He wishes he hadn't said it. He doesn't like the idea of leaving his brother and Claire alone together while he drives off to Mike's. If she's only going to be there another hour, less even, he wants to spend all of it in her company. He wishes he could have said, *Probably not.* But of course Al would know that wasn't the case.

For a few moments none of the three speak. Claire looks down into her cup. Al drinks his coffee in small, quick, breathy sips. His head's splitting, and he has a growing urge to urinate. His cheeks and forehead feel warm to his own hand's touch.

Bob is also hungover. He doesn't mind, though. He likes the sight of Claire at their kitchen table. He likes the way she looks down into her cup as she drinks. He looks down into his own and tries to imagine what she might see—if she's actually looking, that is, and not thinking about something else. He holds his breath until the black coffee stops moving. He first sees the dark bottom of his nose, wide and flat as a pig's nose, a band of light across his cheekbones, his familiar anxious eyes, darker in their reflection, another band of light across his forehead.

He notices that Claire, in her quietness this morning, seems shyer than she has the whole time since they met yesterday afternoon. She keeps pushing her wet hair behind her ears, but it keeps slipping back out again.

Al notices this, too. Her hair, on the sides, is the same length as George Washington's in the portrait of him that hangs in the auditorium of the school he and Al attended. From kindergarten until they graduated high school, all of it in the same building. They'd spent a lot more time with girls in those years, but never, during or since, had he done with one what he did with Claire last night.

"I'll go with you to get the fuse," Claire says to Bob.

"Great," Bob says.

Claire gets up and walks into the living room. When she walks back into the kitchen, she's wearing her man's sport coat and her sneakers.

Bob gets up, leaves the room, then quickly returns wearing his own jacket.

"Why don't we make it a trio," Al says. "I want to buy a lottery ticket anyway." He smiles. His forehead is throbbing. "I can never trust Bob to pencil in the numbers I ask him to."

9

Less than half an hour after Claire drives off, Al and Bob are back out at the culvert. Bob is cutting up the maple branch that had gotten stuck inside and handing the pieces out to Al.

"I can't believe it's that simple," Claire had said, after Al had put in the new fuse and her car started right up. She looked enormously sad—both brothers had noticed this—when she'd said it.

Bob realizes that he hadn't once, in the twenty-four hours since he'd last crawled into this culvert, noticed that time was passing. He had squeezed his entire self into this last day, *his* day, so that time itself was barely larger than himself. Like this maple branch he is now sawing into pieces, it didn't move an inch while the rest of the world underwent its last rotation.

Al, piling the branches and leaves on the bank beside the small streambed, is thinking that everything that happens, *while* it's happening, is simple. It's only afterwards that it gets complicated. If when you look back in time to before a thing happened, you look right through the thing itself, as if it were a window or a lens, it becomes the last part of all that earlier time, and not just the first part of everything that has happened since.

Often, on the nights he slept in his recliner, he'd switch the TV back on after Bob went to bed. He'd turn the volume all the way down, and with the remote, he'd keep flipping channels until a woman appeared on the screen. The moment the woman's image was replaced by a man's, or by something else, he'd change the channel again until he found another woman. He preferred scenes where there was just one woman, rather than several. It's not difficult to watch TV this way—the way he does it without his brother—because there are more images of women than anything else. What he discovered this morning, looking through last night into his past, is that this is also true of his own separate life. The parade of images inside the TV is exactly like the passage of his own changing thoughts: though every single thing he's ever seen or done is somehow *in* there, there are more women than anyone or anything else.

After they finish clearing the culvert, Bob crawls out and crosses the road to see if anything has gotten stuck on that side. Stopped by a rock, floating in some new, green reeds, he finds a butter dish. It has a white plastic bottom and a clear plastic top. It's the kind that fits a quarter-pound stick. It's like the air car the Jetsons drive around in; it's like the basket that carried the baby Moses.

He squats beside it. Watches it bobble in the rising water, now moving around the rock since the flow has been restored, and just before the quickening current takes it into the culvert, he picks it up. Further back from the road, moving like a snake in the current, he finds a bathrobe sash. At the moment his eyes find it, it begins to be carried toward him—the effect of clearing the culvert has just gotten back that far—as if it had been the last in a line of cars waiting for a light to change. It's a wet, dark red. He imagines that when it's dry, it will be the same bright red as Claire's sneakers. He walks back toward their side of the road, carrying the butter dish in one hand and swinging the wet cloth belt, in a wide circle, with the other.

The appearance of these two objects reminds him of what Al doesn't know, nor anyone else, which is that his essay "Meat" isn't all of what he has written. That's just what he shows to other people. He also writes sentences. He keeps hidden a growing list of them. They just come out of him: they appear as mysteriously as the two objects he now holds in his hands, and after carrying them around in his head, sometimes for days, he writes them down. There are nearly a hundred now.

They aren't just strings of words. Each time he reads them, a life grows around them, like the lives of the people who owned this butter dish and this bathrobe sash.

Last summer he wrote: *The apricots in the Greenville Super-*

market are the same size and the same shape as the vaginas of young deer.

When he was ten he became more and more uneasy, being at school: *It's hard to be friends because I can't hear what they're saying when I smell their hair and skin and clothes.*

When he was thirteen he wrote this one about his father: *No one else sees the wrinkles, like strong blood vessels, that form in the front of his blue jeans and then disappear each time he squats to pick up another bale.*

"Never know what'll wash down," Al says to him.

Bob hands him the butter dish.

Al holds it, looks down at it, turns it over. There's a price sticker on the bottom, but the price has washed off. All that's left is a dollar sign and the faded remains of a bar code. "Nobody's ever used this," he says. He turns it right-side up again, sets the lid in place, holds it up to his face, and looks through it at his brother, who smiles back at him. Bob's cheeks—his whole face—look rounder, like their mother's when she was a young woman. He lowers it now to look directly at Bob.

Bob feels uncomfortable, being looked at by his brother. He drops the smile from his face.

"I guess we'll never know who owned it," Al says.

"Or how it found its way to us, or *why* they never used it," Bob says.

"It's a mystery."

"It's like a quarter you get in your change at Mike's," Bob says. "Last month somebody could've dropped it into a slot machine in Las Vegas. A month before that, somebody grabbed it out of a cash register during a holdup in New York City. Maybe somebody even got killed for it. . . ."

"A butter dish?"

"*No,*" Bob tells his brother. "The quarter."

"You think somebody'd get themselves killed for a quarter?"

"Forget it." Bob grabs back the butter dish.

"It's just a piece of plastic," Al says. His anger rises suddenly. He knows Bob thinks he doesn't understand something. His anger swells. "Somebody living at a higher altitude must've dropped it," he says. "Or threw it out the window. Or their house burnt down and the fireman's hose washed the damn thing into a brook."

He gathers the maple branches into a neat pile. He then takes the bathrobe sash from his brother's hand and ties them up with it.

They have brought the saw, along with the pile of branches, back to the house and have returned to the field. They are each on opposite sides of the road, reaching into the culvert with rakes and pulling out the last of the smaller branches and leaves and muck. Each spring, since they were children, since their father was younger than the two brothers are now, they have cleared out this culvert. If they didn't, a pond would form and swallow the road shoulder on the mountainside. Then, by late spring, the hay would have taken on a pale, weak color. By early summer, it would be three inches shorter than everybody else's. By midsummer it would be dead.

Bob finishes his side and walks back across the road to help his brother on the outflow side of the culvert, where most of the small stuff builds up. He tells Al they should save the butter dish. They can boil it to get out any germs. Then wash it in dishwashing soap. "Who knows," he tells his brother. "Claire might pass this way again. If she doesn't permanently relocate to Germany, that is. I bet she'd like it. A butter dish is just the kind of thing she might like."

Al's gaze meets his eyes as he says this. His stare is even more direct, more focused than before. The two of them are quiet for a while afterwards. They rake the last of the mucky debris up the graded sides of the embankment that holds the culvert in place.

Al then says, "She's now got a whole pack of those fuses in her glove compartment." His voice is sharp. He wants to sound surer of what he says, and more final, than anything his brother might say in response. "And *I* showed her how to change them. We won't be seeing her again."

Bob suddenly realizes why, earlier, he didn't want to leave Claire and his brother alone together. He'd had a series of dreams the night before, a flow of quick, changing images, like a too-fast slide show, like the windows of a train speeding past, like sentences coming out of him too fast to read. At first he thought it was the flickering play of light and dark against the back wall of the bedroom when his brother, sitting in the recliner late at night, holds down the channel-changer button. Last night, in bed, after he and Claire went all the way, something had happened between them, too. In his sleep, he'd sensed it. He kept himself from fully waking by holding his eyelids shut like clenched fists. What he saw was a raging parade of images that flew by too quickly for him to comprehend or remember a single one.

Al has begun to think the same thing. It hadn't, until now, even occurred to him that he might not be the only one. He half remembers, in the emptier part of last night, before Claire woke him, that he'd sensed something happening in bed. Something beyond the unusual state of a third person sleeping between them. It might have been a dream, but if it was, it was a dream that didn't have a story, only a feeling. It made him angry at Bob, who can be such a goody-goody boy, does just what he thinks he's supposed to, and never has a thought of his own— like just before, with that stupid butter dish: *Just the kind of thing she might like . . .*

Al watches Bob pull the sludgy leaves off the tines of his rake and drop them into the irrigation ditch. When he's done he just stands there, holding the rake handle, looking into the brown, slow-moving water. Briefly, he looks back at Al, then he kneels down, moves the leaves into the current with his hand. When all the leaves have moved downstream he keeps moving his hand in the water, parting it, as if to get a closer look at something on the bottom.

"Anything interesting?" Al's voice isn't loud, but it's growly and sharpened to a point. "Salt and pepper shakers, maybe? . . . A butter knife? Look down there, see if you can find us something else we don't need. How about some napkin rings."

Bob, watching his brother, rises to his feet. His grip tightens on the rake handle. This time he looks back into Al's eyes.

Al crosses the ditch to Bob's side. He bends his knees and slowly lowers himself, holding his eyes firm to Bob's stare. He picks up the butter dish and returns slowly to a standing position. He moves his eyes downward, first to Bob's hands, one just above the other, clenched and white-fisted on the rake handle, then lower, to his own hand, bending the bottom of the butter dish, like a playing card, between his fingertips and the heel of his palm. He closes his hand, pressing the two ends together. Without a sound, it snaps in two.

Al never takes his eyes off Bob's face. His skin had become hard and wrapped tight as bark, but now it begins to loosen. His face grows longer, then relaxes into a sheepish smile. "This morning I *really* had to take a leak," he says. "Bad."

Bob blushes deeply. He looks down at his two wet shoes, at the dark, mucky streaks in the grass. "Me too," he says.

Al then asks, "You think she'll really get back together with that guy?"

Bob thinks a moment. "I don't think she'd travel all that way if she didn't think it was likely." He finds the sides of his mouth rising into a smile. He then says, "It really wouldn't matter . . ."

"They'll be together. They'll be happy."

"It really wouldn't matter," Bob says again.

"What we're saying here," Al says, "what it boils down to, is how much we really care if this woman has a baby."

Bob looks back at him.

Al reaches into his pocket. "Do we?" he asks.

"Nah," Bob says.

Al pulls out his hand, then opens it and shows Bob the condom, molded into a sloppy, wet ball. "My bladder was about to burst," he says.

Bob, now laughing, says, "After breakfast, I tore off the bottom part of mine—you know, the balloon part—and left the ring part on." He takes a smaller, waxy-wet latex ball out of his own pocket and shows it to Al. "I thought if I left that part on, like a wedding ring or something, it would be enough. But you know what happened? It slipped off."

Al is now doubled over with laughter.

Bob lifts his pants, one leg at a time, and shakes them. "Maybe it came out the bottom," he says.

"Stop," Al says, hugging his stomach and stomping his feet. "It hurts to laugh this hard."

"Seriously," Bob says. He looks at his brother. His laughter is abating, but he's still smiling. "What if Claire and her husband don't get back together. I mean, they probably will, but what if they don't?"

"If they don't," Al says, his laughter slowing too, "and if she has a baby, she'll still be all right. That Claire is one smart cookie."

"That's for sure," Bob says. He's looking back at the outfeed now, at the wet piles of mud and twigs and dead leaves.

"You can believe that," Al says.

"I do," Bob says. He drops his rake and nods toward the water, falling smoothly off the metal lip of the culvert onto the streambed, already beginning to raise the level in the channel of the ditch.

Epilogue

Al is looking at his father through the fogged driver's-side window of his car. The door handle is colder than ice in his hand, but he doesn't release his grip. When he presses the button, he says, *Okay*. This is in a dream. He has to do this, open the door, because no one else will.

People are all over the place, all of them here because his father's car's here, and because his father, who is dead, is inside it. But none of them will open the door.

A state trooper is trying to measure the snow-covered tire tracks that lead from the car back up to the road. Another is kneeling on the hood—*that close to him, for God's sake*—reaching through the broken windshield and moving a pencil around in the snow and broken glass on the dashboard. A man and two women from the volunteer ambulance service are just standing there, off to the side of the car. They have with them a folding stretcher, with its wheels buried in the snow so it looks like a big letter N with the bottom missing and the sides crushed together.

There's a tow truck idling up by the side of the road. Sometimes the voices coming from its radio seem to be talking to the voices coming from the radio in the ambulance parked right in front of it. They're all here, yet none of them will open the door.

Okay, he says, and pulls it open. It tries to swing closed again, as car doors will, but Al blocks it with his body, like you do when you reach in to lift a bag of groceries off the seat. He bends slightly at the knees so he can lean in. His father's face and his fingers are the color of the inside of tree bark. He can see the nose and closed eyes and the forehead, but the mouth is pressed into the backs of his hands. It's open, his mouth, but pressed down. Like he was saying something right up to the moment the car hit the tree, but then had to stop because his teeth got pressed against his knuckles.

Everything in the dream is the same as it was in real life—
except that the car, when he leans into it, has the new-car smell
it had years before this time, when he and Bob were children
and his parents had bought it. That's how he knows he's
dreaming.

He backs away from the smell. From one step back, it looks
like his father had never been alive. *Okay*, he says again. He
tries to wake himself. But he wakes into another dream. The
new dream also has the new-car smell. It's like the second dream
had been going on the whole time the first one was and he just
stepped out of one and into the other. Not like changing channels; like climbing into another boat that, for a moment, rides
in the water next to yours. In the new dream he's lying across
the front seats of Claire's car and he suddenly notices the small
bright gleam that is the cigarette lighter. He reaches under the
seat for it. He can't wait for the moment when he sits up again
and shows it to her. He then realizes the lighter wasn't there
when he'd first leaned his head down below the seats. It was
dark down there. He had been staring into the darkness below
the driver's seat, his arm twisted above him, his fingers trying
to open the fuse-box casing, when it flared into existence. Then
it was just there, this small, bright glow. Reflecting the light
that enabled him to see it, where there was no light to reflect.

This is what he wants to tell her when he sits up again, but
she's gone. She was just here. A minute ago, she was here.
Wasn't she? The car's still here. He's got the lighter in his hand.
Wasn't she just here? If she doesn't come back soon, it will become like she was never here.

It's six A.M. Early July. Bob is sitting on the porch, drinking
his coffee from a glass with ice cubes in it. He hears, from inside,
the sound of Al's voice. A deep, drawn-out moaning that stops,
briefly, each time he inhales. He'd done this a minute ago, and
then it stopped. Bob knows it's the sound Al makes when he's
trying to wake himself up, and didn't give it a thought the first

time. But Al's never done it more than once, and this time, between two of the moans, he says something that sounds like the word *Okay*. Bob decides to go inside and help his brother wake up.

Al has kicked off the blanket and is lying with his hand across his forehead, as though he'd raised it to see something at a distance, under bright sunlight. But he seems peaceful, lying still. Perhaps the dream has passed. On his way back out to the porch, Bob gets more ice from the freezer and pours more coffee into his glass.

The first hay is thick and high and ready. Today they'll start to mow. Bob looks down and sees Norton, their puppy, chewing on the toe of his bedroom slipper. He scoops him up and sets him on his lap, facing the field. Norton's three months old and is beginning to seem like a permanent member of the household. Mike's grandchildren had him in a cardboard box, along with his mother and four brothers and sisters, in the All-In-One parking lot. This was in May. They'd set the box on the hood of Mike's truck and leaned a cardboard sign across the windshield: *Free Dogs*. The mother is Mike's collie. The father, Mike told them, came and went without introducing himself. Al named the puppy Norton after the character in *The Honeymooners*. His paws are a bit smaller than a pure collie's would be by now, and his coat's a lot darker.

Before Al's moaning had distracted him, Bob had been thinking about Claire. Sitting here, with Norton on his lap, he returns to the exact point he'd left off at. Like his thoughts were a train, stopped briefly at a station. He'd gotten off, then climbed back on.

He'd been thinking that since Claire left, his life prior to her arrival—his memory of it—has come to seem less like the memory of real occurrences and more like the memory of a long dream. Like he'd been asleep a dozen years, even longer.

It's as if, since his parents died, he'd been dreaming, and in the dream he'd been living the first part of his life over, making that part easier to understand and more pleasing to remember.

He'd been filling stuff in. . . . Like he gave the first part of his life a second coat of paint, instead of going on to the next part.

The thought occurs to him that Claire's visit was an event as large as when his parents died, only a good event.

They didn't save a thing from her visit. Not a crumpled cigarette pack, not the empty wine bottle, not even the burnt-out fuse. They returned the lighter fluid to Mike's the next morning when they picked up the new fuses. They threw the condoms —he never found the ring part of his—into the irrigation ditch. They could be out there, in the field, disintegrated back to their basic molecules, or they could have stayed intact, carried along by the current to the point where the water slips underground at the edge of their field, to where it reemerges and feeds the huge cow pond on Mike's brother-in-law's property, a half-mile south, to where it flows out the other side, cascades a sheer five hundred feet at White Falls, into a stream that loses itself in Green River, then crosses the county line. . . . Maybe next spring someone at a lower altitude, clearing the thaw debris from their culvert, will briefly note, and as quickly forget, their presence: two rounded, nacreous lumps, trapped with the branches and leaves and muck, unnoticeable but for their clearly not being products of nature.

Norton has lain down, facing forward, his forepaws on Bob's knee. Every few minutes Bob stops scratching his head, and he begins fidgeting and wagging his tail until Bob starts again.

Maybe she is three months pregnant by now. And maybe, by taking off the condom, he somehow allowed something to take root in *him*. Something that has continued to grow. As if he were traveling back in time instead of forward and the memory of her visit was growing larger, like Norton. As if for a second time he were moving nearer and nearer to Claire's actual presence—this time he was moving toward *her*, instead of her toward him—and this time he could *see* the moment, its actuality, as he approached it.

The screen door whacks shut, and Al, holding a glass of iced coffee, shuffles out onto the porch in pajama bottoms and slippers. Norton jumps off Bob's lap and runs up to him, wagging his tail wildly. Al pats his head, then stands at the porch railing and faces the field. He takes a sip of his coffee. "It's about that time again," he says.

"I haven't seen it this thick in years," Bob says.

Al smiles. "A two-hundred-acre crew cut." In emphasis he moves his hand closely over his own scalp, but he doesn't take his eyes off the field. "That's what we'll give it."

Bob watches his brother. He looks for some sign, some remaining presence of whatever it was he'd dreamed about that caused him to moan and try to wake himself, but there's nothing to read in his appearance. He seems happy, calm, a bit groggy.

"I'd bet the farm we do over three thousand bales," Al says to Bob.

"I wouldn't take that bet," Bob says, "because I believe you're right." He looks down and sees Norton, on his hind legs, chewing at the knee of his pajamas. He feels one of his sharp puppy teeth break through the cloth and lightly poke at his skin. He lifts his leg and pushes the dog. Norton stumbles backward onto his rump, then rears up again and sets his forepaws on Bob's other knee. Bob looks back out at the field and wonders if the hay would have grown as thick and as tall if Claire hadn't passed through. The two brothers have rarely spoken of her since the morning she left, but Bob can't stop himself from speaking this thought aloud.

"I can't help thinking that this year's hay, a crop as good as *this*, has something of Claire in it."

Al smiles, then turns to face his brother. He sees Norton, chewing at Bob's pajamas, and Bob smiling back at him, and starts to laugh. "Maybe," he says. He returns his attention to the field, then says, "It's a funny thought, but you might have something there."

He's thinking that the funniest part of it is that their experience with Claire, even though it happened in the same house, in the same bed, is, for both of them, the first important thing they've ever done separately. He's looking out into the hay, his eyes aimed at the center of the field so he can't see the road, the edges, the horizon: just hay. Its healthy growth has to do with rain—a lot of it but not too much—a warm spring, and plenty of sunlight.

In most ways, Al thinks, life is returning to the way it was before her visit. It's beginning to feel like she wasn't actually there. And that's okay with him. He lets his eyes follow the road—its surface growing vague and wavy in the bright morning light—up to the point where it tops the hill and disappears. Except for the telephone poles, it would have looked exactly the same a hundred years ago: nothing ever changes here. He remembers a story about a mermaid who could leave the ocean, but just for a single day. If Claire were that mermaid, this valley's the place she would choose. Nobody on the outside would ever know she was here. This is the kind of place flying saucers choose to land in, and ghosts can appear in complete privacy. A whole armada of butter dishes could navigate the irrigation ditch from one end of this field to the other, the deer could wear bathrobes, the rain, if it chose to, could fall upward, *into* the clouds, and no one outside this valley would know or, for that matter, care.

Claire's not in the hay. Her presence is nowhere in the whole valley. However, one actual effect of her visit, one that feels more and more real, and true, is that from here on in, he and Bob will probably be doing a lot more things separately.

Norton lets out a sharp, high-pitched bark. Al picks him up, sets him on the porch rail, holds him standing on his rear legs, balanced back against his stomach. "Nah," he says aloud, but nothing else.

Bob watches his brother to see if he'll say more. But Al remains silent.

That's just the kind of crap people like to believe is true, Al thinks to himself. That crops grow better when something special happens. It helps them understand what they feel, by imagining the hay feels it. If he and his brother hadn't cleared the culvert this year, and the hay came up sparse and dry, he'd still be feeling all the things he's felt since Claire was here. He lifts Norton up in front of him. He wants the dog to see what he sees, from *his* eye level.

Life is beyond this valley, Al thinks to himself. *My life.* He's always been unable to think that thought, because he's been too afraid to consider leaving. Three months now since Claire's visit, a whole season of days, and in that time he's steadily become more afraid of staying. If he woke up one morning, walked out onto the porch, and discovered the hayfield had become a parking lot, or an airport, or an ocean, nothing *else* will have changed. He'd still have to live the life he's always lived because he's here.

Three months and Al still wouldn't tell this to his brother, but he doesn't miss her at all. It's like the Claire he remembers has become the Claire he tried to imagine on the afternoon she sat beside him on the porch and he looked out into the field, the way he is right now, instead of directly at her. He began to assemble an image of her, mostly his, and since she was actually here less than a single day, continued assembling it after she left. It's nearly complete.

Norton barks again. Bob imitates his bark in response. Al sets him down. He runs back over to Bob and jumps up on his lap.

Bob can feel that his brother has changed since Claire's visit, and that whatever he'd dreamed this morning was part of it.

Bob hasn't changed at all. In fact, he's become more himself. He's come to understand—no, *not* understand—he's come to name what it is that he most often feels, what he has always, most often, felt: desire. It is the most consistent part of himself, the largest part of what he feels like *to* himself—for his whole life up until now and for as long as he'll be on the planet. It's yearning, and it's horniness, and its more, because it's more than any feeling he's ever known the coming and going of. It isn't seasonal, desire. It's a light that never goes off, a constant arrival of sensation. No one ever told him that.

He wonders if people outside this valley ever talk about it. If

they don't, well then, their lives aren't so different after all.
There's nothing they know that he doesn't.

Al is smiling.

Bob has no idea what he's smiling about.

Al's facing the field and his eyes are closed and he looks like
he's picking up radio waves, like he's an antenna, a smiling
antenna, and whatever he's receiving is not coming from out in
the field, or anywhere else nearby, for that matter.

"*Enterprise* calling Al," Bob says.

"We're receiving transmissions from beyond Federation
Space," Al says. He doesn't turn or open his eyes.

Norton jumps off Bob's lap, runs down the porch steps and
out into the grass in front of the house. He faces the field and
barks.

"It appears you *both* are," Bob says.

A rabbit suddenly appears on the grass in front of the house.
Norton leaps up once, then chases it to the point where it runs
under the barbed-wire fence and into the hayfield. He stops
there and keeps barking.

Al turns, faces his brother. "It's going to be a hot one," he
says.

Bob looks at him, then toward the sun rising over the field.
"We'd better get started, then," he says. "See how much we can
get done before noon. Valley'll be an oven after that." He gets
up, brings his coffee glass into the house.

Bob stops the door just before it closes, opens it again, and
follows his brother inside.

The Beginning of the End of the Cold War

But in spite of my soul's leap out to him, at the end of its elastic, I saw him only darkly, because of the dark and then because of the terrain, in the folds of which he disappeared from time to time, to re-emerge further on, but most of all I think because of other things calling me and towards which too one after the other my soul was straining wildly.

—Samuel Beckett

1

8:30 P.M.

Nazzarino Jacobs leans back against his car, half sitting on the ledge of the open driver's-side window, with his elbows on the faded blue roof, looking up. The evening sky, above the rooftops and antennae, is supernaturally empty. His stomach is clenched like a fist. He will accept whatever comes.

He is searching the heavens for a neutron bomb. Any moment now, one released from the belly of a high-altitude bomber, concealed in the highest reaches of atmosphere, or carried in the nose of an intercontinental missile, will pierce this helmet of pure sky. Earlier today, he learned that both sides have developed systems that can outwit radar and, though they're still required by the Geneva convention, the last thing he'd expect is a whistle. Why would someone attach one to an explosive intended, specifically, to destroy life? The thin metallic whines that threaded the skies over World War II bombing objectives were warnings: *Get out of the way. We just want the railroad bridge and the ammo dump.* However, when a weapon is not designed to mangle steel, and demolish brick and mortar, but to undo life at a molecular level, a whistle would be a cruel joke. There'd be no place to hide and nothing worth doing once you heard it. The truth of the matter is, if a neutron bomb were falling,

191

and if you wanted to know about it, you'd have to look up. It could happen anywhere, anytime, and there'd be no whistle. The absence of warning would be a small kindness, the last you'd receive.

An hour earlier, for no apparent reason, his right front tire blew out. Before he knew it, he'd skidded across two lanes. There was a white Chevy cruising in his blind spot when the tire blew. As he skidded, he watched it sail across his rearview mirror. If its driver's reflexes had been a hair slower, it wouldn't have mattered if a neutron bomb was falling or not. He's now parked in an island of unused pavement at the foot of the overspan of the Williamsburg Bridge. He has a spare tire and he has a jack, but the jack has no handle. Manhattan-bound traffic passes on both sides. He tore the sleeves off a red sweatshirt and tied them to the door handles—his SOS.

It's Saturday, June 12, 1982. In the hour he's been here, no one has stopped. It's taken him nearly that long to stop shaking. The sun is quickening its descent. The traffic slows and thickens as it approaches the bridge. Interior light sharpens in the windows of the tenement buildings that face the roadway from both sides. The aerosphere—indoors and out—is boiling invisibly with electromagnetic waves: Saturday prime time. The sun is about to touch the horizon. Despite the exhaust fumes and the smells rising from the East River, despite the whole abrasive chemistry of the evening, the air is calm, even sweet.

Two children, a girl and a boy, wave from the back seat of a Volvo station wagon. They're stopped in traffic less than twenty feet from where Nazz is standing. He wishes their parents would wave, too, but they don't. The forlorn appearance of people standing beside disabled cars in inconvenient places causes a sensation of deep sadness. Adults have learned not to look.

Nazz lives in the East Village, a mile or so uptown from the other side of the bridge. It's not a difficult walk, but he's afraid to leave the car. Even so, if no one stops soon, he'll have to. When the traffic begins to move again, the boy leans out the window, blows against the side of his hand, and makes a fart noise at Nazz.

He walks around the front of the car and stares into the open trunk. Perhaps a jack handle, or some kind of lever good enough to substitute, will appear. This is the first time he's opened the trunk in two years, and the sight of the belongings he's been traveling around with makes him uncomfortable.

If clothes make the man, if possessions define their owner, the collection of objects before him belong to a total stranger. They're his. He somehow acquired and kept each one. But here and now, these things, restored to existence when he lifted his trunk hood an hour ago, are not just *being* there, they are actively describing someone else's life.

He looks back up at the sky.

He spent the day at the Anti-Nuke Rally in Central Park. One of the dozens of leaflets handed to him along the five-mile march up to Eighty-sixth Street delineated the various effects of existing nuclear weapons. It was laid out in columns under these headings: TYPE OF WARHEAD, MEGATONNAGE, DISTANCE FROM POINT OF IMPACT, WIND DIRECTION AND SPEED. If, on a day as calm as today, Nazz were within a half-mile radius of where an intercontinental missile carrying a nontactical (big motherfucking) neutron warhead fell, absolutely nothing would remain. Not even the concrete to hold his shadow. At one mile, little that would be recognizable. At two, the car and its contents would remain intact. Where Nazz now stands there would be a gray-brown shadow about the size of a Frisbee. The gray, clothing; the brown, Nazz.

If that were the case, and if fifty years from now a team of archaeologists from another planet happened onto the scene, they would look into the open trunk of a faded blue Karmann Ghia and see the following: softball mitt, softball, an incomplete set of Volkswagen tools in an army surplus gas mask bag, a tennis racket, an unopened can of Billy Beer, a telescopic fishing rod, a rusted Boy Scout knife, a child's beach pail and shovel, and a magnetized statue of St. Christopher, still in its box, which could serve the extraterrestrial archaeologists as a kind of Rosetta Stone, since it says, on each side, in four different languages, *St. Christopher: Patron Saint and Vigilant Protector of All Who Travel This Earth.* Everything but a jack handle.

In the sunlight, this confluence of objects brings to mind words like *gentle, Pepsi Generation, cheerful, casual, relaxed, integrated.* And if Nazzarino Jacobs knows anything about himself, it is that he is none of these things.

He bought the softball mitt and softball in a fit of enthusiasm when he and some of the other business agents who worked for Local 613, Distributive Employees Union, decided to organize a team. That was three years ago, and they haven't yet played their first game. The tennis racket was a gift from Regina, his ex-wife, for his twenty-ninth birthday. They were married at the time. He's now thirty-three and has only used it once, hitting balls against the wall of the schoolyard across the street from his apartment. The statue of St. Christopher was a gift from Helen, who cleans the offices of District 613. One morning he found it sitting on his desk. She gave one to all the business agents. He used to get an annual use out of the fishing rod, the knife entered his life during his Boy Scout years, and he has no memory of how the Billy Beer got there.

The beach pail and shovel are the only items in the entire inventory that are not his, and the only ones it gives him any pleasure to look at. They belong to his daughter, Theresa, whose name, over the years, has evolved to Tuna. The refining process began when she was seven. They were reading the names of countries on the globe he had given her that year for Christmas. If she couldn't pronounce one correctly, Nazz would sound it out for her.

"Tu-*nee*-sia," he said, slowly.

"That's beautiful," she said.

"It *is* nice."

"I bet if they had a contest for the country with the beautifulest name, Tunisia would win it. *Tunisia.* What do you think, Nazz?"

She never calls him Daddy, but calls her mother Mommy.

"First prize."

"Can *I* be Tunisia? I mean my name. . . ."

"Your name?"

"It's not that different from Theresa. And I hate Theresa. There's a girl in my class called Montana, and that's her real name."

Within two years the name streamlined itself to Tuna. She's now eleven and no longer plays with the beach pail and shovel. He sees her every other weekend.

If the interplanetary archaeologists who came upon this car would assume—as do most earth archaeologists when they unearth shards of pottery and stone axes at grave sites—that the characteristics evoked by the collection of possessions found in this trunk were, by extension, those of their owner, if they made this equation: *These things = Nazzarino Jacobs*, then these scientists, in the parlance of Planet Earth, would have their heads up their assholes. But if they were to assume that the owner of these artifacts obtained them, over a period of time, because each, at a specific moment, represented some element of an identity he would like to have, or someone near him (the person who gave it to him) would like him to have, they would be getting warmer.

Finally, the wisest archaeologist, making the first in a series of deductions that might have the whole thing cleared up in another fifty years, might add to the previous thought, *Well, that might be the key; then again, it might not.*

It's beginning to get cooler. The bridge's understructure and the soot-brown fronts of the nearest buildings have become darker.

Nazz looks directly into the setting sun, then closes his eyes.

There are now two suns, both black, one beside the other. It's as if he can see, separately, the image held by each eye. One of the suns begins to move toward the other, leaking inky tendrils into the pale light. Just before it reaches the other sun it veers off. Then it rises, slowly, until it climbs above the screen of his perception. He is left calm and sad. Were he an astronaut returning home after twenty years in space, he'd be as happy to land right here, or in Tunisia, as in his own backyard. He's on Earth: beyond that, how could anything else matter?

He begins to wave at the passing cars. Most people look, but no one stops. He imagines himself as he appears to them. Untouchably forlorn, comic, forgettable. Just another schmuck stranded for a time among the cables and stone and hubcaps and pigeons. Nazz has driven past this person more than once.

If a neutron warhead had exploded and you were out of range of the shock and flash, but within range of its eddying radiation, when it reached you, you would feel it as you would feel sunlight on a June evening, which is to say, not at all.

2
Memorial Day

As if they'd agreed to notice each other at the same moment: Nazz, turning his head as he slows for the light, and this man, witless and filthy, standing one step from the curb on Houston Street, holding a roll of paper towels and a bottle of Windex. He walks up to the open driver's window and smiles at Nazz. "Brand-new," he says, holding out the paper towels. He then pokes his middle finger into the end of the cardboard spool, rips off the cellophane wrap, and shoves it into his pants pocket.

"I used to be a florist," he tells Nazz. He's wearing a thread-worn flak jacket. On the lapel is a maroon button with the words *I'm a Pepper*. "Know what happened?" he says. "The cops just strolled in one day and broke up all my showcases." He sprays the windshield and then begins to wipe in a circular motion. The crumpled paper gets darker and darker. He watches Nazz through the widening circle of clear glass. When their eyes meet they smile at each other.

Nazz has just driven Tuna home, to Queens. They spent the three-day holiday weekend together. They saw two movies: *Return of the Jedi* and *Bladerunner*; went to the Festival of St. Anthony in Little Italy; and had all three lunches in a Ukrainian coffee shop—Tuna's favorite restaurant—on First Avenue. Earlier today, they went to the parade.

When he picked her up on Saturday, he gave her a Monopoly game.

"Who gives Memorial Day presents?" she asked. "I never got one before."

He also gave her one of the red sweatshirts that the Local 613 contingent would be wearing to the Anti-Nuke march in two weeks. "I'm starting a new tradition," he told her.

She held the sweatshirt up to herself. It came down to her knees. "I can wear it as a nightgown," she said. "Or I can wait till I'm your size and wear it in gym class." She threw it over

197

her shoulders and tied the sleeves around her neck like a cape. "Isn't Memorial Day for soldiers that died in wars?"

"That's right," Nazz said.

When the guy finishes the windshield he walks back to the driver's window. "You want the back one done?"

Nazz tells him no.

"My shop was in Detroit. You know, the Motor City . . . De *twa* . . . Ever been there?"

"Never have."

"I was right off Woodward Avenue. Carried fresh-cut and potted. I had *some* walk-in trade."

Nazz hands him a dollar. He takes a step back from the car, pokes a finger into the buttonhole of his breast pocket, opens it, looks down into it.

"I have two kids," he says, still looking downward into his shirt pocket. "A son and a daughter."

"I have a daughter," Nazz tells him. He watches the light change, but he doesn't take his foot off the brake. "An ex-wife, too."

"The latter," he tells Nazz, "ex or not, goes without saying."

Nazz smiles, turns, looks at him.

He reaches over and sprays the windshield again. A light flurry of suds, and only on Nazz's side. A taxi pulls up and hovers behind the car. Its driver honks.

He stops wiping, hands Nazz the paper towels and the Windex, backs away from the car, and waves the driver on.

"There are two empty lanes," he says. "A cabdriver . . . You'd think he would know."

Nazz looks out the window at the guy, at his face, his eyes. Nazz wants to ask him something, but he doesn't know what.

A passenger jet, flying low, heading west, passes overhead.

"Look at that," he says to Nazz. He takes a step further back, looking up. Flying toward the sun, the nose and the fronts of the wings are the color of fire.

Nazz has no idea what would come out of his mouth if he began to ask his question. He knows only that the act of asking it would be like putting his hands against both sides of the moment and pushing outward.

The man looks at Nazz, suddenly lurches toward him, and yanks the bottle of Windex from his hand. He's furious. He rocks himself back and forth. He won't speak. He glares at Nazz, at the paper towels he is still holding, propped against the steering wheel.

Nazz hands them back.

He examines the roll, holding it from the bottom, then points it at the sky. "What's your favorite airline?" he asks. He's smiling now. He has stopped Nazz from changing the script, kept the conversation on course.

"My oldest," he says, without waiting for an answer, "he's in college. Full scholarship. That one's a real brainiac. I tell you . . ."

The light changes to red again. The next time it changes back, Nazz will drive on.

"And the youngest . . . Before she could walk she was making flowers with crayons. Now she paints pictures. Cars, houses, trees. She also likes to travel all over the place. I tell you . . ." He points the roll of towels toward the sky again. "That one's going places."

3
History

On May 9, 1970, Nazz and several other demonstrators were trying to overturn one of the buses that had been parked, front to back, around the White House lawn. Prior to that moment, he would never have believed that any number of people, using only their bodies, could possibly lift something that heavy off the ground.

Two weeks earlier, police and demonstrators clashed violently at a Black Panther rally in New Haven. On May 1, Richard Nixon announced that American ground troops, supported by air cavalry and B-52s, had crossed the Cambodian border. Three days later, four of the demonstrators protesting that expansion of the war were killed, suddenly and inexplicably, by gunfire from National Guard troops at Kent State. That morning, just before dawn, a bomb blew out the ground-floor windows of the National Guard headquarters in Washington.

They rocked it. Each time, the outside wheels reached an inch or two higher. Nazz pressed his shoulder against the side just over the rear fender. He could feel it lose weight at the top of each upswing as it neared its center of gravity. He could almost see the bottoms of the tires.

Then the canisters hit. There was too much noise to hear the thuds of the guns that launched them. Each one hit with the flat conk of a half-filled beer can dropped onto the sidewalk. The air suddenly felt hotter. Although the cloud didn't appear thick, the air abraded his skin like coarse sandpaper. It stung unbearably when he closed his eyes. He kept running until he sensed the people around him weren't running.

There was a red plastic pail filled with water on the sidewalk. People were dipping their gas-soaked bandannas into it. Nazz scooped out dripping handfuls of water and poured it over his head. His eyes, nose, and lips were on fire. It wasn't like sunburn or being touched by flame; it was the way hot food burns the inside of your mouth but much worse. It was inside, under the skin.

He rubbed his eyes on his shirtsleeve.

"Don't do that."

His eyes were tearing and clouded, but he could see the woman who had spoken. She wore a faded blue work shirt and cut-off denim shorts. She looked familiar. He threw more water on his face. He wiped his eyes again.

"You're making it worse," she said.

"Do I know you?"

Before she answered he remembered that he'd seen her that morning, on the bus that brought them to Washington from CCNY in Manhattan.

"I don't think so," she said. "Regina Genarro." She reached out her hand.

"You were on the bus from New York," he said. "You were sitting up front, next to that guy who kept giving everybody instructions. *Stay with your affinity group. Carry a bandanna in case of tear gas. If you hear gunfire, hit the ground. . . .* What an asshole . . ."

"That was Jeff." She pulled a handkerchief out of her shoulder bag, dipped it into the water, and handed it to Nazz. "Here, use this." Then she said, "Jeff isn't so bad. He just wants to be helpful. One of the things he said—which you apparently didn't hear—was to *not* directly touch your skin where it burns from tear gas."

Nazz wiped his face with the cool wet handkerchief. Then he pointed over his shoulder, in the direction he had just run from. "It didn't fall over, did it?"

"What didn't fall over?"

"The bus."

"No. But *they* believed it would. That's why they fired the gas."

"It was about to go. I'd never have believed it. . . . Like some dumb-fucking elephant. I could feel it. We could have turned them all over."

"Sure looked that way," Regina said. "Does it still hurt?"

"What?"

She pointed at his face.

"How does it look?" he asked her.

"How does it feel? That's what's important."

"Like shit."

Regina laughed. Nazz thought her laugh was graceful and calm. Her shirt collar hung open. The sun had reddened the small well of skin between her neck and shoulder.

"Where's Jeff?" he asked.

"I don't know," she said.

In early spring 1971, Regina discovered she was pregnant. She and Nazz had been living together since the fall, working part time to pay the rent on their East Village apartment and studying full time. They were both in their senior year. They loved each other. They wanted a child. They got married.

The following autumn, Nazz became a graduate student—comparative literature—and an instructor—remedial reading and writing—at CCNY. At the end of his first semester Theresa was born.

It was around this time, it seemed to Nazz, that the pull of gravity, perhaps the only consistent factor in all of human history, began, finally, to weaken. As things started to drift upward, they also began to drift apart.

The elements of the comprehensible world, the world of our invention—TV, government, the arts, headlines, the outsides of buildings, the hours of the day, clothing, music, food, medicine, hairstyles, everything, every *thing*—began to detach themselves from every other thing and slowly walk off in their own separate directions. The events that touched the lives of everyone continued happening, but in their own time and space.

The world we built after the Second World War, which, for Nazz, had been the whole world, was now just one small planet in an inconstant and unchartable solar system. All the men who came home from that war, and all the women they married, were now giving up the last of their youth. And they were doing it separately. No generation had done this before. Their children, who had served in Vietnam, or hadn't, began to build their homes, and live their lives, as if they'd all just returned from somewhere. But there was no clear or shared idea of *where* they had returned to.

As the past dismantled itself, the separate worlds became dreams that hovered like clouds over the days of Nazz's life.

People wore wide, bright ties and nodded smiling agreement with other people before they'd even finished speaking, but were quietly unhappy. Archie Bunker's joyless, claustrophobic living room only begins to give you the picture. You felt it when you bought a car, walked in the park, got high with friends, painted the kitchen. It became a very sad time. And now it seems a very long time ago.

Nazz's teaching job paid his tuition and a bit more. It was with a student loan that he mostly supported his family. At the end of his first year of graduate school, Vice President Agnew made the headlines: IN NEW YORK'S CITY UNIVERSITY, DIPLOMAS ARE MEANINGLESS—THE PRICE OF OPEN ENROLLMENT.

Agnew's statement, as it turned out, was part one of a two-part communication. The second part was an enormous budget cut. As the message traveled northeast from the White House, through the Lincoln Tunnel and into New York, it got decoded. The unscrambled version read: *We don't want you getting educated, moving out to our neck of the woods, taking our jobs, and marrying our children.* Over and out. Nazz was laid off before the beginning of the next semester.

By then Theresa was almost a year old. Nazz quit school, passed through a series of low-paying jobs, and found work as a stock clerk in a department store on Fifty-seventh Street, which turned out to be a Local 613 shop. He liked being a union member. The people he met were also aware that the world was coming apart and were interested in putting it back together. He attended meetings and discovered that he indeed slept better, having a family medical plan. He quickly learned to read contracts and write grievances. In this one way his education had paid off. When the shop steward quit, Nazz was elected. Three years later, he left the stockroom and became an employee of the union: a business agent to three shops of his own.

He now serves a chain of bookstores in Manhattan, the clerical staff of a community college in Westchester, and the employees of a commercial printing firm in Brooklyn.

In the mid-seventies, when Nazz first started, the older business agents would speak of the old days, after the war: a two-year strike in Buffalo, fighting scabs in Brooklyn, burning cars in Detroit. But things had settled down in the last twenty years. "We took care of the hard part," they'd brag to Nazz.

However, a new *hard part* was just beginning. In the years since he began, it had become increasingly harder to get reasonable raises for the employees in the shops Nazz represented, and impossible to stem the erosion of benefits. Employers began to watch clocks more closely, monitor sick days, lunch hours, coffee breaks. Workers who had only a vague idea of who their employers were began learning their names. They wanted to know who was to blame.

In 1976, Theresa entered kindergarten, and Regina began substitute teaching in the same public school. A year later, Regina was offered a full-time job teaching at a junior high school in Queens. She accepted it.

She began to prefer the neighborhood she now commuted to, to the Lower Manhattan neighborhood they lived in. Many of their friends had moved. The people who replaced them wore suits to work. She and Nazz spent less and less time together. She said all he seemed to care about was the union.

Nazz began to hate coming home. He and Regina had less and less to say to each other about their daily lives. He had an affair with the woman who sublet the apartment downstairs while the dancer who lived there went on tour. It came to be that he and Regina both spoke more to Theresa than to each other.

Christmas, 1978. Nazz gave Theresa the globe. Regina gave Nazz the tennis racket.

"What do I do with this?" he asked.

"Keep it in the car," Theresa said. "You never know when you'll have to walk on snow."

"If you don't want it," Regina said, "I can return it."

That summer Regina and Theresa moved to an apartment in Queens, near the school Regina still teaches in. Nazz remained in their railroad apartment.

Nazz understands it this way: As they grew older, they grew different. In the years since they separated and divorced, their relationship has eroded into a vague, angry, deep tension. Nazz tries to feel as if more time has elapsed and a surer, clearer distance has grown between them. There is nothing in the world he can love more than his family.

Over the years Nazz has been a business agent, he's become completely at home in the places where people work. So much so that wherever he is, people think he works there. People come up to him in the supermarket and ask, *How come the cottage cheese isn't marked two for ninety-nine like it says in the paper?* In department stores people want to know if they have *this* in blue, or in a size eight.

Sometimes, during his workday, he sends a postcard to his daughter. He recently sent her one with a 3-D picture of King Kong bestriding the World Trade Center, which said:

Dear Tuna,
You're always telling me how lucky I am because I get to eat lunch wherever I want to while you have to eat in the yucky school cafeteria. Well, listen to this. I was coming out of the

men's room in Burger & Brew when this big galupe, no smaller than the character on the front of this card, grabs me by the arm and yells, HEY MACK, I ASKED FOR MY CHECK TEN MINUTES AGO! He was even wearing a cowboy hat. No kidding. Cross my heart.

4
Lunch

Two junkies are sitting across from Nazz at the horseshoe-shaped lunch counter at Woolworth's. They're sipping Cokes from white paper cone cups that sit in aluminum holders. The salt, pepper, sugar, and the ketchup and mustard containers, are crowded against a little aluminum fence at the far edge of the countertop. Two clips hold an open menu above them, for display, like a music stand. On the right side is a list of sandwiches and side dishes. The left side is a full-color photograph of to-matoes, cucumbers, radishes, carrots, onions, and potatoes. They are perfect and glossy, and drops of water cling to them. It's like looking through a window into a Technicolor garden after a light rain has fallen.

It's two-thirty, and the lunch crowd has gone. One of the waitresses is refilling creamers, the other is setting dirty coffee mugs into green mesh trays and then carrying each tray through a set of swinging doors. The two junkies, who face Nazz from the opposite wing of the counter, are the only other customers. They are waiting for someone or something. Periodically, one of them squeezes open a red plastic change purse and pokes at his coins.

Nazz reads the menu without taking it out of its stand. He stares into the photograph until he loses sense of the rest of the room. It's like looking into a TV screen at the moment the world stops. Not ends, just stops.

The junkie with the change purse gets up, stands behind his friend, and tries to convince him of his loyalty.

"Look, man, you know me. Anybody ever comes at you, I'm on em. Like *that*. You're covered. You know *me*."

Nazz is impressed with how strongly and how truly he appears to believe what he's saying. It's the same sincerity employers often use when explaining how a temporary layoff will benefit everybody. They appear to believe what they're saying just as much. Maybe they do.

The other junkie scratches his chin and his thin mustache and sucks Coke and watery ice up his straw.

This morning Nazz had the first session of contract negotiations for the employees of the StreetBookMart chain. Their current contract expires on June 1. That's in three weeks. The ninety-some-odd employees are not happy with the way things are. He and Sandy Newman, shop steward to all four stores, spent the morning sitting across the table from the owner, his three partners, and a stenographer. The first order of business was to set up a schedule for the first week of negotiations. Management wanted a two-week schedule, but Nazz wouldn't make plans beyond one. If they were to become unreasonable, and if there were another week of meetings on the calendar, he'd have to show up or risk that the union be charged with refusing to negotiate in good faith. He'd then lose any leverage gained by allowing the contract expiration date to grow dangerously near. Sometimes the only response to an odious proposal, such as urinanalyses, or salary reductions, or requiring new employees to take lie detector tests, is absolute silence.

Finally, both sides exchanged proposals for non-financial amendments and additions for the new contract. Financial matters—raises, cost-of-living adjustments, medical benefits—the hottest items, are saved for last. This first exchange is how both sides tell each other what they want by how much they are willing to ask for.

When the session ended, Sandy went back to the shop she worked in to tell her coworkers how things went, and Nazz walked over to Woolworth's to pick up a Monopoly game for his daughter.

After he finishes his grilled cheese sandwich, he'll head up to the Local 613 offices on Twenty-first Street, look over both sets of proposals, and see where things stand.

The last time Nazz picked up Tuna, she was playing with a

tabletop Ms. *Packman*. It was a gift from Regina's boyfriend, Delmore. She's been seeing him nearly a year now.

He's the first man Regina has gotten close to in the years since their divorce. Until now, Nazz hadn't given their new lives, their *next* lives, much thought. Their separate existences would continually assemble themselves; changes and additions would be inevitable, and the difficulties that arose would be handleable at the times, and places, in which they arose.

What drives Nazz up the wall is the idea of this guy giving his daughter such an expensive gift. He doesn't want him getting any closer to Tuna. He doesn't want him having any influence. And worse, Regina and Delmore are going to Italy this summer and have invited Tuna to come along. Who could have seen this coming?

While Tuna was playing with Ms. *Packman*, Nazz asked her if she didn't prefer games you played with people.

"Like what?"

"Chess, Scrabble, Monopoly?"

She told him Scrabble was boring, it never ended, and she couldn't play chess. Neither could Nazz. That left Monopoly. The ideal gift for a labor representative to give to his daughter.

Nazz finishes his sandwich. He holds his coffee mug up for the waitress to see. She arrives in front of him and refills it while, with her other hand, she shakes the near-empty creamer sitting beside it. She takes it with her when she returns the glass pot to the hot pad on the coffeemaker, then replaces it with one she's just refilled.

He looks at the menu again, then around the room. He remembers an episode of *Twilight Zone* in which some guy is given a stopwatch that doesn't measure time but stops it. Each time he presses the button on top, the life around him freezes. Someone speaking on the phone, a car passing on the street: the whole world stops. And nothing starts moving until he presses the button again. It's great. The guy can go shopping and then just stroll past the cashier, kiss any woman he wants to, arrange things so that the pretty secretary who'd spurned him in the opening scene and his demeaning boss find themselves in a very compromising position when the clocks start again. At the end he accidentally breaks the watch while the world is in *stop* position. He's the only one *in* time, and he'll have to spend the rest of his life in a frozen, timeless world. In the last moments you see him among a bunch of statue people, and Rod Serling tells us of the fate that awaits him and the lesson he has learned too late. Then the commercial comes on and you forget about it until one day twenty years later when you're sitting at a lunch counter in Woolworth's, eating a grilled cheese sandwich and staring at a photograph of a pile of wet, perennially fresh, chemically dyed vegetables.

Another junkie walks in and stands behind the other two. His short, recently cut hair is combed neatly like Frank Sinatra's or Jerry Lewis's. He's about seventeen, and his eyes are as pale and blue as a Siberian husky's.

The other two are glad to see him, but he tells them he's angry. He's been wandering around for half an hour because they didn't tell him exactly where, in Woolworth's, they would be.

"We been *here*," the one with the change purse tells him.

"And I been walkin around downstairs with the toys and the parakeets and then over by the flowers and shit. . . ."

The one with the mustache smiles at him.

He tells them that if next time they didn't tell him *exactly* where to find them, he wouldn't bother looking.

It's mid-May, and the first truly warm spring weather has arrived. Nazz walks uptown along the sunny side of Broadway. The sides of the buildings are brighter, their textures and colors clearer, than they've been for months. When he reads over the proposals, he'll decide which of their first requests to give up in exchange for concessions by management. Both sides laced their proposals with freebies. These aren't things you don't want; they're things you'd like to have but know you won't get. For example, the employees will withdraw their request that coffee breaks be extended from ten to fifteen minutes if management withdraws their proposal that only one of the three annual sick days can be taken on a Monday or a Friday. Once both sides get started it'll sound like: *We'll eat number seven if you withdraw thirty-two, parts A and B.* These things are the first currency exchanged at a collective bargaining session.

Nazz takes the elevator to the fourth floor, then walks down the long hall to his office, a square, classroom-size space with file cabinets and metal shelves along the walls and three sets of two desks, set facing each other like Ferrante and Teicher's pianos, down the middle.

As he came in from the bright afternoon, it occurred to him that the building could really use some renovations, especially a new coat of paint. It also occurred to him that Helen, the cleaning woman, is nowhere in the hall. He's hardly ever aware of her presence; why should he notice her absence? Who knows why something might come to mind? Who has time to know?

Murray Lewis, who sits at the desk facing Nazz's, is the only other person in the office. Business agents spend most of their time in the field.

When Nazz sits down, Murray lifts up a copy of the *New York Times*, folded to the crossword puzzle, which he has completed.

"What number is that?" Nazz asks.

"Seventy-one."

"Couldn't be." Nazz smiles. "Last week you were only at like fifty-something."

"Seventy-one," Murray says again. "I've already broken my last record. Just twenty-nine more . . ." He puts down the paper, picks up his desk calendar, and points to a date with a bold red dollar sign written on it. "On June tenth you'll be fifty dollars lighter than you thought you'd be."

They have a bet that Murray can't complete a hundred puzzles in a row.

"How do I know you're not just writing in letters?"

"They're all right here." Murray slides a cardboard box out

from under his desk. "And each one available for inspection on the day it comes out. The day *before* the answers are printed. Read em and weep."

"Who's got the time?"

"There were two interesting hints today," Murray says. "Especially from a political/historical point of view."

"I got work to do," Nazz says.

"Just listen. The answer to one is 'Lenny Bruce.' The other was the word 'mantra.' Know why that's interesting?"

Nazz opens the proposals and uncaps his Bic pen. "Why?"

"Cause twenty years ago, when I was your age, the word 'mantra' wasn't in our vocabulary—nowhere near it—and Lenny Bruce was a criminal. Hardly anybody knew who he was. Certainly not enough people for him to be in a crossword puzzle. They didn't even have comedians in crossword puzzles. You had people like John F. Kennedy or Ed Sullivan. Or famous people from the past, like Calvin Coolidge or Winston Churchill or Admiral Halsey. Know who Admiral Halsey was?"

"I've heard the name."

"Goes to show you how things change."

Murray then notices the Monopoly game on Nazz's desk. He points to it. "What's that?"

Nazz holds it up.

Murray gets up and walks over to Nazz's side of the desk. "I love it." He starts laughing. "That's another thing people never used to say. *I love it.* At least not sarcastically. You had to actually love something to say you loved it."

"What is it you *sarcastically* love?"

"Management giving free gifts with their first proposals." He picks up the box and holds it against his ear. "I just want to make sure it's not ticking."

"It's for my daughter."

"I figured," Murray says. "My youngest has one, too, but he never plays with it. He prefers the new electronic shit." Then he asks Nazz, "How was the first session?"

"Uneventful. But I expect it won't be an easy one."

"They're all getting harder. Harder and nastier. Only the crossword puzzles are getting easier."

Nazz begins reading the proposals.

"That's why I think it would be great if management greased the wheels. You know, a *lagniappe*."

"A what?"

Murray opens his desk drawer and pulls out a paperback dictionary. " 'Lagniappe: A small gift given to a customer along with a purchase, something given gratuitously, or by way of good measure.' "

"You use a dictionary when you're doing the puzzle?"

"That ain't cheating."

Nazz points at the Monopoly game. "If management gave them—lan yaps—I guess this is what it would be."

"The perfect complimentary gift," Murray says. "Like TV game shows where all the contestants get the game in a box so they can play at home."

5

8:45 P.M.

This morning, before the rally, Nazz and a contingent of about twenty members of Local 613 met on the corner of First Avenue and Fourteenth Street. They all wore red sweatshirts like the one whose sleeves are tied to his door handles. Front and back, in bold white lettering, they carried the words:

WE SAID *RAISE*—NOT *RAZE*
LOCAL 613
DISTRIBUTIVE
EMPLOYEES UNION

The sweatshirts were Nazz's idea. He organized a hundred and twenty dollars from the union to have them made. The copy was thought up by Sandy Newman.

By the time they reached Twenty-third Street, tens of thousands of marchers had squeezed onto First Avenue. As they headed north and west toward Central Park, their numbers swelled. It was a clear, hot morning. People marched in groups of two to a hundred, carrying signs and banners, wearing buttons and legends on their shirts: *Single Parents Against War; Keep the Skies Friendly—Retired Airline Employees of Greater New York; Ninth Graders for Peace; Midtown Residents for the Future* . . .

After the rally, Nazz had dinner with Sandy. The contract negotiations had gone badly. The management of Street-BookMart were hanging tough. They'd offered unreasonable raises and no cost-of-living adjustment. At the last minute— against Sandy's wishes—both sides agreed to a two-week extension of the existing contract. That means things have to be settled Monday, the day after tomorrow, or the employees at all four stores will go out on strike. Sandy invited Nazz over to her apartment, in Brooklyn, to eat Chinese takeout and discuss strategy.

As a rule, Nazz doesn't make house calls, but he's been in-terested in Sandy for months, and this is the first opportunity he's had to get any nearer than their working relationship has allowed. He's never quite known what to say to her. She's twenty-three, and so unlike him—incomprehensibly and beau-tifully so.

Two weeks ago, she showed Nazz the copy for the sweatshirts. She could have recited the words, but instead she had typed them out and handed him the sheet of paper. She then stood there, self-conscious, all business, and watched his eyes. WE SAID *RAISE*—NOT *RAZE*. You can read five words faster than you can read the time off a clock, but he kept his eyes on the paper. He wasn't at all thrilled with it—nor was he sure people would understand it—but knew she was and wanted him to be. Nazz, in his blue jeans, sports jacket, and permanent-press shirt, standard uniform of the business agent; Sandy, in a black T-shirt, her thick, crew-cut short hair hennaed the rich red of clay, with a pure white streak tracing a single, longer curl up from her forehead.

"I like it," he said.

"Do you?" She looked at him. She squinted and focused, then slowly began to smile.

"It's short, to the point. . . . We'll use it."

He wants to know how she thinks. Beyond this small part of what she wants, or wants from him, she is unreadable. At these times it seems that the decade between them has suddenly yawned into a light-year. He knows there is more to the mystery. There is its first cause: how much he wants her.

Today the business at hand was marching, listening to Bruce Springsteen sing, to Buddhist monks chant, to speakers from all over the world. Today, for Nazz, the business at hand was ex-periencing the pleasure of being angry, along with 750,000 other people, at the same thing.

He and Sandy were waiting on one of the endless lines to the Portosans lined up along the edge of the Sheep Meadow. The enormous crowd extended on both sides and in all direc-

tions, out into the park and beyond. Nazz told her that for anyone who's done any organizing, it was a great pleasure to see so
many people in the same place at the same time. Sandy stood
up on her toes to see if the long, snaking line had grown any
shorter. She then suggested they find a secluded bush.

They walked through the dense, endless crowd until they
came to a thick cluster of brambles at the uptown edge of the
zoo. Sandy got down on her hands and knees and crawled in.
Nazz followed. A small path wound through the roots of the
bushes into a quiet, hollowed-out circle. They were at about a
twenty-foot radial distance from the rest of the crowded world.
They found a clamshell filled with cigarette butts and burnt
matches, a red, white, and blue headband, a clear plastic cassette
box in which there was a pencil, sharpened down to a stub.

"Can you believe this?" Sandy said. "Using an ashtray in
here."

They were kneeling, facing each other. There was a dome of
branches and new leaves less than a foot above their heads.
There was a sweet, human dirtiness in the hard-packed soil.

Nazz said, "I bet there isn't one square inch of this city that
somebody hasn't walked on, sat down on, slept on. . . ."

"Or pissed on," Sandy added.

They could hear the loud vague wind of electric guitars and
amplified voices.

"We're in the heart of an enormous beast," Sandy said.

"Like Jonah—two Jonahs—inside the whale."

"Not like Jonah. He was in the stomach . . . with all that
half-digested food."

"And there must have been a lot of it," Nazz said. "Whales
have big appetites."

Sandy then stood up, as much as she could, until her bowed
back was cupped in the lowest branches. She unclasped her belt
and slid her jeans down to her ankles.

"Well?" she said.

"You're beautiful," Nazz said.

She smiled at him.

To Nazz her skin seemed calm, if skin can be calm, and it was smooth.

Sandy squatted, then said, "What about you?"

Nazz straightened his legs and leaned over, opened his fly, and aimed his penis out into the bushes. "I feel like Adam and Eve," he said. He loved the sound of her piss, spattering the ground, and his own, spritzing into the leaves and branches. "It's been a wonderful day," he said.

After they found their way back out of the maze of brambles and stood up, they kissed. Softly, and just longer than a peck. Sandy smiled, but didn't say a word until they'd worked their way back to the spot where the Local 613 contingent were eating sandwiches, drinking beer, and reading aloud to each other a list of antipersonnel warheads, aerial bombs, and artillery ordnance from a pamphlet titled "How to Destroy Life."

They sat down.

"I find it interesting," Nazz said to her, "that in the language of weaponry, the opposite of *nuclear* is *conventional*." Then he pointed his finger outward, moved it in a circle indicating the endless sea of people they were in the middle of, and said, "Today could mark the beginning of the end of the Cold War."

That was when she invited him over.

After the rally, they took the subway downtown to where Nazz's car was parked, then drove into Brooklyn. He liked having Sandy in his car. It preserved the feeling created by their sudden intimacy. The sun was high and bright over the river when they drove across the bridge.

After dinner, however, they fought. Not over the nature of any changes they might have begun to bring to their relationship—not officially—but over labor politics.

Had dinner gone any differently, he wouldn't be standing here now, leaning against his car, watching the sun go down, waiting for a neutron bomb to fall silently from the top of the sky.

Sandy saw the potential strike at the StreetBookMart stores

as the first step in a series of events that would change the entire political system under which she, her coworkers, and everyone else in the world must live. Being both naive and sophisticated, and angry, she wants the strike. In sympathy, she expects the Con Edison linemen to cut off the juice and the postal workers to refuse to deliver.

Nazz told her they must first do everything possible to avert a strike. Workers rarely win anymore. To gain anything, she'll have to narrow her sights.

"Unions must unite to smash the system," she said.

"I truly wish they could."

"You've given up, then."

"Like it or not," Nazz told her, "in our day and age the unions are alone. They can't change the system. At best, they can somehow adapt workers to it."

"And you're happy with that . . . ?"

"Give me a fucking break."

"Working for the enemy and you're *happy* about it."

Fifteen minutes later, Nazz was pulling onto the Brooklyn-Queens Expressway. Sandy no longer seemed unlike him. She was just like other people, himself included, when they're not interested in hearing a damn thing anyone else has to say.

Why stop at cutting off the electricity and stopping the mail? Why not ask the books in the store to refuse to be opened and allow their pages to be read? How about asking the networks to stop broadcasting? I've got it: a solar eclipse that will last for the duration of the strike. . . .

What could he say to her? *We'll both dream our private little history and live happily ever after.* What could anyone say to her? She doesn't want *me.* . . . She wants Alexander-Fucking-Berkman.

Most people he knows think he is, or want him to be, someone else. That's why Regina gave him the tennis racket. She wanted him to be someone else, but he didn't get the message. They were both twenty-one when they got married. As they neared thirty she wanted different things from him. Be someone interested in tennis, is what he heard her say, which to him seemed like the first step on a path that led to a clubhouse filled with middle-aging men whose priorities included the maintenance of the calm, healthy, untouched-by-life appearance of senators. Maybe it was not so much what she wanted him to become, but that she'd grown tired of what he was.

Nazz didn't walk out of Sandy's apartment because he was angry; he left because he couldn't say another word. Not unless he slid away from himself. Not unless he performed, which meant dropping out of sight and lying low until he and Sandy had passed through the entire moment and come out the other side.

He only performs on the job, and since earlier, in the park, his relationship with Sandy, as he understands it, however dreamed-up or tentative, is no longer limited to the workday. Had she asked him since what he thought of the words on their sweatshirts, he would have told her.

He only performs on the job. When it gets him something important and only when it suits him. He only performs for management.

Right then the tire blew.

Only for management and only when it suits me.

He didn't hear the blowout, nor the scream of the tires, nor the horn of the car he'd cut off. These sounds hovered in the spot his car had suddenly leapt out of while Nazz drifted through silence. When he came to a stop they broke against him like a wave.

You prepare your performance, decide which character you'll play, by watching how the management representatives walk into the room on the first day, each one of them, and how they sit down at the table. That's what Murray had taught him, his first year as a business agent. You look for the ones who appear to genuinely believe that they aimed at what they hit. That they became senior vice president, or head of personnel, *not* via a series of fortuitous accidents, but as the inevitable manifestation of a superior class intellect. They're the easiest to perform for, because you're helping them nurture the identity that comes with their paychecks. "You give em a pissed-off Jimmy Hoffa when you wanna assure em there's order in da universe, by speakin in da true voice of labor; you give them Marcello Mastroianni in *The Organizer* when you want to woo them with the romance of their own humanity."

The fact that they have all the marbles does most of the talking, and the only consistent truth—now or back in Murray's day—is that they are not willing or happy to share. Nothing is even fifty percent effective, and the percentages are going down. Even in the best of years, it's dreaming to *expect* results, no matter how good a performer you are.

It's getting cooler.

The sun has lost half of itself below the horizon. Only when it rises or sets can you actually see the sun moving. It moves quickly.

He walks to the front of the car and looks at the flattened tire. It must have blown out for a reason. There is no effect without a cause. Perhaps, ten years ago, someone fired an artillery beehive round (antipersonnel; limited range; nonexplosive) due east, against a hillside near Khe Sanh, and one of its darts lofted the hilltop, picked up a tailwind, and spent the next decade crossing the South China Sea, the Pacific Ocean, and the continental United States, then finally began to lose its wad somewhere over New Jersey, and came to its last rest in the left front tire of Nazz's 1974 Karmann Ghia as it cruised toward the entry ramp of the Williamsburg Bridge. That must've been it.

He pulls his sleeveless sweatshirt on over his regular shirt. He wishes that he and Sandy had simply gone to bed the first thing upon arriving at her apartment. No talking. No tampering with the spontaneous, sexy affinity they'd felt earlier.

A blue Mustang flies past, trailing a concussive salsa beat from its open windows.

Nazz decides he will wait until the moment the sun has completely set. If no one has stopped by then, he'll leave the car and walk across the bridge. He's afraid that if he stays here much longer, especially after dark, he'll disappear entirely. At this moment he feels tired and just barely visible. At this moment he feels the frailest degree above never having existed at all.

6
The Beginning of the Morning

Nazz is walking down the long, narrow hall leading to his office. He's thinking that he's the only one in the whole place, but then he sees Helen, the cleaning woman, sitting in a folding chair beside one of the dark-wood office doorways. This is in a dream. When he wakes, he will remember it whole, but gradually, as the morning wears on, it will erode down to a sediment of two or three images, an odd fragment of memory that every so often will rise to the surface of consciousness, for no apparent reason, and communicate nothing.

But now he's walking down the hall and getting nearer and nearer to Helen. She's a heavyset woman in her mid-fifties. Quiet, friendly, impersonal. At work, her bearing tells you that the most important parts of her life are lived elsewhere. Her right leg is crossed over her left knee, and Nazz can see the dark bottom of her tennis sneaker.

The doors and doorframes are scratched and battered, and it occurs to Nazz that they are the same ones, or exact replicas, of the ones he walked past every day in the public school he attended twenty-five years ago. He alters his course so he's headed directly toward Helen. He's getting nearer.

But then he says to himself, *We only know each other to say hello to. Beyond that, what could I mean to her? She has her own world.*

Just before he reaches her he changes his course again and walks past her down the middle of the hall.

He is aware that Helen watches him, curious about his sudden change in direction.

Nazz is beginning to wake up. And he's afraid. What if he doesn't get to wherever it is he's walking toward?

The motions of the dream continue into his gradual waking, but the fear begins to recede.

He has the odd feeling that in the dream he might have been

Helen, too. She wasn't Helen, though, or *just* Helen, but another part of him. There was no one else in there.

Beyond these thoughts, he accepts the dream whole. He never questions his dreams. It would be like listening in to a phone conversation in a language he barely understands.

His life is *of* the world, and when his eyes are open he's usually too busy to think about anything beyond what he's doing. His understanding of himself, if it ever rears its head in his lifetime, will be as a citizen, will be in terms of the body he is one cell of.

He's not curious as to why he chose Helen to costar in this particular dream, or about the familiar doorways, or about his own strange behavior.

As he realizes it is Monday morning, he says, aloud, "shit." This first spoken word carries him across a border to a place where he's more awake than asleep. He suddenly has the feeling that he's had this dream before. The next thought, one he often has, is whether he actually *had* the dream before, or only dreamed that he had.

On the Saturday of the weekend just past, he'd learned about Tuna going to Italy with Regina and her boyfriend. He is angrily thinking about it in the shower. This was something they could never have afforded when they were married.

Regina had answered the door, quickly kissed him hello. She was wearing pajama tops and jeans. She had a toothbrush in her hand. "I'm running late," she said, and rushed back to her room.

Nazz has rarely gone farther into the apartment than the living room. Tuna usually meets him there.

The TV was on. *B.J. and the Bear*. A fat state trooper pulled B.J. over to the side of the road, climbed onto the running board of the cab of his semi, leaned his face close to B.J.'s, and told him he couldn't get away with something or other in *his* county. It all happened in front of the same hills the helicopters fly over every week at the beginning of each episode of *M*A*S*H*.

Nazz waited awhile, standing in front of the TV. Then he walked into the kitchen. Tuna was sitting at the table, playing *Ms. Packman.*

"Hi," she said.

She hadn't looked up from the screen. He wondered if she'd recognized his footstep or his smell. He sat down next to her.

"Sssssshhhhhit!"

"What happened?" Nazz asked her.

"I just got eaten by a monster."

"You?"

"Well . . . *Ms. Packman.*"

He kissed her hello. "Is this game better than humans?"

"It's fun. Try it."

That was when he asked Tuna if she didn't prefer games you played with people. The question began the process of elimination that left them with Monopoly.

He turned the screen so it faced him, took the control knob, and asked Tuna to start her up. "Contact." In less than sixty seconds he'd lost all three players.

"What do you want?" he said. "My first time. It's working right, isn't it? How come they don't call it *Packwoman?*"

Tuna took over the game and began eating power dots like crazy. She leaned and rocked as if she were having real physical contact with what was happening on the screen. Nazz was amazed at her concentration and dexterity.

"You're great," he told her. "You handle those controls like a pilot."

She didn't answer. A new grid of dots appeared on the screen.

"Speaking of flying . . . Before, when I was in the living room, I was watching B.J. and the Bear, and you know what? B.J. got pulled over by Smokey in front of the same hills the choppers fly over every week at the beginning of M*A*S*H."

"Have you been dreaming, Nazz?"

"No, I mean it."

"You mean B. J. Hunnicut."

"No, I mean B. J. with the big truck and the monkey."

"Can't be. M*A*S*H is in Korea." She eats a power dot. Then, in quick succession, a monster and two cherries.

"But it's filmed in California."

"It looks like Korea to me, Nazz."

"How do you know what Korea looks like?"

She let out a small belch. It made a sound like a fingertip tapped against the bottom of an empty paper cup.

Then she said, "I've seen about a hundred M*A*S*H's."

"But that's TV. That's not being there. It's like looking at countries on the globe."

That's when she told him she might go to Italy. At first Nazz didn't believe her.

"This summer," she said. "Del's taking Mommy, and they invited me to come along."

"What?" Nazz stood up. "When?"

"End of July. When he takes his vacation."

Delmore, along with his family, owns a chain of drugstores on Long Island. Tuna has been to one of them. "They're enormous," she said. "They don't just sell medicine. They got bathing suits, video games, jewelry. Do you believe it? They even sell hanging plants. . . . In a *drug*store."

Nazz had asked the appropriate people at Local 613 to find out if the employees of these stores were organized.

Tuna looked at him. "You don't want me to go?"

"Sure I want you to go. Only I wish somebody'd asked me about it."

"You don't want me to go?" she asked again.

Nazz sat down again and turned the screen back to himself.

He and Regina had tried to soften the blow of the divorce and sidestep the inexplicable by constantly reminding Tuna of how little had changed. In the years that followed, they tried to keep her at a distance from the tensions and frequent arguing that had become their postmarital relationship. But this can backfire. There are times when Nazz truly needs her to know how hard it is.

"I'm getting the hang of this," he said. He'd managed to eat about a third of the dots on the screen. "Will you send me postcards?"

"Sure," Tuna said. "I'll send one with the Pope."

"And one of Sophia Loren."

"I'll write you about everything. Even where I eat lunch."

Nazz is sitting on the bed. He was not conscious of, nor does he remember, the series of small acts that brought him here. Turning off the shower, drying himself, crossing the room, sitting. Another memory had realized itself like a Polaroid. He was walking somewhere. He was walking and then, unexpectedly, he changed direction.

At first the act of walking, and of changing direction, was all he perceived. It wasn't happening anywhere. Then the memory found its time and place. He had just gotten off a train in Grand Central Station. He was twenty years old. Two weeks later, he would meet Regina in Washington.

He had just returned from New Haven. He'd been at a rally for the Black Panthers at Yale.

A row of police, in riot gear, stood facing the crowd who were waiting for Bobby Seale to speak. People were standing, sitting, milling around. Their numbers were quickly growing: twenty minutes earlier, Nazz had been standing at the back of the crowd; he was now in its center.

Suddenly the police and the people in front were running at each other. He never really learned what happened, or why it was happening. It was as if a calm sea had spontaneously begun to boil.

Nazz saw a woman running toward him, being chased by a policeman, the solid mass of bodies trying to part itself as they approached. A ripple of alertness, like nerve speaking to muscle, shot through the crowd around him, and their powerful motion carried him toward one side, then pushed him toward the other.

Then, suddenly, they fell away on both sides and he had no sensation of people against him. He stood in the narrow aisle of space and was now the destination the policeman and the woman were running toward. They both rose and fell with each step. The sunlight ignited the globe of his helmet and face mask each time it briefly rose above her head. She had gotten less than twenty feet from Nazz when he saw the nightstick swing downward against her back. He saw her eyes close. He saw her sink, as if into water, beneath the heads and shoulders of the crowd that began to close itself again the moment her forward motion slowed to a stop.

As Nazz approached her, the crowd began to break up again, thin out, and scatter. Even so, by the time the space around her had emptied, she was gone.

When, hours later, Nazz found himself within the hive-like motion of evening rush hour in Grand Central Station, his lips began to move. Among all these people, he couldn't keep hold of his thoughts unless he spoke them aloud.

He felt afraid. The crowd had an entirely different collective will than the one he was part of earlier, and it channeled differently into movement: fast and urgent, restless yet ordered. It pulled like a strong current.

The desire to do something other than just survive is accompanied by a fear of death. It's costly and it's dangerous. The energy in this enormous concourse would not even allow him to consider it. It would be like slipping out of his body while he was on his way someplace, then watching it continue, unpiloted, drifting off course, losing momentum, losing will. And it needs that will—every being in that whole restless place knew this—to get somewhere and then to get back home again.

Her eyes were closing, he said aloud.

As he was crossing the terminal, heading toward the subway, he suddenly veered off in the direction of a saxophone player he could not, yet, see but whose music he could hear. The tune was magnetic, familiar, pleasing.

He had never known so much life to inhabit a single moment.

As he approached the source of the music, he remembered, with disbelief, what it was. The theme from *Candid Camera.* But being played so sweetly, it had become a different song. He squeezed into the small crowd that was watching the guy play. His music was beautiful and generous. This Jiminy Cricket handful of notes, the sound of coins jingling in a pocket, and he had transformed it into a mournful history of vowels.

But this isn't the heart of the memory.

There was something more in that moment that he needed, even more urgently, to remember. Then he could go on automatic pilot, get dressed, leave for work.

It was the tea.

The tea . . . The warmth and smell of it, rising above the top of the open paper bag held by the woman standing next to him.

7

9:00 P.M.

The darkness came on suddenly. The sun had remained at a thousand watts until the last of it fully disappeared.

The car might get towed away, or stolen, or stripped down to the chassis, but Nazz has no other choice but to leave it. He locks the doors, closes the trunk, and heads toward the Manhattan-bound walkway. St. Christopher will have to look after things.

He walks about twenty feet, then stops and looks back at his car. Two motorcycles fly past. One after the other their headlights flash in the rear bumper, then in the passenger-side door handle. Last week, while eating dinner in front of the TV, Nazz watched one of the contestants on *Jeopardy!* tell Alex Trebek, the host, that he had an unusual hobby: remembering the birthdays of friends and relatives and calling them each year on their day. He had already memorized over fifty dates. In that moment, the very fact of his existence infuriated Nazz, who has forgotten about him until now. This man, who had constructed his whole life, right down to his hobbies, so that he'd be what he thought the world called upon him to be—as unthreatening and as immediately comprehensible as someone whose skin was as thin and clear as the screen of a TV—would have that life dismantled, along with everyone else's, if a tide of neutron radiation were to suddenly roll across this portion of the planet. Nazz's heart is aching.

A taxi rolls slowly by, with its trunk tied down over a pile of suitcases, and a couple reclining in the back seat with their heads together. Then another Kharmann Ghia, a red one, slowly pulls off the road and stops right behind his. Nazz stares at it from across the roadway. He doesn't believe it's real.

The driver then honks. Nazz crosses back over and walks up to the car. Across the front bumper are three NO NUKES ARE

GOOD NUKES bumper stickers. The driver is a small elderly black woman with short gray hair. She rolls down the window.

"I only stopped because you have a Karmann Ghia," she says.

"I love you," Nazz says.

"But we haven't met," she says.

Nazz notices two turtles in a wire cage on the passenger seat.

"I'm Nazzarino Jacobs," he says.

"Olivia Thomas," she says, then introduces the turtles. "Pat and Mike."

Nazz says, How do you do, twice, addressing the turtles individually. Then he again says to Olivia, "I love you."

"Now that we all know each other, I'll accept your devotion. Need a lift?"

"Just a jack handle."

She reaches under the dashboard, pulls the trunk release, and the hood lurches up an inch. "Know where it is?"

"Right where mine would be if I had one."

Olivia gets out of the car. She stands behind Nazz and watches him work.

"What does that mean?" Olivia asks. She reads the back of his sweatshirt. " 'We said *raise*, not *raze*.' "

People have been asking him that all day.

"It means we want a raise in salary, not a nuclear war."

"Were you at the rally today?"

"Yeah."

"Me too. I knew anybody with a Karmann Ghia had to be all right. Funny, I didn't see you, though."

"There were seven hundred fifty thousand people."

"Where were you sitting?" she asks.

"Back of the meadow . . . center." Nazz pulls off the ripped-open tire, picks up the spare, and joggles it over the lug bolts.

"Let's see. . . ." Olivia squats next to Nazz. "How far were you from the Hoosiers for Nuclear Disarmament? Their contingent was back there somewhere."

"I don't know."

"I was about fifty feet from them. Nearer the middle, I think, but it's hard to tell. There were so many people. . . ."

"That's what I mean," Nazz says.

"Were you near the Buddhist monks?"

"Did you like the music?"

"Never answer a question with a question," Olivia says. "Did you see the Retired Teachers for Peace?"

"I did," Nazz says. "Our contingent was pretty close."

"That's my outfit," she says proudly. "Yup, that was us. To answer your question, I didn't think much of the music."

Nazz throws the flat tire into his trunk, slams it shut, and returns Olivia's jack handle. When she walks back to her car, he opens the door for her.

"You could've thought up a better slogan," she says. "I'd never have figured it out."

"You're right," Nazz says. "It's lousy." He shuts the door.

He leans against it for a second, as if to make sure he had closed it properly. Then he says, "I can't thank you enough. No one else stopped. No one else even saw me."

"You still love me?" she asks.

"Yup."

"Maybe you *can* thank me enough." She smiles a gently lecherous smile. "How old are you?"

"Thirty-three."

"Sorry," she says. "Too old." She flips on her directionals. "Men are over their peak at nineteen."

She quickly pulls out into the traffic, right in front of a man driving an Eldorado, who honks at her sudden intrusion in his lane. She looks into the rearview mirror, shifts into second gear, then sticks her left arm out the window and gives him the finger. She points it straight up at the sky.